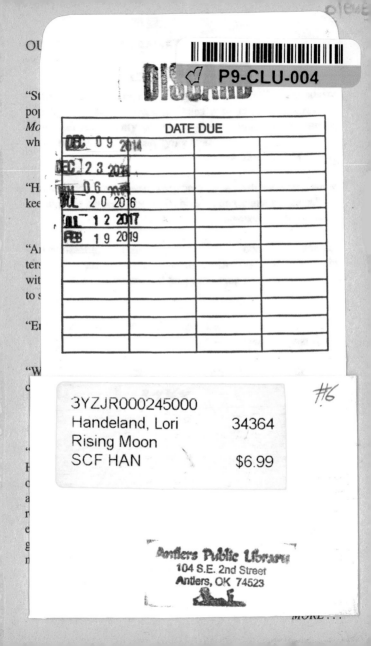

P9-CLU-004

DISCARD

DATE DUE			
DEC 09 2014			
DEC 23 2014			
MAY 06 2015			
JUL 20 2016			
JUL 12 2017			
FEB 19 2019			

#6

3YZJR000245000
Handeland, Lori   34364
Rising Moon
SCF HAN $6.99

Antlers Public Library
104 S.E. 2nd Street
Antlers, OK 74523

OU

"St
pop
Mo
wh

"H
kee

"An
ters
wit
to s

"En

"W
c

H
c
a
r
e
g
n

MORE . . .

"The end is a surprising, yet satisfying, conclusion to this series . . . another terrific story."
                                                          —*Fresh Fiction*

"The characters are intriguing and the romance is sexy and fun while at times heart-wrenching. The action is well-written and thrilling, especially at the end . . . *Dark Moon* is another powerful tale with a strong heroine who is sure to please readers and a hero who is worth fighting for. Handeland has proven with this trilogy that she has a bright future in the paranormal genre."
                                          —*Romance Readers Connection*

"Elise is Handeland's most appealing heroine yet . . . this tense, banter-filled tale provides a few hours of solid entertainment."
                                                     —*Publishers Weekly*

"Smart and often amusing dialogue, brisk pacing, plenty of action, and a generous helping of 'spookiness' add just the right tone . . . an engaging and enjoyable paranormal romance."
                                                             —*BookLoons*

"A fantastic tale starring two strong likable protagonists . . . action-packed . . . a howling success."   —*Midwest Book Reviews*

"Handeland writes some of the most fascinating, creepy, and macabre stories I have ever read . . . exciting plot twists . . . new revelations, more emotional themes, and spiritual awakenings are prevalent here."   —*Romance Reader at Heart*

HUNTER'S MOON

"Another fast-paced, action-packed story of sacrifice and love in the shape-shifting realm . . . a terrific second book in her werewolf series."   —*The Best Reviews*

"A continuation of the perfection that is a fascinating series the author started in her novel *Blue Moon* . . . fantastic and way too hard to put down."
                              —*Romance Reader at Heart*

"Handeland has more than proved herself a worthy author in the increasingly popular world of paranormal romance with these slick and highly engrossing tales and has become an author whose works will always be greatly anticipated."
                              —*The Road to Romance*

"An absorbing, fast-paced story that will keep readers enthralled from start to finish . . . a paranormal delight . . . once you read this, you won't be able to help going back and reading the first [novel]."
                              —*Fallen Angel Reviews*

"An edge-of-your-seat paranormal romance that seizes the reader by the neck and doesn't let go . . . in-depth characterization, an excellent setting, and an exciting storyline make *Hunter's Moon* one for the keeper shelf."
                              —*Romance Reviews Today*

"An incredible sequel to last year's *Blue Moon* . . . fast-paced and full of twists and turns . . . another winner . . . a must-read paranormal."
                              —*Romance Junkies*

"This book and all its predecessors have all the hallmarks of an upcoming classic series; focus is sharply maintained, the heroes are flawed and compelling, the tension level taut, yet lightened with wit."
                              —*Huntress and Eternal Night Reviews*

BLUE MOON

"Chilling and sizzling by turns! Lori Handeland has the kind of talent that comes along only once in a blue moon. Her sophisticated, edgy voice sets her apart from the crowd, making her an author to watch, and *Blue Moon* is a novel not to be missed." —Maggie Shayne, author of *Edge of Twilight*

"Presenting an interesting and modern twist on the werewolf legend, Lori Handeland's *Blue Moon* is an intriguing mixture of suspense, clever humor, and sensual tension that never lets up. Vivid secondary characters in a rural, small-town setting create an effective backdrop for paranormal events. Will Cadotte is a tender and sexy hero who might literally be worth dying for. But the real revelation in the book is Handeland's protagonist, police officer Jessie McQuade, a less-than-perfect heroine who is at once self-deprecating, tough, witty, pragmatic, and vulnerable. She draws you into the story and holds you there until the very end." —Susan Krinard, author of *To Catch a Wolf*

"Handeland sets a feverish pace, thrusting Jessie into one dangerous situation after another, and she keeps readers in delicious suspense . . . What makes this book so compulsively readable, however, is Jessie's spunky narration, acerbic wit, and combustible chemistry with Will. Handeland has the potential to become as big as, if not bigger than, Christine Feehan and Maggie Shayne." —*Publishers Weekly*

"Hold on to your seats! Handeland delivers a kick-butt heroine ready to take on the world of the paranormal. *Blue Moon* is an awesome launch to what promises to be a funny, sexy, and scary series." —*Romantic Times* 4½ stars, "Top Pick"

"A fast-paced and thought-provoking story. Dynamic characters in *Blue Moon* will leave you with no doubt that you are reading something special . . . the beginning of an exciting new series." —*Enchanted in Romance*

"This book has everything—excellent writing, fascinating characters, suspense, comical one-liners, and best of all, a super-good romance."
—*The Best Reviews*

"An incredible werewolf story with a twist . . . full of sass and with a delightful, sarcastic sense of humor."
—*Paranormal Romances*

"The action is fast-paced, the plot is gripping, the characters are realistic, and I absolutely positively cannot wait for the next book in this series."
—*Fallen Angel Reviews*

"A dry wit that shines . . . Everything about this book is wonderful: the sizzling sexiness, the three-dimensional characters, and the sense of danger."
—*Romance Junkies*

"Great intensity, danger, drama, captivation, and stellar writing."
—*The Road to Romance*, Reviewer's Choice Award

"Lori Handeland makes a superlative debut in the world of paranormal romance with *Blue Moon*, first in an enticing new *Moon* trilogy. *Blue Moon* is simply not to be missed."
—*BookLoons*

"If you enjoy werewolves that are linked to folklore with characters that seem to be in every town, whether it is small or big, then pick up a copy of *Blue Moon*. You will not be disappointed."
—*A Romance Review*

"A captivating novel that draws readers in from the first page . . . for a story that will entertain, delight, and have you glancing askance at the full moon, run, do not walk, to the nearest bookstore and grab *Blue Moon* . . . A book guaranteed to please readers of paranormal, suspense, and romance . . . a winner on all counts!"
—*Romance Reviews Today*

ST. MARTIN'S PAPERBACKS TITLES
BY LORI HANDELAND

RISING MOON
MIDNIGHT MOON
CRESCENT MOON
DARK MOON
HUNTER'S MOON
BLUE MOON

RISING
MOON

LORI HANDELAND

St. Martin's Paperbacks

NOTE: If you purchased this book without a cover you should be aware that this book is stolen property. It was reported as "unsold and destroyed" to the publisher, and neither the author nor the publisher has received any payment for this "stripped book."

This is a work of fiction. All of the characters, organizations and events portrayed in this novel are either products of the author's imagination or are used fictitiously.

RISING MOON

Copyright © 2006 by Lori Handeland.

All rights reserved. No part of this book may be used or reproduced in any manner whatsoever without written permission except in the case of brief quotations embodied in critical articles or reviews. For information address St. Martin's Press, 175 Fifth Avenue, New York, NY 10010.

ISBN: 0-312-93850-0
EAN: 978-0-312-93850-5

Printed in the United States of America

St. Martin's Paperbacks edition / January 2007

St. Martin's Paperbacks are published by St. Martin's Press, 175 Fifth Avenue, New York, NY 10010.

10 9 8 7 6 5 4 3 2 1

Thanks to Jen Enderlin
Without her, none of this would make any sense.

1

EVERYTHING WAS ALL right until the photograph showed up in my mailbox.

Actually, that isn't true. Nothing had been all right since my sister vanished into thin air.

I'd never known people could disappear so completely that no trace was ever found. Isn't this America? Land of the free, home of the security camera? Big Brother is watching more often than we think. Unfortunately, he'd been asleep at the switch when Katie went AWOL.

For three years there hadn't been a sign of her despite all the pictures I'd plastered on signposts, store windows, and every missing persons Internet site I could find.

Then I'd gone into the office, started sorting through my stack of mail, opened a five-by-seven manila envelope, and voilà! There she was, standing outside a building named Rising Moon.

It had taken me all of three minutes to determine the

place was a jazz club in New Orleans. I'd shoved a few changes of clothes and my toothbrush into a backpack and boarded the next available flight.

A few hours later, I stood on a street called Frenchmen, listening to jazz wail out an open doorway and wondering how it could be so freaking hot in the middle of February. When I'd gotten on the plane in Philly, fat snowflakes had been tumbling down.

I'd never visited New Orleans, never wanted to. I wasn't the party type; I wouldn't fit in. However, I didn't plan to stay. I planned to get Katie and get gone.

I forced myself to walk through the door, ignoring the smoke, the noise, the people. The inside was sparse, narrow, nothing like the big, airy taverns at home, which boasted lots of tables, lots of space for billiards, darts, and other amusements. Rising Moon was all about the music.

I knew nothing about jazz. Give me some Aerosmith, a little Guns n' Roses, even Ozzie on a really tough day. But jazz? I'd never understood the attraction.

One look at the man playing the saxophone near the front of the room and attraction took on a different twist.

He was tall and slim, and everything about him—his hair, his clothes, even the glasses that covered his eyes—was dark.

I glanced at the ceiling. Not a spotlight to be had.

"Weird," I muttered, and received a few glares from the spectators crowded as close to the man as they could get.

There wasn't any stage. He just stood in a corner and played. From the microphone, the piano, and the abandoned drum set behind him, I assumed the corner *was* the stage.

He held that sax as if it were the only thing he'd ever loved. Despite the need to show the picture of Katie to anything that moved, I found myself watching, listening, captivated by a stranger and his music.

Even with the dark sunglasses bisecting his face, I could tell he was better than handsome. His hair was shorn close, but that only drew attention to the sharpness of his cheekbones and the devilishly well-trimmed mustache and goatee.

His hands were long fingered and elegant, the hands of an aristocrat in a world where such distinctions were long dead. He seemed European, and I guess that wasn't too odd, considering.

New Orleans had always been more foreign than domestic—a city where life moved at a slower pace, where music and dancing were part of every day and every night, where French was as commonly murmured as curse words. No wonder I'd felt itchy and out of sorts from the moment I'd stepped off the plane. I was a peasant, and I always would be.

The tune ended, whatever it was, the last notes drifting toward the high ceiling and fading away. The spell over the crowd broke as they clapped, chattered among themselves, then lifted their glasses to drink.

"Thank you, ladies and gentlemen." His voice was as mesmerizing as his hands—deep, melodious, with an accent I couldn't place. Perhaps Spanish, with a pinch of the South, a dash of the North, and something mysterious just beneath.

The bartender, a tall, muscular black man with eerily

light brown eyes and impossibly short natural hair appeared at my elbow. "What can I get you?"

I wanted to shake my head to clear it of the dopey infatuation with the sax player's hands and voice. I was not the type of woman who went gaga over a guy for any reason, let alone his looks. If I cared about looks I'd be in deep shit. My face certainly wouldn't inspire any sonnets.

I laid the photo of Katie atop the polished wood. "Seen her?"

"You a cop?" The bartender's accent was pure Dixie.

"No." I could have shown him my private investigator's license, but I'd discovered more info was forthcoming when I made my reasons personal. "She's my sister. She was eighteen when she went missing. Three years ago."

"Oh." His face went from suspicious to sympathetic in an instant. "That's too bad."

I couldn't determine his age—maybe thirty, maybe fifty. He seemed both a part of this place and yet removed from it. Muscles bulged beneath his dark T-shirt, and the hand that reached for the snapshot would have made two of my own.

He peered at the picture so long, I wondered if his tiger-eyes were in need of some pretty thick glasses. Then he set it back on the bar and lifted his gaze. "A lot of people go missing in this city. Always have. What with the tourists, Bourbon Street, Mardi Gras, the river, the swamp, the lake—" He spread his big hands and shrugged.

I'd have to take his word for it. I hadn't done much research on the city proper before I'd hopped on the plane. I'd spent what time I had trying to figure out where the manila envelope had come from, although I'd had no luck.

My address had been typed in both the center and the top left-hand corner. There'd been a stamp, but no postmark. Which made me think someone had shoved it into my mailbox when I wasn't looking.

But why?

"My sister went missing from home," I clarified. "From Philadelphia."

"You've come a long way."

I shrugged. "She's my sister."

Sisters can be both the best and the worst—depending on the day, the mood, the sister. Mine was no different. Still, I'd travel to the ends of the earth twice over for Katie. Sure, we'd fought, but we'd also been best friends. I'd shared so many things with Katie, that without her I felt like only half of myself.

"I don't recognize her." The bartender leaned back, nodding at someone who waved for a drink.

"Are you the owner?" I asked.

"No, ma'am. That would be John Rodolfo."

"And where could I find him?"

He jerked his chin toward the rear of the tavern. "Should be in the office."

As I headed in that direction, the murmur of voices and the clink of glasses filled the burgeoning night. The corner of the room was empty; the hot saxophone player was gone.

I was surprised at my disappointment. I didn't have time to hang around and listen to music I wasn't all that fond of. Hell, I didn't have time to listen to music I liked.

My life was my work and I didn't mind. I can't say what I would have done if I hadn't become a private investigator. Back when I was twenty, two years into college and no clue on a major, it had seemed like a good idea to take a little time off and work for Matt Hawkins, the PI my parents had hired to look for Katie. He was old, he needed help, and it was my fault she was missing anyway.

Well, not *technically* my fault. We'd had a stupid sister fight, and she'd walked out. I should have gone after her; at the very least, I should have met her later that night as I'd promised. But I'd been angry; I'd stood her up, and I hadn't seen her since.

I never had gone back to college. Matt had left me his business when he'd retired the previous year. He helped out here and there—like now, for instance, when I had to leave town to follow a lead. I was conveniently between cases, and Matt could deal with anything that might come in during the few days I was gone.

A door marked PRIVATE stood between two others marked MESSIEURS and MESDEMOISELLES. So where did the "Mesdames" pee?

Most people would hesitate before barreling through a door labeled "private" but not me. I'd never been very polite even before I'd applied for my license to pry, so I turned the knob and stepped inside.

The room was pitch-black. I guessed Rodolfo wasn't home. I started to leave, but a single muttered curse from the depths of the darkness had me fumbling for a switch.

The harsh electric glare left me blinking. Not so the man behind the desk. He still wore his sunglasses.

For a minute my mind floundered, wondering why he was in a dark room, wearing dark glasses. Then the truth hit me in a flash brighter than the fluorescent lights.

He was blind.

"Can't you read?" The man came around the desk, his long supple fingers trailing the edge, showing him the way. " 'Private' means just that. The facilities are on either side of this door."

"I—uh—sorry."

"Fine. Get out."

My eyebrows lifted at the rude words spoken in that sexy growl of a voice. "I wasn't looking for the bathroom. I was looking for—"

I stopped. Was I looking for him? I wasn't sure.

"A quick fuck with the sax man. Not today, *chica,* I have a headache."

He crossed the short distance separating us more quickly than a man who couldn't see should. He also grabbed my arm with a minimum of bumbling and yanked me toward the door.

I stood my ground. I was at least four inches shorter than his six feet, and he probably outweighed me by thirty pounds, but I was in shape and determined. He couldn't budge me if I didn't want him to.

"John Rodolfo?" I asked, and he stopped tugging.

Staring at a point just to the left of my face, he demanded, "Who the hell wants to know?"

"Anne Lockheart."

He tilted his head, and I was struck anew by his beauty. Even with his eyes covered so I could discern neither their shape nor their color, he was handsome beyond imagining.

"Do I know you?" he asked.

"No."

He dropped my arm, but he didn't step back. "Let's try this again. What do you want if not a quickie on the desk?"

"I prefer my quickies against the wall, but not today and not with you."

His lips twitched. I wondered what he'd look like if he smiled, then shoved the notion aside. I doubted the expression ever crossed his face, and wasn't that sad?

Come to think of it, sad was how he'd seemed in the flare of the overhead lights in that instant before he'd sprung to his feet and come after me.

"You prefer women." He shrugged. "I could change your mind."

I snorted. A typical macho answer—as if one night with him could change anyone's sexual preferences.

"Not that it's any of your business, but I don't prefer women. What I prefer is to get down to business."

"Which is?"

I still clutched the photograph, but since it would do me no good with Rodolfo, I shoved it into the pocket of my jeans. "I'm searching for my missing sister."

Any trace of amusement vanished. "What does that have to do with me?"

"Someone sent me a photograph of her standing outside this jazz club."

"And you wanted to ask if I'd seen her." He spread his hands. "Can't help you. Haven't seen anyone in quite a long time."

"Her name was—*is* Katie. Katie Lockheart."

I'd made that slip before, talking about Katie as if she were dead. It was hard not to after three years.

I'd worked enough missing persons cases to know that not finding someone in the first thirty-six hours indicated, more often than not, that they wouldn't be found alive. I patted my pocket, praying the photograph meant the statistics were wrong in Katie's case.

"Never heard of her," Rodolfo said.

"That doesn't mean she wasn't here."

"True." He stood so close his breath stirred my hair. Even though the door was open, the lights were on, I felt crowded, lost, and a little bit trapped.

I inched back. "I spoke with the bartender, and I'd like to speak with your other employees—"

"There aren't any."

"Excuse me?"

"No other employees."

"But—"

"We haven't been open that long."

"How long?" I demanded.

If Rising Moon was new, that would date the photo, give me a better idea of when Katie might have been here.

"Less than a year."

"What was the place called before?"

"Same thing. I haven't done much except clean and stock."

"The outside hasn't changed? You didn't buy a new sign?"

"No."

The excitement rushed out of me like air from a punctured balloon.

"We've had a few cocktail waitresses but in the service business . . ." He shrugged. "They come and go. We're constantly shorthanded even though I offer a room as part of the salary. A lot of cheap apartments were washed away by Katrina."

"Anyone who's worked for you still in town, maybe working somewhere else?"

"Not that I know of, but that doesn't mean they aren't."

I sighed and withdrew the snapshot from my pocket, staring at the image of my sister. Katie had always been the golden child, literally. While my hair was an indistinct shade, hers sparkled like a sunbeam at dusk. My eyes were the hue of a mud puddle, hers seemed to reflect the deepest blue sea. Her nose was straight and cute, her skin clear and white. And her body . . . Let's just say that when God handed out bra sizes, he'd given Katie three quarters of mine.

You'd think I would hate someone so perfect, and sometimes I had. But along with all that beauty, Katie was genuinely sweet and a whole lot of fun. We'd played a thousand and one games of hide-and-seek as kids—and Katie always won, but I didn't mind because I'd loved being with her.

I'd become obsessed with the search, to the exclusion of almost everything else, but she was my little sister, and I was supposed to take care of her. I hadn't done a very good job.

"Shut off the light when you leave." Rodolfo turned sharply, as if he couldn't wait to be alone.

I'm not sure why, but I touched his shoulder, meaning to apologize for intruding, or maybe thank him for nothing. He spun around, his hand coming up and snatching my wrist before he yanked me against him.

I gave a little squeak of surprise, then my breath whooshed out as I slammed against his chest. I glanced into his face but all I saw was my reflection in the dark lenses that shaded his eyes. I looked pale, frightened, and somehow prettier than I knew myself to be.

"I—I'm sorry," I managed. "I startled you."

"I don't like to be touched," he murmured.

Which explained his annoyance when he'd thought I'd come for sex. What it didn't explain was the bulge in his silky black trousers, which pressed against my hip, the heat, the pulse revealing that while Rodolfo might not want to be touched, his body had other ideas.

He let me go with an annoyed shove, then stalked to his desk and sat down, effectively removing his lower body from view. But I knew what I'd felt.

Hot guy was attracted to me. I wasn't sure what to think about that.

2

I N DIRECT CONTRAST to my girlie-girl sister, I'd always been a tomboy. I'd liked sports instead of dolls, preferred outdoor games to books. Men were intimidated by my aggressiveness, turned off by my dishwater hair, my crooked nose, and my less than gorgeous face and body. I wasn't fat or thin, neither short nor tall. I was okay—average, plain.

I wore jeans a size too big, extra large men's dress shirts, always white so I could bleach out the stains that never failed to appear, even when I hadn't been near a single thing capable of causing them.

Not that I hadn't had boyfriends, relationships, sex. Just not lately. When Katie disappeared, I'd dedicated my life to finding her. I hadn't considered it might actually take my whole life, but if it did, then it did.

Just because I harbored a secret longing for the kind of love my parents had—one that never faltered despite numerous years and the incredible hardship of losing a child—didn't mean I was going to find it. Women like me usually ended up living with cats. I didn't much like cats, but that was beside the point.

Rodolfo was so out of my league it was scary. However—my gaze was drawn to his sunglasses—he didn't know that.

Still, why so interested so fast? He'd behaved as if he'd been behind bars for several years. I made a mental note to check his background.

"Well . . . thanks," I said.

"For manhandling you?"

He sounded disgusted with himself. I felt kind of bad. He hadn't scared me, much. In truth, I'd enjoyed the last few minutes more than a little. I wasn't the type of woman who brought out the beast in men. I hadn't realized I'd wanted to be until today.

"I'll live," I said dryly, and inched toward the door.

"The lights," he murmured.

My hand hovered near the wall. Why did it bother me to leave him in a darkness he couldn't see any more than he could see my face? I barely knew the man. If he chose to brood blindly in the dark, what was it to me?

I flicked the switch, shut the door, then stood in the hall, unable to walk away. The murmur of the crowd, the clink of the glasses, the warm-up squawks of a new band almost made me miss the sounds from the room marked PRIVATE.

Rodolfo was talking to himself.

I doubted he'd be happy if he found me hovering out here, so I turned and took one step toward the crowded, noisy bar before I stopped.

I didn't want to go through there again; I just wanted out. To my right lay the rear exit. I used it, slipping into a dark back alley strewn with garbage. Maybe the crowd would have been a better idea.

I reached for the door just as it clicked shut behind me. I tugged, but the thing was locked from the inside.

"Dammit." I wished I had a gun.

I'd been certified to carry a lethal weapon in Pennsylvania—I'd taken a class and everything—though I usually didn't bother. Searching for missing persons and sneaking around taking pictures of cheating spouses or fraudulent employees didn't call for a handgun.

I could have brought mine along, but the understandable hassle that went with transporting a firearm on a plane just wasn't worth it. Who knew I'd be creeping around a scary alleyway after dark?

And it was scary—chilly despite the blistering heat of the night, almost navy blue with flickers of silver from a moon too covered with clouds to discern a shape. The stench of rot lingered in the air and somewhere, not too far away, something with more feet than two skittered off.

I might be a tomboy; I might know how to shoot a gun; I could even beat the crap out of someone who outweighed me by thirty pounds—I'd taken self-defense the first time a nut took a swing at me on the job—but I was still woman enough to hate rats. Does anyone really like them?

I forced myself to walk with a confident swagger in the direction of a single dim streetlight. There had to be a way back to Frenchmen Street where I could catch a cab to the brightly lit neon center of Bourbon. Considering I was the antiparty girl, the notion shouldn't be so appealing.

I hadn't taken four steps when the blare of a trumpet and the beat of drums erupted from inside Rising Moon. I jumped a foot, spun toward the sound, and swore I'd caught a glimpse of an animal sliding along the side of the building.

Should I run? I doubted a rat would chase me.

But if that had been a rat, it was the hugest rat ever grown in Louisiana, maybe the world. What I'd seen had looked more like a dog—a big one.

Except a dog shouldn't make my heart thump so hard it threatened to burst from my chest. A dog wouldn't hang in the shadows, just out of sight, but rather run out to greet me, or at least try to beg a meal. Unless there was something wrong with it. Like rabies.

Which meant running—probably not a good idea.

Instead, I walked backward. Keeping my gaze fixed on the dark shadows that surrounded Rising Moon, I vowed never to leave home again without my gun.

The closer I got to the single streetlight, the darker those shadows became. The music spilled through the open windows and into the night, nearly drowning the thunderous beat of my heart. Nevertheless, I could have sworn I heard a growl simmering beneath.

I was spooked. That was all. I knew better than to walk alone in dark alleys. I'd just been so desperate to get away from Rodolfo's muttering that I'd taken the first out I could find. Which was foolish and impulsive—two adjectives that rarely applied to me. If Matt ever found out about this, he'd smack me upside the head, and I'd deserve it. Hey, if I lived to see him again, I'd smack myself.

At last the streetlight glared from directly above.

A small corridor between two buildings revealed a busy Frenchmen Street beyond. I headed in.

The structures surrounding me were so tall they blocked any trace of a glow; I could see nothing but a blotch of gray ahead. I hurried toward it, even as something entered the alley behind me, its bulk causing the shadows to dance. I couldn't hold myself back anymore; I ran.

In the tight, enclosed lane, the harsh rush of my own breath echoed in staccato rhythm with the muted thud of my tennis shoes against the pavement and the clunk of my backpack slung over one shoulder.

The end of the alley loomed, seemingly farther away the closer I got. The space between my shoulder blades burned, as if a bull's-eye had suddenly appeared—a place for the bullet to strike, the knife to plunge, or the wild beast to land, then fall with me to the ground.

I tried to glance around, as all stupid people do when they're chased, and my toe caught on a crease in the cement; there were a lot of them. I pitched forward; my hands shot out and smacked hard into the buildings on each side. A sliver plunged into my left palm, a ragged board scraped my right, but at least I didn't fall.

I burst into the open seconds later, sweaty, wild-eyed, and hyperventilating. Using a shaking hand to swipe my tangled, shoulder-length hair from my eyes, I lifted the other and hailed a passing cab.

If I climbed in a little too fast and nearly shut the door on my foot, the cabbie didn't seem to notice. "Where to?" he asked.

"Bourbon Street."

The moon burst from behind all the clouds, bright

and eerily silver. I threw a final glance at the alley, which was now lit up like Times Square.

Nothing was there.

I forced myself to face front as the cabbie swung a U-turn, the wail of a sax that sounded more like a howl rising toward the navy blue night.

3

W HERE CAN I get a room?" I asked.
The cabbie snorted and glanced in the rear-view mirror. "Mardi Gras parades are gonna start soon. There ain't a room to be had."

"Anywhere?" My voice rose.

He shrugged. "You can try."

He dumped me at the corner of Bourbon and St. Peter. I walked into the nearest hotel, where I heard the same thing. I asked for a recommendation and only got laughed at. Seemed I'd been more than foolish to come to New Orleans without a reservation this close to such a busy time of the year.

Wandering down Bourbon Street, I was fascinated in spite of myself. A lovely, gated restaurant, with gardens and outdoor tables, existed next to a theater that, from the appearance of their posters, didn't show Disney movies. A sports bar with a Dixieland band shared space with a shop that proudly displayed pornographic T-shirts. A gorgeous, nineteenth-century hotel—also booked to capacity—with a row of second- and third-floor terraces accessed by French doors, was positioned directly across the street from a strip joint.

The distinctive smell reflected the nature of the place—stale beer, fresh greenery, and rot.

I stopped at one of the bars, ordered a sandwich, showed Katie's picture, but no one knew her. I was never going to find her this way. I needed help.

The closest police station was on Royal Street, at the heart of the French Quarter.

I explained my situation to the first cop who asked, showed my ID and Katie's picture. A short while later I shook the hand of Detective Conner Sullivan.

"Have a seat." He indicated a chair on the opposite side of his desk.

Sullivan was NFL size—probably six feet five, about two fifty—with blond hair that appeared to have been styled by the Marines and brown eyes that did not jibe with his name or match his fair coloring.

I especially liked his tie, which sported a Harlequin clown tossing heart-shaped confetti. The contrast of the shorn hair, crisp suit, and flat cop eyes with the amusing tie intrigued me more than it should.

I'd spent the earlier part of the evening lusting after a slightly crazy, blind jazz musician; I didn't need to be curious about the great big, well-dressed detective. I had more important things to worry about.

"I'm looking for my sister." I laid Katie's picture on the desk. "Her name's Katie. Katherine Lockheart."

His large hands enveloped the snapshot. He stared at the photo for at least thirty seconds, and I started to think he might recognize her, then he slowly shook his head. "Haven't seen her, and I don't recognize the name."

I took a deep breath, swallowed my fear, and plunged ahead. "Any Jane Does?"

His gaze flicked from Katie to me. "Always. But none that match this." He returned the picture. "You'll want to check the hospitals."

I nodded. I knew the drill.

"Are you in missing persons?" I asked.

"Homicide." At my confused expression he continued. "We've had a lot of people go missing around here. Quite a few of them turned up dead. An equal amount haven't turned up at all."

"When you say a lot . . ."

"Dozens."

My eyes widened. "And you haven't been on CNN?"

"Not yet," he said dryly. "Though the dozens have been over a period of several years, lately the tally's increased to a disturbing level."

"How disturbing?"

"Double the usual amount of missing and dead in the past six months."

"You thinking serial killer?"

He blinked. "Why would you say that?"

"It didn't cross your mind?"

"Crisscrossed several times and settled in for a nice long stay. I just didn't figure anyone else would agree."

"Why not?"

"For one thing, the multiple methods of death."

"Multiple?"

"Yeah." His disappointed sigh said it all.

Serial killers followed a pattern, almost anally so.

They found a way to do the deed that worked for them, and they stuck to it.

"Some died by strangulation, others had knife wounds, a few gunshots. We've even had several deaths by animal attack."

"Which wouldn't be attributed to a serial killer."

He grunted as if he were unconvinced.

"Did you call the FBI?" I asked.

Two bright spots of color flared beneath his cheekbones. His Irish skin probably fried like bacon beneath the Louisiana sun.

"They sent an Agent Franklin. He went over the cases and decided we couldn't possibly have a serial killer."

"Because the methods of death were so dissimilar?"

"That and the victims were nothing alike—women, men, young, old."

Serial killers were also a bit anal about whom they killed, sticking to short, sassy blondes or big-boned redheads, basically anyone who reminded them of Mommy.

"My boss wasn't happy that I brought in the Feds on a case that was so obviously not Federal."

Bosses were funny that way. I was glad all over again that I didn't have one. I'd never played very well with others—except for Katie and sometimes not even her.

"I'm not supposed to be treating the murders as connected. But—" He shrugged.

"You've got a hunch."

"I've got something," he muttered. "I can't believe that we've suddenly had a rash of killings from a dozen different people, or that another dozen have suddenly disappeared without a trace. That's just too much of a coincidence."

People disappearing without a trace—that was right up my alley. I had to admit I was intrigued.

"You'd rather believe that one person has killed them all," I said, "in defiance of every truth we know about how mass murderers behave?"

"It'd be tidier."

My eyes drifted over his blue suit, pristine white shirt, and neatly knotted tie. I could see where tidy would appeal to him.

"So how come I was brought to you?" I asked.

"I've got an agreement with Missing Persons. We exchange information, and if someone comes in when they aren't here and I am, I take the report, then give them a copy."

"And vice versa?"

"You got it." Sullivan opened a drawer in his desk and yanked out a huge file. "I've been nosing around on my own. But lately, I haven't had any extra time to spare."

I wasn't sure why he was telling me this, except I'd been told I was easy to talk to. The trait was a handy one since a lot of my work involved trying to get information, a confession, a name.

"Why do you keep at this when there's no connection between the victims?" I asked.

He lifted his gaze to mine. "Because I found one."

I leaned forward. "What?"

"The majority of the victims were missing before at one time or another."

Silence settled between us, broken only by the distant ring of a telephone.

"Let me get this straight," I said, "the sudden influx of dead and missing were all previously missing?"

"Not all, but that may just be because no one noticed or no one reported it."

"Which still doesn't mean they're victims of a serial killer."

"No. But it is a connection."

"Did you tell your boss? The FBI?"

"I need more information before I make a fool of myself again." He stared at me for several seconds. "Would you like to look into this?"

"Me?"

"Everyone who's turned up dead or missing was missing before," he said slowly, as if speaking to a half-wit.

"I got that."

"Your sister is missing."

"She's been missing a long time."

"Seems she went missing here last. Like a whole lot of other people."

I frowned. I didn't like what he wasn't saying.

Sullivan shoved the file over to my side of the desk, opened it and pointed to a list of names. "These are the missing and the dead; next to them is the last place they were seen."

My eyes skimmed the page, then I straightened as if I'd been goosed.

"As you can see," Sullivan said, "quite a few got on that list after visiting Rising Moon."

4

I DON'T UNDERSTAND."

"It's not that hard, Miss Lockheart."

"Anne," I said absently, staring at the list, biting my lip, then glancing at the picture of Katie standing outside Rising Moon.

"Anne," Sullivan repeated. "People have disappeared, some have turned up dead, and the last place they were seen was that jazz club on Frenchmen."

"Coincidence."

"Coincidence is just another word for clue. Especially when *you* show up with a picture of a missing person in front of that cursed bar."

"Cursed?"

New Orleans *was* the voodoo capital of America. If a police detective who believed in curses existed, I had no doubt he'd work here.

"Figure of speech." His lip curled, revealing his disdain for the whole idea. "Although there are rumors the building's haunted. I swear everything is around here."

"That's common in very old cities."

He lifted one shoulder. "Something's weird there; I just don't know what. The place reopened under new ownership about six months ago."

My head went up as I recalled Rodolfo saying he'd been open less than a year, but six months . . .

Sullivan dipped his chin, answering the question I had yet to ask. "Just when the dead and the missing began to double."

"You can't . . ." I trailed off.

"What?"

"Think that Rodolfo is a serial killer."

"You met him?"

"Yes."

His lips tightened. "Just because he can play the sax and the piano—"

"Piano?" The image of those hands caressing the keys made me a little light-headed.

Sullivan's eyes narrowed. "He's a talented pretty boy, that doesn't mean he isn't dangerous."

"He's also blind. I doubt he's capable of chasing people around the city and murdering them."

"Maybe he has an accomplice."

"Because he's so damn gorgeous anyone would be happy to be his murder buddy?"

"You never know," Sullivan muttered. "I've seen crazier things than that."

I was certain he had. I'd dealt with my share of cops. They saw a lot, most of it bad. That Sullivan was even pursuing this when he'd been slapped down by both his boss and the FBI meant he cared. I had to admire that.

"Did you check him out?" I asked.

Sullivan gave me a long look. Of course he had.

"And?"

"He's a native of the city. Creole background."

I'd heard the word, but I wasn't exactly certain of its meaning.

Sullivan noted my confusion. "Creoles are descendents of Europeans born in this country. The Spanish and the French settled New Orleans. The place feels French, but a lot of the architecture is Spanish, and Rodolfo is an old Spanish name."

Which explained his slight accent, although he didn't seem to be speaking English as a second language.

"How far back were his Spanish ancestors?"

"A few branches on the family tree, but around here they like to keep the past alive."

Understandable when the past lived and breathed on every street corner.

"So Rodolfo's got family in New Orleans?"

Sullivan shook his head. "He's the last of them according to the records. He left years ago, before he even graduated from high school."

"Why?"

"No one knows. Probably the usual stuff—his parents didn't understand him; he wanted to be a rock star."

"Where did he go?"

"He drifted, which made it damn hard to find out what he's been up to. I tried to track his Social Security number—"

"And were there a rash of unexplained deaths or disappearances in any city where he lived or worked?"

Sullivan lifted a brow. "You've done this before."

"A little."

"I couldn't find a trace of him. He didn't file a tax return until last year."

That *was* odd, but not unheard of. Especially for a runaway who'd probably lived on the streets.

"You gonna call the IRS?" I asked.

"Maybe."

"I'm sure Rodolfo was working for cash, playing sets in bars, getting paid under the table. People do it all the time."

"Still illegal."

"Boy Scout," I muttered, ignoring the glare he sent my way. "How did he lose his sight?"

"Couldn't find anything on that either."

Strange. The loss must have been caused by an accident or an illness, maybe even a tumor. Incidents like that would leave a paper trail, Somewhere.

Unless he'd been too down and out to go to a doctor and that's why he'd ended up blind in the first place.

"Will you help me?" Sullivan asked.

Since the detective was right about Katie fitting the profile, such that it was, and I didn't have any more leads, or any pressing business in Philly—

"Can I take the file?"

Sullivan grinned; the expression made me realize he was years younger than I'd first thought—late twenties instead of mid-thirties. Not that it mattered.

"I'll make copies." He disappeared into a back room, and seconds later the whir of a machine drifted out.

I'd agreed to stay, but *where* would I stay? Maybe Sullivan had a suggestion.

When he returned, he tossed the file onto the desk, and the sheet with the list of names spilled onto the floor. As I reached down to retrieve it, my eyes stuck on the repetition of the words "Rising Moon," almost as if the place were calling to me.

Rising Moon was short handed; I had hands. The salary included a room, which I needed. And, conveniently, people were disappearing from there in droves. I should really keep an eye on things.

I doubted Sullivan would agree that I needed to be that close, so I just wouldn't tell him about it.

How crazy could Rodolfo be? He was running a successful business; he had employees, customers. If he talked to himself in the dark, not my problem.

Besides, we'd already established that Rodolfo couldn't be the killer, but there might be someone at Rising Moon who was.

"How can I reach you?" Sullivan asked.

I scribbled my cell phone number on a corner of a page, tore it off and handed it to him, my mind already moving ahead, trying to figure out how I'd get a job in a jazz club when I knew nothing about jazz, and I'd never been a waitress or a bartender in my life.

I left the police station after promising to stay in touch. Once outside I relished the coolness of the air just before dawn.

I had to call my parents, make up something. I couldn't tell them I was investigating a possible serial killer. They'd flip about that even before I told them why.

Until I knew for certain Katie was a victim, I'd keep my mouth shut. However, I did need them to send me more clothes.

I glanced at my watch—five A.M.—if I added the time difference they'd be up in half an hour. I'd just check out the Café du Monde until then.

By the time I reached the café near the river, exhaustion threatened. Not that I hadn't pulled some all-nighters in my life, but everything that had happened since yesterday—the envelope with Katie's picture, the travel, the emotional ups and downs—had combined to make me dizzy with fatigue.

I discovered chicory coffee and beignets cleared that right up. By the time I ran up the staircase to the elevated walkway near the river, I was wired. I gazed at the sleepy city and wondered what had possessed the founders to build in the crescent-shaped bend of the Mississippi. Back then the place had to have been a mosquito-infested swamp.

My mother answered on the second ring, as if people called at dawn every morning. Of course, since Katie, every phone call could be "the call."

My choice of career hadn't thrilled my upper-middle-class parents. My dad was an accountant; my mother had been a nurse. Once Katie was born, she'd stayed home and she'd never gone back. I'd think our family was lost in the fifties, except in that gilded decade daughters didn't often disappear and women didn't become private investigators.

"Mom, hi—" I began.

"Where are you?"

Sometimes I swore the woman was psychic. Then again, they did have caller ID.

"New Orleans," I answered, and quickly told her as little as possible.

"Anne, you don't even know if the girl in the picture is Katie," my mother said.

"Yes I do."

"Why would someone send you a photo and not tell you who they were or why they took it?" my father asked. As usual he'd gotten on the extension the instant my mother said hello.

"I'm sure the person saw Katie's picture on a Web site or a poster and was surprised to remember her face from their vacation pictures."

My father grunted, as unconvinced of that as I was.

"Not knowing when the photo was taken means it could date from before she disappeared and not after," my mother pointed out.

"But Katie never went to New Orleans."

"You're certain of that?"

"Aren't you?" I demanded. "She'd just graduated from high school when she disappeared. Did she turn up missing at any other time I'm not aware of?"

"Only the one time," my mother whispered.

I wanted to smack myself for upsetting her, even as I fought not to break into a happy dance.

"Don't you see?" I said excitedly. "The picture had to have been taken after Katie disappeared, and that means she was alive longer than the last night she was seen."

I hadn't realized until right then that I'd been se-cretly afraid Katie was at the bottom of the Delaware River.

"Annie."

My mother was the only one who called me that. I was not the "Annie" type. I didn't have curly red hair, couldn't sing a note, and in my opinion the sun did not always come out tomorrow. Tomorrow was usually a day full of clouds.

"You need to give this up now," she continued.

"Give what up?"

"Your obsession with finding Katie. She's gone, honey. She isn't ever coming back."

I collapsed on one of the benches and stared at the Mississippi flowing peacefully by as if mocking the sudden gurgling, coffee-laced turmoil in my gut.

My parents had given up. They thought Katie was dead.

"You've changed so much since we lost her," my mother murmured.

"Haven't we all?"

Before, my parents had seemed young. They'd laughed during meals, danced beneath the stars on warm summer nights, there hadn't been a speck of gray in their hair.

Afterward, they'd aged, almost overnight. They never went anywhere, just in case Katie called. Later it was just in case someone found her. Lately . . .

Lately they'd started going places again. They'd even taken a vacation to Florida last month. Why hadn't I understood what that meant?

"I need you to FedEx me some clothes," I said, ignoring what I didn't want to hear. "Warm weather stuff, okay?"

"How long are you staying?" my father asked.

"I'll let you know."

"You should come home, Anne."

"I can't."

Silence drifted over the line. Finally he murmured, "Be careful."

I wasn't sure I could do that either.

"Where should I send the clothes?" My mother scrabbled about for paper and a pen. She might despair of me, but she'd always be there for me. Just as Katie had always been there.

Until she wasn't.

5

T HE ONLY ADDRESS I knew was the one for Rising
Moon, which I'd written on the back of the photo.
I recited it to my mother before we said, "I love you"
and "Good-bye."

The sun spread down the streets ahead of me like a
golden carpet. Soon heat would rise from the pavement.
Though Frenchmen Street had no doubt been rocking
until only a few hours before, plenty of people still
strolled the sidewalks.

The big windows on the front of Rising Moon were
dark and uninviting. What had been sparkling and lively
last night had turned dull and quiet, the unlit neon sign
nothing but empty glass. Las Vegas must look like a real
dump in the daytime.

Figuring the place would be empty until midafternoon at least, I almost went back to the Quarter. I'd
peer in the shop windows and see if I could find a few
cooler things to wear until Federal Express arrived.

Then a flicker of movement from beyond the glass had me reaching for the door. The knob turned beneath my hand. The scent of stale beer and old smoke wafted over me. I wrinkled my nose and went inside.

"Not open till five."

The same buff bartender lifted chairs onto the tables. The floor was littered with cigarette butts and sticky from too many spilled cocktails.

"I didn't come for a drink." I grabbed a nearby broom and began to sweep everything loose into a pile. "I came for a job."

He didn't pause, didn't even glance my way as he continued to lift chairs at a brisk pace. "I thought you were searching for your sister."

"I need a place to stay and something to eat while I'm doing it."

He stopped lifting chairs; I stopped sweeping crap. "Ever worked in a bar?"

"Nope."

"You're hired."

I blinked. "What?"

"Mardi Gras is breathing down our necks; we need help. You got a brain; you'll catch on."

I thought that might be a compliment, but I wasn't sure. "I'm Anne," I said. "Anne Lockheart."

"I'm King."

"Of what?"

"That's my name."

I wanted to ask if King was his first name or his last but figured that would be impolite.

He smiled at my obvious confusion. "My mama liked Elvis."

"Oh, *the* King."

"Right." King tilted his head. "You want the job?"

"Don't I have to talk to the owner first?" Not that I wanted to or anything.

"He don't have much to do with the day-to-day nonsense. That's what I'm here for."

"When do I start?"

King indicated the broom. "You just did."

IN TRUTH, I didn't have to work until that night around eight P.M. when things got busy. King ran the bar. I would take drink orders for the tables. How hard could it be?

"Minimum wage, plus tips," he said, as he led me upstairs. "And this."

King pushed open a door to reveal a single room: bed, chair, nightstand, dresser; the empty closet gaped without a door. Though the color scheme screamed mid-seventies—gold and olive green—at least it was clean.

"Bathroom's here." He crossed the hardwood floor, not an area rug to be had, and flicked on a light. Bright white tile, a claw-footed tub framed by what appeared to be a brand-new shower curtain.

"Second floor's empty but for you right now. If we're lucky, more help will stumble in. If not, I'll get temp workers from out of town for Fat Tuesday."

"What about you?" I asked. "I thought a room was part of the deal."

"I work so much that when I get away, I need to get away."

I could relate. My apartment in Philly was above my office. Talk about a one-track life.

I was tempted to ask where John Rodolfo lived, but I didn't want King to think I was a groupie.

"You trust me enough to let me live here alone?"

"You plannin' on stealin' from us, *cher*?"

My eyebrows lifted at the casual endearment. "Uh, no."

"Didn't think so. 'Sides, I take the money with me. You want to steal booze, it's your headache."

"What about food?"

"No kitchen. All the soft drinks and coffee you want are free for the askin'. No alcohol when you're working."

"Fine by me." I wasn't much of a drinker. Never had managed to acquire a taste for it.

"Otherwise," he continued, "you're in New Orleans. We got food on the street corners, at the grocery store. You can't throw a stick and not hit someone cooking."

"I've heard that."

"You'll want to get some sleep. You'll be on till the place clears out. Could be early or late dependin' on how much the folks like the music."

The idea of lying down on that bed, drawing the shades, checking out for a while, was enormously appealing, as was the allure of a shower and a change of clothes.

"Are there different bands every night?" I asked.

King nodded. "Locals mostly. Play for tips."

"That's it?"

"New Orleans has always been more about the music than the money."

"Which musicians bring in the most customers?"

"The crowd depends on Johnny."

Johnny? Rodolfo looked the least like a Johnny of any Johnny I'd ever known.

"If he decides to play," King said, "people come in off the street after just a few notes, word gets around, other bars clear out—"

"He's that good?"

King lifted one bushy black brow. "You couldn't feel it?"

If I hadn't heard Rodolfo play the night before I wouldn't have known what King meant. But I *had* heard him and I *had* felt it. A tug from deep inside, a part of me that recognized the beat and wanted more, a pull that was almost sexual. No wonder women followed him into the "private" room for a quickie.

"Sometimes it seems like he's possessed by the music," King murmured, "or maybe it's just the music possessing everyone else."

What a strange thing to say.

"You seem to know him well," I ventured.

His gaze flicked to mine, and I was struck again by the oddly light shade of his eyes. "Johnny and I are two of a kind."

I AWOKE TO a darkness so complete I wasn't quite sure where I was. Then someone laughed, a drum went *ba-bump*, and a horn gave a tentative toot.

Rising Moon was open for business.

With all that noise, I doubted I'd be doing much sleeping during normal sleeping hours. But beggars couldn't be choosers, and by next week my days and nights would be all turned around anyway.

Which was probably why the last person who'd lived

in this room had purchased curtains so heavy they blocked out every scrap of light. There'd been a lot of day sleeping going on.

I showered, pleased to discover the water pressure didn't suck, then pulled out a change of clothes, which were pretty much the same clothes I'd had on before, only cleaner. After twisting my hair into a French braid, I was ready. Never had worn makeup; I didn't own any. Putting paint on my face was like putting paint on a two-story Colonial—still the same old, same old underneath—a little color couldn't change the structure.

The stairs outside my room spilled out near the rear door, which stood open tonight. The scent of something spicy and dark, almost burned but not quite, made my mouth water. I hadn't eaten since the Café du Monde.

I didn't have time now, but for a minute I just took in the scent, so tantalizing it was almost a taste. I had to force myself not to follow my nose like a cartoon dog floating on the trail of a delicacy.

The band of the evening played a slow, earthy tune and I swayed with the rhythm. My eyes closed; a breeze blew in through the screen door, both cool and warm at the same time, smelling of sun and water and midnight.

I heard a shuffle out there in the dark, and my eyes snapped open. I peered through the screen, even though common sense shouted for me to retreat to the busy, loud area where all the people were. Too bad one of my best, and worst, traits had always been curiosity.

What was out there? A rat? A dog? Or something more dangerous?

The glow of a cigarette flared; steamy white smoke

trailed toward the sky, and twin moons appeared in the center of Rodolfo's sunglasses as he turned in my direction.

"What are you doing out here in the dark?" I blurted.

"It's dark?"

Okay, that had been a really stupid question. What difference did the dark make to him, and I could see very well that he was smoking. But—

Where had he come from? At first glance, I'd seen nothing out there but the night.

He took another drag from his cigarette, one of those long, slim, antique-looking cigarillo types I imagined plantation owners had smoked as they watched their slaves toil away in the tobacco fields.

"Smoking is bad for you," I said.

He actually laughed. One quick bark that didn't sound amused. "*Chica,* the whole world is bad for me."

Rodolfo continued to stare in my direction, the flat reflection of the moon in his glasses unnerving. "What were you doing upstairs?" he murmured.

For an instant I wondered how he had known I was up there, but then, my mother always told me I came down steps like an elephant.

"I live there, work here."

He tossed the cigarette with a lazy flick, the burning tip sailing downward like a scarlet falling star. Though his footsteps thumped slowly against the pavement, he reached the door so fast I didn't have time to escape. Not that I had anywhere to go.

"Why would you want to work here?"

"Money? The room? Your charming personality?"

He ignored my attempt at humor. It hadn't been much of an attempt.

"You should go home."

"I am home. For now."

"I meant go back wherever it is you're from."

"You don't want me here?"

I'd meant to be sarcastic, but the question came out sounding anything but. What I'd sounded like was a lost, frightened little girl, and lost, frightened little girls often disappeared.

Rodolfo took a deep breath, almost as if he were smelling me. Maybe it was just an intensification-of-the-senses thing—he couldn't see me, so he smelled me? It should have been weird, but what it was, was exciting.

"What I want—" he said tightly, and took a step closer.

I stepped back, and he cocked his head, pausing. When he spoke again, his voice was normal—or as normal as that sexy voice ever got. "I want you gone."

Funny, I didn't think that was really what he wanted, and despite his strange behavior, I didn't want that either. Everything about him fascinated me.

"King said he was in charge," I began.

"Oh, really?" Rodolfo crossed the short distance to the screen door and, after minimal fumbling, opened it and strode past me into the tavern. As soon as the crowd saw him they began to cheer. He raised a casual hand but didn't stop, going straight to the bar and waiting for King.

Rodolfo said a few words; King said several back. I inched closer.

"We need her," King snapped.

"No we don't."

"Trust me, Johnny, the girl will be useful."

"You're crazy," Rodolfo muttered, then turned and headed for the performance corner amid backslapping and welcoming shouts.

I didn't understand what was going on. Rodolfo seemed both attracted and repelled by me. Why, when he couldn't even see me? Maybe it had something to do with my smell.

King beckoned, and I met him at the end of the bar.

"Whad you say to him?" he asked.

"What did *he* say?"

King glanced in Rodolfo's direction. "He said your voice calls to him."

"Is that bad?" I asked.

"For Johnny it is." King glanced at Rodolfo with a worried expression as he began to play the piano.

"Why?"

King walked away without answering.

I stared at John Rodolfo and remembered last night. Him in the dark on one side of the door, me in the hallway listening to him talk to himself.

Maybe he heard a lot of voices. Maybe they told him to do things I didn't want to know about. Like kill people.

Suddenly leaving didn't sound half bad.

King shoved a notepad and pencil into my hand. I stared at them for a moment, then lifted my gaze. "I thought I was fired."

"Haven't even started yet."

"But—" I flicked a glance toward Rodolfo, who was

now doing something to the piano that made me think of tangled sheets and sultry Louisiana nights.

"Johnny might own the place, but he don't own me. Besides." King shrugged. "We got no one else."

"Gee, thanks," I said. "What do I do?"

"Write down orders. I fix the drinks. You take them back."

"That's it?"

"I tell you how much they owe. You get it. And remember whose drink is whose. They like that."

The evening progressed. I'd figured I wouldn't have too tough of a time remembering which person got which drink, but when you're trying to write down one thing while someone else is telling you another, people are laughing, chattering, music is playing, and you've got three other tables waving at you . . . it's easy to forget.

I started to write short descriptions next to their drink. Vodka tonic—red shirt. Miller Lite—blue eyeshadow. That worked pretty well.

What didn't work was showing Katie's picture. Some people barely looked, some refused to. They were on vacation; it was almost Mardi Gras, and they didn't want to hear about missing sisters.

Laissez les bons temps rouler!

At any rate, no one in Rising Moon that night would cop to seeing her. The more I thought about it, the dumber the showing of the picture seemed to be. What were the chances I'd stumble across someone who'd met Katie?

Pretty damn slim. Of course, that didn't mean I was going to stop doing it.

Rodolfo played a long time. First the piano, then the sax; he sat in with one band and stayed for another.

The crowd swelled. Everyone was thirsty. My ancient athletic shoes, chosen for comfort rather than support, were not suitable for the job. My feet ached all the way up to my eyeballs.

I was so busy I didn't see him leave. But suddenly the crowd thinned, and when I glanced at the performing corner, a woman played the piano and there was no saxophone to be had.

6

THAT NIGHT I fell into bed exhausted and was asleep as soon as my head hit the pillow, only to come awake with a gasp and a start in that darkest of hours just before the sun appears on the horizon.

My heart was thudding so hard my straining ears could hear nothing but *ba-bump, ba-bump, ba-bump.* What, if anything, had woken me?

I'd lived alone in Philadelphia; I shouldn't be freaking out about being the only living soul inside Rising Moon.

Except Philly was home. New Orleans was a strange place, with an emphasis on strange.

Something scraped across the floor above me. I sat up; my neck creaked when I lifted my chin toward the ceiling and squinted. I don't know what I expected to see. I didn't have X-ray vision.

Holding my breath, I waited, but I didn't hear anything else.

Still, something had woken me, made me nervous,

even in dreamland. I wasn't an easily spooked person, but I doubted I'd be able to sleep again until I made certain all I'd heard was a mouse, or a loose shutter, or the wind rippling through the eaves.

A few moments later, dressed and creeping barefoot up the back steps, I wished like hell for a flashlight, but there hadn't been one anywhere in my room.

A scrabble, like fingernails against wood, sounded just ahead.

"Hello?" I called.

Something shot down the stairwell, something dark and small that screeched like the banshees of legend. I flattened myself to the wall as it flew by.

Only when it had disappeared into the well of black below did the sound the beast had made register.

"A cat," I managed. "Only a cat."

Thunk.

My eyes lifted. "Or not."

A cool breeze seemed to swirl in from nowhere, turning the sweat on my body to ice, and along with the breeze traveled an all too human whisper.

I'd never believed in ghosts; I was too practical for that. Of course, I'd never been confronted with one either. Seeing has always meant believing in my book.

Sullivan had referred to Rising Moon as "that cursed bar." He'd said there were rumors the place was haunted, though from his manner he didn't believe it. I hadn't either.

However, standing in the whispering night all alone, I was forced to rethink my opinion.

I had to know the truth, so I took the remaining steps to the door at the top, turned the knob and walked in.

Despite my wide and staring eyes, I saw nothing, the darkness so complete it surrounded me like a velvet curtain. In the depths, something growled.

I flung out my arm, fingers groping along the wall. One flick and light glared down on the tiny room from the single bare bulb in the ceiling.

Near the heavily shrouded window stood a bed. In it a figure tossed and turned, moaning, muttering.

John Rodolfo seemed caught in the grips of a nightmare. He'd thrown off the covers; he wasn't wearing any clothes.

I couldn't help but see; I wasn't blind. I couldn't help but admire; I wasn't dead.

His skin glistened with a fine sheen of sweat, which only emphasized the rippling muscles and smooth olive skin. For a musician he sported some mighty nice pecs and a decent set of abs. Had he been bench-pressing pianos?

Embarrassed to have walked in on him like this, I started to back out of the room, but he continued to thrash and moan as if in horrible pain and I hesitated.

I couldn't leave him like this. I'd had nightmares—a lot since Katie disappeared—and I knew I'd rather be woken than forced to finish one.

"Rodolfo?"

The only response was another moan.

"John?" I spoke a little louder as I stepped a bit farther into the room.

"No!" he shouted, thrashing and straining upward as if someone were holding him down.

Now what? The sound of my voice seemed to be making him worse.

I stood in the doorway, uncertain. Should I shake him awake? That seemed forward, even for me. I bit my lip, shuffled my feet, sighed, and he stopped thrashing, turning his face toward the door. "Anne?"

I considered escaping to my room and saying nothing, but that would be cowardly, and I refused to allow it.

"Sorry," I said. "I heard a noise. I didn't realize you lived here."

He sat up, reaching for the sheet, then drawing it across his lap. The motion only caused my gaze to slide there ahead of the white cotton, and I got an eyeful of something else that was mighty nice. I needed to get laid—soon—before I did something, or someone, really stupid.

"I—uh—" He put a hand to his forehead; he wasn't wearing his sunglasses. This was the first time I'd seen him without them, and he looked younger, even with his eyes shut.

Strange. Why keep them shut? Unless—

Before I could stop it, my mind flashed on an image of him opening his eyes to reveal gaping sockets. I winced and turned away. Just because the man couldn't see me didn't mean I should stare at him while he was undressed and dopey from sleep.

"I get headaches," he said. "I come up here to lie down."

"Migraines?" I glanced back as he patted the nightstand, found his glasses, slipped them on.

"Mmm."

I needed to leave; the poor man was recovering from a migraine. I'd never had them, but my mother did and whenever she woke up she was woozy from the pain if not the meds.

Nevertheless, I found myself moving closer. "Have you always had migraines?"

"No." His lips turned up ruefully. "They're a recent development."

Ding-ding-ding! A head injury might cause blindness, which would also explain the headaches.

"Did a trauma cause you to lose your sight?"

He choked, the sound one of surprise and . . . amusement? "Trauma?" he repeated. "I guess you could call it that."

I waited for him to be more specific, and when he remained silent, I asked. I couldn't help myself. "What happened?"

"Nothing I can explain," he muttered.

I opened my mouth, shut it again. I couldn't make myself keep pressing him. I guess there was a limit to how far even my curiosity would take me.

"Will the headaches go away eventually?" I asked.

"Not if they're penance for my sins."

"What?"

"A joke. Never mind."

He got to his feet, wrapping the sheet around his hips and securing it with a quick, practiced twist. Then he padded to the sink, splashed his cheeks with cold water and slicked his hair back so sharply droplets of liquid flew, pattering against the ancient wooden floorboards like rain.

"Does it make you uncomfortable to be alone with me?" he asked.

I lifted my gaze from the floor to his face. The

sunglasses shrouded his eyes. Whoever had coined the phrase "windows to the soul" had known what they were talking about. Not being able to see Rodolfo's eyes was really starting to bug me. The mirrored glasses made it seem like he had no soul.

I let out a short, derisive laugh—at both my thoughts and his question. "No," I said. "And even if it did, this is your place. You can stay here if you want to."

"I have an apartment on St. Ann. I don't use it much. It's easier . . ." his voice trailed off.

I understood. He worked here, why traipse several city blocks, especially when getting there couldn't be all that easy for him? The convenience of this third-floor room had to far outweigh any need he had to get away.

"I should thank you for letting me stay," I said.

"With Mardi Gras coming up." He shrugged, the muscles in his arms and chest flexing, rippling beneath the skin like smoothly flowing water. I hoped I wasn't drooling, but at least he couldn't see me if I was. "Beggars can't be choosers, *oui*?"

His use of French startled me a bit. "I thought your ancestors were Spanish."

"I am what I am. My family is long gone." He turned away. "Everyone I ever knew here is dead."

The desolation in his voice called to me. I understood loss and grief, the nostalgia that both helps and hurts. Which was the only reason I crossed the room, reached out and touched him.

He'd warned me not to. Why couldn't I learn?

At the first hint of flesh against flesh he spun so fast my eyes detected only a blur. His hands closed over my elbows, his palms so hot I flinched at the sensation if not the pressure as his fingers tightened just a little too much.

"John," I began, and he cursed, the words a jumble of Spanish and French, muttered too low to be understood even if I'd ever been any good at either language.

I stared at my reflection in his glasses; I didn't look as frightened as I felt. Once again I appeared prettier than I was, both alluring and enticing. No wonder he kissed me.

My mouth opened on a gasp as he yanked me onto my toes and covered my lips with his. He didn't hesitate; he took; he ravaged; I liked it.

I was not the type of woman men devoured. Or at least I hadn't been before today. Today John Rodolfo kissed me as if he'd been waiting to do so his entire life.

He savored my mouth as if he planned to memorize every inch. His teeth scraped my bottom lip, the slight pain a bloom of pleasure even before he laved the tiny hurt, then suckled. His grip on my arms gentled; I didn't run away. Instead, I sighed, surrendering.

The short, neat mustache and goatee were both sharp and soft, a new sensation that tempted me to rub my cheek against his face—and several other places.

The sheet slithered to the floor, and I barely noticed, my mind and body centered where we touched. My skin tingled as if static electricity flowed from him to me. I'd never felt so alive.

He tasted like midnight. He smelled of summer rain. His hair beneath my fingers was slick and wet and far too short. I couldn't help it; I ran my hand from his neck over his shoulder, down his chest, then lower still.

Right before I reached his belly he stumbled back, bending to grab the lost sheet, then covering himself, though nothing was going to disguise the erection that made a pup tent of white cotton just below his hips.

He cleared his throat. "I shouldn't have done that."

"I didn't mind."

His head went up. "This is a bad idea."

"What is?"

"You. Me."

"Seemed like a terrific idea from my end."

"There are things you don't know—" He shoved his fingers through his hair, pausing when he encountered the stubbly strands.

I opened my mouth to ask "What things?" then shut it again as the bright light from the ceiling bulb hit Rodolfo's raised hand.

A thin white scar bisected his wrist.

My gaze flicked to his left hand, twisted in the sheet around his waist. I couldn't see if there was a corresponding line there, but it didn't matter. One was enough to reveal the truth.

Once upon a time, John Rodolfo had tried to kill himself.

7

SUDDENLY I WANTED to get as far away from the man as I could. Not only were there things I didn't know about him, there were things he didn't know about me. For instance, I wasn't working here out of the goodness of my heart. I was trying to discover if someone at Rising Moon was a serial killer.

Uneasy, my gaze flicked again to his wrist, then away. What could have enticed him to suicide? Too many murders?

I doubted it. Serial killers liked to kill. They felt no remorse. That was why they were *serial* killers. They killed again and again and again until someone stopped them.

I had enough problems in my life. I didn't need to be involved with a man who had a death wish—even if he kissed like the devil and looked like an angel. I let my gaze trail over his well-trimmed goatee and perfect, half-naked body.

Or maybe it was the other way around.

"You're probably right," I said, backing toward the door. "Bad idea. Employer, employee. All sorts of trouble."

One black eyebrow lifted above the sunglasses. "I'm so happy you see it my way."

His voice was cool and sarcastic. If I hadn't just been swapping spit with the man I'd think he had no emotions at all.

But I had been and he did. I'd felt the desperation in his embrace, tasted the lust on his tongue. He'd wanted me as much as I'd wanted him, and he'd also been frightened of it. Wanting someone that badly for no reason at all wasn't quite sane.

So who was crazier? Him? Or me?

"Will you be all right?" I asked.

"No."

The question had been a courtesy. Kind of like asking, "How are you?" upon meeting someone. You didn't really want to know.

"Never mind." Rodolfo waved a hand toward the door. "Go away."

That was more the answer I'd expected, yet still I hesitated.

"I've been alone for eons, *chica,*" he said softly. "I prefer it."

I imagined year upon solitary year in the dark, thinking, brooding. No wonder he talked to himself.

"I need to sleep a while longer." He touched his fingers to his forehead.

How could I have forgotten his migraine? I suppose being kissed senseless was a good excuse—or maybe a poor one.

"I could bring you some aspirin."

"The only thing that helps is sleep." Rodolfo returned to the bed. "Turn out the lights. Shut the door."

He reclined, removing his glasses, setting them on the nightstand with nary a fumble, keeping his eyes closed the entire time.

He'd dismissed me. Slightly annoyed, I did as he asked. Or should I say as he'd ordered? There were times he reminded me of some lord of the manor, ordering his servants about, expecting them to obey without question.

My watch read five-thirty A.M. I was exhausted. Maybe I could catch a few more hours of rest myself.

As I hurried toward my room, one of the doors along the corridor creaked open, and I paused. No one else was supposed to be in the building.

I looked up. Or so I'd thought.

I stepped closer to the gaping doorway. "Hello?"

No one answered. No kidding. Did I expect an intruder to pipe up and say, "I was hiding in preparation to kill you, but since you caught me, never mind?"

Before I could think about how dumb the action was, I opened the door all the way to the wall, just in case someone was lurking behind it, and flicked on the light.

The room was empty, musty, and unoccupied as promised. However, a single candle glowed in the corner.

I hadn't lit it. I peered at the ceiling. I also kind of doubted Rodolfo had. Then again . . .

I crept closer, planning to blow out the flame— definitely wasn't safe to just leave it here—and I noticed several things.

The wax had melted into a glistening puddle, which indicated the wick had been lit hours ago. The candle was set on a low table and surrounded by stones, feathers, tiny carvings—a dog, a cat, a pig, and a chicken. If I didn't know better, I'd think I'd stumbled on a child's playroom. Except there was something vaguely unsettling—both sinister and saintly—about the whole thing.

The low table, the candle, made me think altar, while the other items brought to mind—

Voodoo?

Maybe.

I knew next to nothing about the religion; this could be it. Or something else entirely.

Though my unease increased as I neared the candle, I forced myself to cross the room, lean over and blow.

Poof. Out went the flame.

Then I saw the dark, wet streaks marring the wood surface of the table. In the bright light, they resembled blood.

"Can't be," I muttered, and the way my voice shook made me realize it could be, probably would be.

I should call the police, but Rising Moon wasn't my place, and what if, in New Orleans, an altar like this was commonplace? What if it was for protection or success or even to welcome Mardi Gras?

I backed away, resolving then and there to show King before I did anything foolish. It wasn't as if the altar could walk away. Slowly I shut the door behind me and headed for my room.

The candle and all the trimmings would still be there come morning.

• • •

EXCEPT THEY WEREN'T. I don't know why I was surprised.

I got up as soon as I heard a door close downstairs, threw on my now crusty clothes and left my room, stopping at the door of the one where I'd seen the altar the night before.

Nothing was there.

Just to be sure, I checked every other room too, even my own.

Zilch.

Now who was slightly crazy?

I considered telling King what I'd seen, but what good would it do? The events of last night had begun to take on a surreal quality, including the embrace with John Rodolfo. Maybe I'd imagined everything.

I kept what I'd seen to myself. For all I knew King could be a serial killer—though the odds were against it. For some reason no one can quite figure out, serial killers tended to be white, middle-aged men.

However, he *could* be the owner of the altar. If the thing was religious, it was none of my business. If it was sinister, I didn't want to know.

I should probably tell Sullivan, though without proof that the altar had ever existed . . . why bother?

Without a burning need to see King, I returned to bed. When I awoke about midafternoon, a Federal Express box sat outside my door full of lovely, clean clothes. I took a shower and donned some denim shorts and a T-shirt. Then I grabbed Sullivan's file, and without even checking to see if anyone was puttering around Rising Moon, I headed for an Internet café I'd spotted on Chartres Street.

Set back from the main thoroughfare, the tables within a walled garden were occupied by an assortment of locals and tourists. Inside, next to the coffee bar, a long, narrow room was full of computers.

I paid for a latte, a bran muffin, and an hour of Internet use, then got down to business.

I did my usual search of names, background, credit information. I found nothing that Sullivan hadn't already.

As I sipped my coffee, I took out the list of victims, complete with the locations of the disappearances and deaths, as well as the dates. There was something about the dates of the earlier victims that bugged me. They seemed to occur at regularly scheduled intervals.

I pulled up an astrological Web site and typed several of them in.

"Ding-ding, we have a winner," I murmured. People seemed to disappear and die more often than not on the nights of a full moon.

That really wasn't so odd. Ask anyone who works the night shift anywhere and you'll learn that a full moon equals crazy time. I wouldn't be surprised if a lot of serial killers preferred to do their work beneath its glow. I had a bad feeling that a full moon made blood shine more brightly.

Out of curiosity I continued to type in dates. As they became more recent, the pattern fell apart. Six months ago, when the murder/disappearance rate doubled, only a few had occurred on a full moon night.

And there went my theory.

Nevertheless, I typed "full moon" and "New Orleans" into the search engine. What I got back was—

"Voodoo." That figured.

"You interested in voodoo?"

I lifted my head. The girl who'd waited on me at the counter—her nametag read MAGGIE—was stuffing empty cups into the trash and sterilizing abandoned computer kiosks.

She didn't appear a day over sixteen, though I figured she must be. Her hair had been dyed an impossible shade of black, which matched the liner rimming her light blue eyes. She'd be pretty if she didn't try so hard not to be. I didn't much care for the tattoo of a snake on her skinny pale arm either, but it wasn't my arm.

I glanced at my watch. My time was almost up.

"I don't know much about it," I said.

"I do."

I straightened. Wasn't that convenient?

"There are several voodoo shops in town," she continued, "some are just for the tourists, some are the real thing."

"The real thing?"

My skepticism must have been evident in my voice because Maggie stopped cleaning and met my gaze. "Voodoo is a legitimate religion. There's an initiated priestess with a shop and a temple on Royal Street, though she hasn't been in as much since she had the baby."

"The voodoo priestess had a baby," I repeated dumbly.

Maggie's lips quirked. "About eight months ago.

A boy. All his fingers and toes—not a scale or a tail to be found."

"Ha-ha," I said, really hoping she was kidding.

"There are a few other places I can direct you to, if you're interested."

"No, thanks." Nice Protestant private investigators did not visit voodoo priestesses, even for fun. It gave us a rash.

The girl craned her neck to see past my shoulder. "If you aren't interested, why are you looking up voodoo on the Internet?"

"I was just messing around. You said you know a little about it?"

"I've studied some."

I gave a mental shrug. What could it hurt to ask? "I typed in 'full moon' and 'New Orleans' and got back 'voodoo.' Any idea why?"

Her brow creased. "Certain ceremonies take place under the full moon."

I returned to the astrological Web site and wasn't surprised to discover that last night there had been one.

"What kind of ceremonies?" I asked.

"To be honest, any ceremony works better under a full moon. There's incredible power there."

"Uh-huh," I said, unconvinced about the power of the moon. "I saw a low table with a candle, feathers, stones—"

"An altar."

I'd thought as much. "There were also red streaks—maybe paint."

"Probably the blood of a chicken or a pig."

God, I hoped so, but since the blood had been as

gone as the altar when I'd come back, I'd never know for certain.

"What would an altar be used for?" I asked.

"To contact the loas."

"Which are?"

"The immortal spirits of voodoo, they act as a bridge between God, known as the Gran Met, and humankind. Think of them as the saints, angels, and demons of Catholicism. The candle's flame represents a bridge between our world and the next."

"Why would anyone want to contact voodoo spirits?"

"For help."

"In what?"

"Whatever is asked. Did you notice anything else on this altar? Each of the loas has a particular item they prefer as an offering and each one has a specialty— something only they can grant us lowly mortals. An altar for Aida-Wedo might have drawings of rainbows or other items that represent the sky, which are offered in exchange for fertility."

Note to self—do *not* leave an offering for Aida-Wedo.

"There were just the stones and feathers," I said slowly.

"Which are common elements to all voodoo altars."

"And tiny animals."

Maggie frowned. "Animals?"

"Carved. From wood, I think."

"Odd."

"They reminded me of—" I searched for the word. "Totems. But those are Native American, not voodoo, right?"

"I've never heard of carved animals being placed on an altar, though sometimes there are dolls."

"Voodoo dolls?"

Maggie shook her head. "Voodoo dolls aren't true voodoo. They came from Europe not Haiti and were part of the witchcraft traditions there. Any voodoo dolls you see in New Orleans are for the tourists."

"Then what are the dolls on the altars for?"

"They represent the loa and have nothing to do with curses."

Interesting that she brought up curses, considering I'd found the altar in a supposedly cursed, haunted bar.

"Could what I saw have been an attempt to remove a curse?" I asked.

"Maybe." Maggie thought a minute. "Might also have been an attempt to place one."

8

THIS WAS ALL foolishness. I didn't believe in curses; I thought voodoo was a joke. But someone at Rising Moon obviously didn't share my opinion.

"You should really talk to a person who's more knowledgeable than me about the religion," Maggie said.

"You seem to know quite a bit."

She smiled, pleased. "As I said, I'm interested. You can't live here and not be."

I probably could, but that was just me.

"I bet if you called Priestess Cassandra," Maggie continued, "she could help you figure out what those animal carvings were for."

"I hate to bother a voodoo priestess with a new baby."

I'd had a couple of friends in the same situation. After a few weeks of sleep deprivation they resembled Linda Blair, croaking obscenities as their heads spun round and round. And they'd just been regular old new moms. I did *not* want to mess with a cranky voodoo priestess.

"She's the most knowledgeable voodoo practitioner in the city from what I hear," Maggie said. "She even went to Haiti on some kind of pilgrimage. You should see her snake."

No, I shouldn't.

"I'll keep that in mind," I said as I gathered Sullivan's file.

"Cassandra's on Royal," Maggie called as I left the café. "Shop by the same name, you can't miss it."

I lifted my hand in good-bye and kept going.

My phone rang as I headed toward Frenchmen; a glance at the caller ID revealed a local number.

"Anne, can you meet me?" I instantly recognized Detective Sullivan's low clipped voice.

"Now?" I stopped walking and turned toward town. "Where?"

"There's a place called Kelly's on Orleans. Do you know it?"

I knew none of the places here, but I had a feeling I was going to learn. "I'll find it."

With Bourbon Street as a center point, locating things wasn't hard. The French Quarter extended from Esplanade to Canal in one direction and from Rampart to the Mississippi in the other—a total of about ninety-eight blocks.

I found Kelly's without any trouble—a small, narrow tavern among a host of others. Sullivan was already at the bar, nursing something clear and sparkly, with ice. His big hand enveloped the smaller container, and he downed the drink in a single gulp, then nodded at the bartender for another.

"Long day?" I asked, sliding onto the stool beside him.

The man behind the bar filled Sullivan's glass with clear soda. Interesting. Most cops I knew would have been drinking straight vodka, and I wouldn't blame them.

"Not bad," Sullivan answered. "What'll you have?"

"Same." I smiled; so did he, the expression starting a warm glow just below my breastbone. Conner Sullivan was a nice man, and I met so damn few of them.

My mind flashed on last night—make that early this morning—Rodolfo and I in the attic, him naked, me wanting to be. My face flushed, and I downed my drink in several large gulps.

"Long day?" Sullivan repeated.

"Oh, yeah." I motioned for another.

"Where are you staying?"

"Rising Moon."

His lips, which had still been curved appealingly upward, turned in the other direction. "What?"

"I got a job at Rising Moon. The salary includes a room on the second floor."

Sullivan blinked, several times, long and slow. "You're serious."

"Most of the time." I emptied half my second soft drink. I should probably have ordered water, but the sugar really tasted good after a night with so little sleep.

"When I told you I wanted your help on this, I didn't mean—"

"For me to actually do something?" I interrupted.

"I don't think sleeping in the lion's den is classified as anything other than suicide."

"No one's going to kill me."

"No? Does he know who you are?"

I knew precisely whom Sullivan meant by "he." "Of course."

"You told him you're a private investigator, looking for your missing sister and working for me because I think he's a serial-killing psycho?"

When he put it like that— "Not exactly."

"What, exactly?"

"Rodolfo knows I'm searching for my sister."

Sullivan waited, but I didn't elaborate, because there was little else to tell.

"This is a bad idea," he muttered.

"If people are disappearing from Rising Moon, someone should be there."

"If people are disappearing, you could be next."

I shrugged and took another sip. I didn't care.

"Have you been undercover before?" he demanded.

Setting my glass down slowly so I wouldn't slam it, I faced him. "Yes. My license isn't just for show."

"Do you have a gun?"

"Not on me."

"Where is it?"

"In Philly."

"Which will be so much help if you're dragged into the swamp."

"I can take care of myself, Detective."

He didn't answer, just signaled for another round. We were both going to be hopped up on sugar before this was through.

"Why did you call me?" I asked.

"I wanted to make sure you had a room. It didn't occur to me last night that the city was filled to the brim." He shook his head. "I wasn't thinking."

"Where were you going to suggest that I stay?"

"With me."

Silence fell between us. Dull red crept up his neck. "I have an extra room."

"That's very nice of you," I said. "You don't even know me."

"I checked you out."

"Oh?" I wasn't surprised. "And what did you find?"

"You're exactly who you say you are. You're single-minded in your devotion to finding your sister. No black marks on your record. You'd make a good cop."

"Thanks." For a man like him, who seemed to live and breathe his job, that had to be the highest praise. "How did you end up in New Orleans?"

"You don't think I'm from here?"

"No."

"What gave me away?"

"Lack of an accent?"

"Maybe I got rid of it."

"Why would you do that? You've got to take heat every day for being a Yankee."

He shrugged. "More when I first came than now. People got used to me."

In a city that had tallied more than its fair share of police corruption, Sullivan had to be an icon, or maybe a curiosity. In the wake of Katrina, at least fifteen percent of the NOPD had deserted their posts and many were caught looting. I doubted Sullivan had been one of them. I was certain that those who valued honesty and integrity and devotion to duty were able to overlook Sullivan's lack of Southern charm.

"Did you have a chance to read the file?" he asked, neatly turning the subject away from himself.

"Yeah. Did you notice a pattern in the dates of the disappearances and deaths?"

"What kind of pattern?"

"I typed them into an astrological Web site."

He straightened. "And?"

"Until six months ago, the majority of disappearances and deaths in New Orleans took place on the night of a full moon."

"So you're thinking we've got a werewolf?"

I snorted. "What?"

"Full moon, disappearances, deaths. Doesn't that equal werewolf to you?"

"If I'm Lon Chaney Junior. You don't actually think werewolves exist."

"No, but there might be someone who does."

"Someone who thinks he's a werewolf?" I asked.

"It could happen."

Not a bad theory, except—

"The full-moon connection falls apart about six months ago."

"When Rodolfo showed up."

"True. Except the full-moon madness *stopped* then."

Sullivan grunted. "Weird shit has been going on around here for a long time. I told you there were several deaths by animal attack?"

"Uh-huh."

"From what I've gathered, there've been whispers of wolves in and around this city for over a century."

"A century," I repeated dumbly.

"The wolves that have been seen are big—timber-wolf size, even though this climate doesn't support timber wolves."

"Of course it doesn't."

He cast me a quick glance. "I'm just trying to tell you what I know."

I waved my hand. "Lead on." Into loony tunes land.

"A lot of the earlier reports were attributed to red wolves, which we had at one time, though they were declared extinct in the wild around nineteen eighty."

"You've done your research."

"Someone had to."

"What about coyotes?"

"Those we have. They were brought in to deplete the nutria rat population in the swamp."

"What's a nutria rat?" It didn't sound like anything I wanted to meet in a spooky, overgrown bog.

"Rodents that resemble beavers with a ratlike tail. They got out of hand a while back and had to be depleted."

"Hence the coyotes. You think your animal deaths might have been them?"

"Coyotes don't attack people."

"And wolves do?"

"Not really, unless they're starving or rabid."

"Swell," I muttered. Just what every big city needed—rabid wild animals run amok.

"After one of the animal attacks, when a swamp

guide's throat was torn out, I called in an expert."

"What kind of expert?"

"Wolf hunter."

I gave a short, sharp bark of laughter. "Where the hell did you get one of those?"

"Department of Natural Resources."

"Oh." That made sense. "And then what happened?"

"Scary old German guy went hunting in the swamp for a few days."

"Did he have an explanation for a wolf where one wasn't supposed to be?"

"Said it happens all the time. People make pets of wild animals—usually get them when they're little and cute. Then they grow into something not so little and far from cute, and they dump them. The animals can't survive in the wild; they're starving, but they also have no fear of humans, a bad combination."

"Did the hunter find anything?"

"One wolf, which he killed."

"And then?"

"Then we had another suspicious death by animal attack, but this time it was in the Quarter."

I jolted. "A wolf came right into town?" That did not sound like any wolf I'd ever heard of.

"Not a wolf. A big cat."

"I take it you're not referring to a twenty-pound tom."

"They don't kill full-grown women. This had to be some kind of wildcat."

"How do you know?"

"I had a zoologist look at the crime scene. The animal left spore. Marking territory as animals do.

"Have you got wildcats in Louisiana?"

"Bobcats."

I frowned. "They aren't that big."

"Big enough, and if the animal was rabid—"

"Then it would be violent and aggressive," I finished.

"Exactly."

I stared into his face. "But it wasn't a bobcat, was it?"

Sullivan shook his head. "I had the spore analyzed. Leopard."

"As in brown with black spots, not native to this country?"

"That would be the one."

"You think someone had a pet?"

"Could be. We've seen the news stories of tigers turning up in Manhattan apartment buildings."

I never had been able to figure out how people could be that stupid. Sure, a tiger cub is cute—all babies are—but they grow up, grow teeth, and then they turn on you.

"What happened after the death by leopard?"

"Nothing." Sullivan's shoulders slumped. "We never found the leopard—dead or alive."

"Bummer."

He shot me a glare. "There've been reports of wolves here and there. Always are."

"People must mistake coyotes for wolves all the time."

"Probably."

"Did you ever confirm what kind of animal killed the other victims?"

"Not really."

"I would think that would be something easy enough to figure out."

"Probably. If the bodies didn't keep disappearing."

"You've got disappearing bodies." I was starting to wonder how sane Sullivan was.

"Not disappearing exactly. They're in the morgue, and then they're not. Some are never seen again. Some are seen all over the place." He cast me a quick glance. "You don't believe me."

"It does sound a little far-fetched."

"I'll get you a copy of the reports."

I stared into his eyes for several seconds, then shook my head. "That's not necessary."

Why would he lie? Why would he offer to get me reports if there weren't any reports to get? And if there were, that made the disappearing, reappearing dead people true.

The jukebox in the corner changed tunes with a thunk and a slow metallic whir. As if on cue, Patsy Cline began to sing "Crazy," and Sullivan snorted. "My boss actually sent me to the local voodoo priestess to see if she knew anything about the bodies."

"Cassandra?" I asked.

His gaze sharpened. "You know her?"

"Heard of her. She seems to have quite the rep around here."

"She seems to show up a lot when things get weird, but I guess that's to be expected."

"What did the priestess say when you confronted her?"

"She denied raising any zombies."

My eyes widened. "I thought we were talking about werewolves."

"Zombies. Werewolves." Sullivan rubbed between his eyes. "This place messes with your head."

"Did you ever find any of the bodies that disappeared?"

"One." He dropped his hand. "Turned up barbecued in St. Louis Number One."

I'd walked past that cemetery at the edge of the French Quarter. Since New Orleans is below sea level—a fact everyone learned too well in August of 2005—citizens are buried inside brick monuments known as ovens. All those chalk-white markers and above-ground tombs were pretty creepy, but they didn't explain a barbecued corpse.

"You lost me," I admitted.

"Body disappears, a day or so later we've got two flaming corpses in St. Louis Number One. DNA tests revealed one to be our missing victim."

"And the other?"

"A recently deceased elderly woman who'd been buried a few days before."

"Cult?" I asked.

"Maybe. Hell, probably. Voodoo is rampant around here."

"From what I've heard, voodoo isn't a cult."

"Not usually, but who's to say what some nut might make it into?"

He had a point. Take a person on the edge of reason, combine with a religion that walked the line between natural and supernatural, and you might come up with a body-stealing cult.

Sullivan finished his soft drink, then set down the empty glass with a click. "There's something going on just below the surface," he murmured. "Like a whole other world exists that most people aren't aware of."

I frowned. Now who sounded crazy?

9

LET'S GET OUT of here." Sullivan stood and tossed some money onto the bar.

I thanked him and glanced at my watch.

"Got an appointment?" he asked.

"I'm supposed to work tonight."

We stepped onto the street. Dusk had arrived, giving the Quarter a sleepy air that would disappear quickly when complete darkness fell and neon lit up the sky. No one could be sleepy then.

"I wish you wouldn't." Sullivan stopped me with a hand on my elbow.

"I know. But I have to."

He hesitated, and for a minute I thought he meant to argue, then he gave a quick grin. "I'll walk you over."

"That's probably not a good idea."

Sullivan tilted his head. "You got a boyfriend back home in Philadelphia?"

The question was so out of place after what we'd been discussing, all I could say was, "Huh?"

"I like you, Anne. I wouldn't mind spending time with you. Is that so bad?"

"Uh—no."

"I thought I'd walk with you, maybe buy us a po' boy on the way. Ever had one?"

I stared into his open, honest brown eyes. No secrets there. The lack of them was very appealing.

"Not yet," I answered.

A po' boy turned out to be a sandwich—kind of a submarine, but better. A huge slab of French bread stuffed with shrimp and oysters, sausage, or roast beef. Pretty much whatever you asked for.

We stood in line at a window on Decatur. I ordered mine with ham; Sullivan opted for medium rare roast beef, undressed, which meant plain. I wanted dressing, which got me lettuce, tomato, and an unbelievable mustard that made my taste buds twinkle.

We ate as we walked, like so many others. I was amazed at how many people carried plastic cocktail glasses, or even beer bottles on the street. That combined with the amount of to-go windows at the bars made me think the laws on public alcohol consumption were virtually nonexistent.

"Must be hard to keep things under control," I murmured as we passed another weaving, two-fisted, drinking tourist.

"The mounted police on Bourbon really help. The officers can see over the crowds, and people give way to a horse. It's also pretty hard to outrun them."

"Still, there have to be fights."

"Wouldn't be Mardi Gras season without them. But most people are here for a good time; they're happy. If not, we throw them in jail and by morning they see reason."

I had a feeling it was a bit more complicated than that, but I let it go.

By the time we neared the less touristy section of Decatur Street, we'd finished our po' boys and washed them down with a bottle of water. I had to work, and Sullivan didn't appear to be much of a drinker. I liked that about him. Among other things.

I stopped walking. "It's probably not a good idea for anyone at Rising Moon to see me with a cop."

"You're probably right." He swept a wisp of hair from my eyes, his fingertips trailing across my brow. "Be careful."

"Always am."

"Really?"

I didn't answer. When it came to looking for Katie, I was often reckless.

Sullivan leaned in, brushing my lips with his own. The kiss was sweet, soft; he smelled really good, like sunshine and cinnamon. I was so shocked, I just stood there; I didn't even pucker up.

"See you." He turned and headed back in the direction of Bourbon.

I stared after him, wondering what had just happened. Had that been a date or a meeting? An end or perhaps a beginning? More importantly, what did I want it to be? I wasn't quite sure.

Darkness had fallen and what appeared to be a full moon shone. I knew that a true full moon lasted only one night and that what I observed was slightly lopsided, though not enough to be seen by the human eye.

Which made the long, low howl that rose toward the silver orb even weirder. If there were no wolves in New Orleans, and werewolves only came out under a full moon, then what the hell was that?

I gave a little snort of derision at my thoughts. There was no such thing as werewolves, and that howl had most likely been a coyote. I was a city girl. I had no idea what a coyote, a wolf, or even a dog howl sounded like.

The wind ruffled my hair, amazingly chilly despite the fading heat of the day. I glanced around uneasily. Where had all the people gone?

Behind me, farther down Decatur, there were plenty. Ahead of me, on the shady street that was Frenchmen, a small knot milled. But right here, no one.

"Hell," I muttered, and hurried along the broken sidewalk in the direction of Rising Moon.

The howl came again, but this time I got the impression a pack of furry beasts serenaded the bright, shiny moon. Strange, but it sounded as if they were just down the street, back in the direction Sullivan had gone.

I spun around, eyes searching the steadily descending gloom. Where was he? I should be able to see him walking away, but I didn't. How could I miss him? He was huge.

Uneasy, I started after him. In my peripheral vision I kept catching a hint of shadows in the alleyways. Shadows with decidedly canine shapes. However, when I glanced directly at them, nothing was there.

I reached the busy section of Decatur. Tourists, tourists everywhere and not a cop to be had.

I forced myself to draw several calming breaths. Sullivan had used a shortcut, that was all. I was certain there were a hundred of them, and a New Orleans detective would know every one.

Now that I was no longer alone, all I heard was the beat of the music pouring from the open door of every tavern; all I saw was the neon. I was tempted to grab the nearest person and ask them if they'd seen any really big dogs or heard strange howling, but considering the intoxicated euphoria of everyone around me, I wouldn't be able to believe them regardless of what they said.

I jogged toward Rising Moon, passing nothing but empty, glistening alleyways, until I reached the bar.

At the end of the long, narrow gap between buildings a man stood smoking. Even before he turned his face and the nearly full moon glinted off his glasses, I knew who he was.

My heart went *ba-boom*. Sullivan's sweet and gentle kiss was forgotten as memories spilled into my mind— the taste of his mouth, the feel of his skin, the scent of his hair. The stark, white line across his wrist.

I should avoid John Rodolfo like the shadowy wolves that ran in the night. Instead I took a single step toward him, and he disappeared around the corner. Before I could stop myself, I plunged into the alley, hurrying along until I burst out the other side.

The only thing left was a whiff of cigarette smoke on the wind.

10

RODOLFO NEVER SHOWED up that night, and the resulting crowd was thin. By midnight, King told me to get lost.

"Don't know where the boss man has gotten himself to," he muttered.

"I—uh—saw him out back when I came in," I said.

King, busy filling a pilsner glass from the tap, glanced up with a frown. "You talk to him?"

"He took off before . . ." I let my voice drift into silence. He'd taken off before I could ascertain it was actually him—although who else would have been standing outside the bar wearing sunglasses beneath the moon?

"Strange." King slid the beer to the customer, then slid the money into his huge hand. "He don't usually disappear so early."

"Maybe he had another headache."

The big man's lips thinned. "There's nothin' you can do for him when he's like that. 'Cept leave 'im alone."

"I know."

"Girlie, that boy's got troubles galore."

"I know that too." I handed him my tray and note-pad. "You said no one else lived here but me."

"No one does."

"Who has a key?"

His head tilted as he considered the question. "Me, you, Johnny. A weekly cleaning crew. The accountant."

"What about former employees?"

"I always get the keys back."

That didn't mean someone hadn't made a copy.

King frowned. "Why?"

I still didn't want to share the disappearing altar with anyone, but—

"You know anything about voodoo?"

His expression chilled, making his oddly light eyes appear even lighter. "You think because I'm black I know voodoo?"

"That's not what I meant. I was just curious."

"Be curious someplace else. I'm a Baptist, born and bred. I don't hold with that hoodoo shit."

"Sorry," I muttered. "Forget I asked."

I headed to my room, stepping gingerly on the stair-case lest the black cat show up again. I should have asked King what its name was.

My cell phone beeped. I checked the message, figur-ing it would be from one or the other of my parents, calling to make sure my clothes had arrived safely. I was right and wrong. The first was from my mother asking just that. The second was from Sullivan.

"Just wanted to make sure you got back okay." A long silence followed before he murmured, "Call me."

I dialed his cell, left my own message. "I'm fine. Thanks for the sandwich and the—" I wasn't sure what to call it. "Conversation," I decided. "I'll be in touch."

The scent of smoke clung to my hair and clothes so I took a shower, let the hot water beat on my sore shoulders and slightly achy feet. Waitressing wasn't for sissies.

Strangely enough, I kind of liked it. I got to talk to people, show Katie's picture. I felt like I was doing something, when for months I'd been doing nothing. I wasn't having any luck, but at least I was trying.

Who knew? The phrase "like finding a needle in a haystack" actually contained the word "finding." It could happen.

I glanced around my rented room and was surprised by the wave of loneliness that washed over me. Sure, I was far from home, but I'd often felt the same in Philly where I lived only ten minutes from my parents. I was alone in a way only a twenty-three-year-old single woman can be. I ached for someone, but there was no one.

I forced myself to turn off the lights, get into bed. The music ended downstairs, but I could still hear the thrum of voices, the occasional high-pitched laughter. Not enough to keep me awake if I'd been at all tired.

I stared at the ceiling. While I should have been thinking of Katie, or even the case, coming up with some sort of plan, instead I found myself thinking of John Rodolfo, wondering where he went when he walked the night, what he did, who he was.

I drifted in that place where time can both fly and crawl, when we're not quite asleep, but we aren't awake either. I saw him wandering in the fog, as alone as I was, wanting someone with whom to share the darkness.

I jerked upright. Rising Moon had gone completely silent below me. I glanced at my watch. Three hours had passed.

The moon shone through my window, creating a silver path between it and my bed. The distant howl of a train, the wind, or something with fur, split the night.

I listened as it died away and an odd tap-tap took its place. Curious, I slipped out of bed and followed the silver trail to the window.

The street lay deserted except for a solitary figure moving slowly in my direction, weaving a bit as if drunk, tapping a white cane tipped with red along the pavement in front of him.

I don't know why I was surprised to see Rodolfo with a cane. Without a dog or a companion, how else would he traverse the city? Still, the apparatus made him seem more vulnerable than he ever had before.

As if in answer to my thoughts, he stumbled, nearly going to his knees before righting himself. Was he drunk?

Before I could think better of it, I left my room, flying down the back stairs and out the door. It wasn't until the warm wind brushed my bare arms and legs that I remembered I wore nothing but a pair of boxers and a thin tank top.

I hesitated for only a moment, then left the shadow of the building and hurried across the street. No one was out here but the two of us, and he wouldn't be able to see anything.

"What are you—" I began, then stopped when I saw the blood on his shirt.

Cursing, I ran the remaining steps to his side, grasping his elbow, gentling my hold when he winced. "What happened?"

"Mugged," he said softly.

His jaw sported a darkening bruise, as did his cheek. I wondered momentarily how he'd managed to keep his glasses from getting busted, then became distracted by the way he held his body, protectively, as if he'd cracked a rib. The fingers curled around the cane had lacerations on the knuckles.

"Where? Why?" I demanded, and he smiled, just a tiny uptilt of his lips, but I was done for. He was so damn beautiful he made me dizzy.

"I believe the why of it was money, *chica*. Isn't it always?"

"How could anyone mug a—"

"Blind man?" he finished. "You can say it. I know that I'm blind."

My mouth twitched. The better I got to know him, the better I liked him. Which wasn't good. If I was going to be attracted to a man for the first time in forever, why couldn't I be attracted to someone like Sullivan?

Because that would be too easy.

"All right," I said shortly. "How could anyone mug a blind man?"

"Much more easily than they can mug a sighted man. Some people are desperate." He tried to take a breath, but thought better of it when pain made him grimace. "I understand desperate. I can't fault them too much."

"I can," I muttered, wishing the culprits had tangled with me instead. "We need to get you to the hospital."

"No." He stiffened. "No doctors. I've had enough of them."

"But—"

"I just want to go upstairs." He indicated Rising Moon with a jerk of his head.

I wondered momentarily why he'd come here instead of going to his apartment, but maybe he'd been closer. Or maybe he'd just needed help, and he'd known I was here.

The thought caused a flutter in my belly. I don't know why I enjoyed being needed. Maybe since I was unable to help Katie, I helped everyone else that I could. Or perhaps it was just because I was good at it.

As Rodolfo stepped off the curb, he caught his cane in a crack and wobbled. I snatched his free hand, and he jerked back. I tightened my fingers around his. "Let me help."

After a few seconds, he did.

Minutes later we reached the third-floor room. He sat on the bed as I hurried into the bathroom. He had very little in the way of first-aid supplies. He had very little in the way of anything—some soap, toothpaste, a few washcloths and towels.

I came out with the cloths. "I'm going to get some ice and some whiskey." He tilted his head quizzically. "Alcohol for those knuckles. Can't hurt. Actually, it probably will hurt, but less than an infection. Did you catch those on someone's teeth?"

"Could be," he said, and I realized he probably didn't

know what he'd hit. That he'd hit anything was pretty damn amazing.

Hurrying into the tavern, I found a few empty plastic bags and filled them with ice, then grabbed a cheap bottle of whiskey—the alcohol content was the same regardless of the price—and ran back up.

I stopped dead just inside the door. Rodolfo had removed his shirt and was dabbing at his chest with one of the washcloths. His back to me, I was momentarily captivated by the play of muscles beneath smooth, bronzed skin. I wanted to run my tongue all over him.

He reached for his shirt, and I caught a glimpse of his chest before he covered it. Several raw slices marred the once perfect flesh.

"They had a knife?" I demanded.

He buttoned a few of the lower buttons, shrouding his abdomen from view before I stopped him with a hand on his. "I should clean those."

"They're just scratches. I'll be all right."

"You could get an infection."

He snorted.

"Let me—" I took a step forward; he took a step back.

"No." He held out the stained washcloth. "I can do it."

I stared at him for several seconds, but my evil eye had no effect. Finally I doused the cloth with whiskey and handed it to him. He turned away, dabbing at the injury.

He seemed almost shy, as if he didn't want me to see him, was afraid to let me touch him, and that did not fit with the man I knew. Although how well did I really know him?

"Why do you go out alone?" I asked.

John glanced over his shoulder; the reflection from the light bulb bounced off his sunglasses, making me blink. "This is my city. Always has been." He tossed the red-tinged washcloth aside and spread his beautiful hands. "I love her. I can't stay away."

"Even if she kills you?"

"Even then," he said. "But I doubt it'll come to that."

"Why?"

"Because"—he finished buttoning his shirt—"I am very hard to kill."

"Oh, really." I moved closer, careful to make enough noise so he knew I was coming. "Why's that?"

"I don't want to die."

I had just reached for his hand, preparatory to wiping his skinned knuckles with alcohol, but paused at his words and rotated his wrist upright.

"No?" I asked, and traced the thin white line that shone starkly in the light from the bare bulb hanging above us.

His skin twitched beneath my touch, and he tried to pull away. I held on.

"That was a long time ago," he murmured. "Things are different now. I'm different."

I wished I could see his eyes, maybe then I could tell if he was lying. But it seemed too forward to tug his sunglasses from his face as I held his scarred wrist in my hand.

"You don't believe me?" he asked.

I frowned, surreptitiously casting a glance at his other wrist. No scar. I wasn't sure what that meant.

"This is really none of my business," I said. "Unless you'd like to talk about it."

"No," he said, biting the word off sharply, giving the intonation a foreign twist. There were times when he spoke like a European gentleman from years gone by, others when he spoke like any other guy. John Rodolfo was a mystery in more ways than one.

I turned his hand back over, holding on tightly when he tried to pull away. "I need to clean these knuckles now."

He stopped struggling. The alcohol on the scraped, bleeding mess had to have stung, but he stood stoically and let me do my worst—or maybe it was my best.

Now that I got a good look at them, they weren't as bad as they'd first seemed. The dimmer light of the moon must have made the scrapes appear deeper. "You don't even need a bandage," I murmured, and he pulled slowly away.

"I'm okay."

"You should put ice on your cheek, those ribs."

"I'll be fine. I've always been a fast healer." He took a slug of the whiskey, making a face as he swallowed. I wasn't sure if it was from the taste or the quality. Maybe both.

"You might have a broken rib. Let me check."

I placed my palm against his side and he froze, his body going as still as his face. Beneath my hand, his chest barely rose and fell, the movement as shallow as the cuts on his knuckles.

"Do you know what you're doing?" he asked, his voice a bit hoarse from the alcohol.

"Hell, no," I said, and he laughed, the sound so foreign, so startlingly sweet, I lifted my head, captivated. Then I was caught, staring into his glasses, mesmerized, as my fingers pressed one rib, then another. I didn't think either one of us was breathing anymore.

"Does this hurt?" I managed.

"Not as much as it's going to," he muttered, and kissed me.

11

HIS TONGUE TASTED of whiskey and though I'd never been a fan, I wanted to suck on it, on him, and draw every inch of the flavor within.

I burned, yet his skin was hotter than mine, my fingers seemingly ice-cold against his heat. He moaned into my mouth, began to lift his head, end the kiss, and I wrapped my fingers around his neck, holding on.

He hesitated, even stopped kissing me for a minute, but when I nipped his lip, pressed my breasts against his chest, then slipped one finger beneath the waistband of his trousers and over the tip of his erection, the hesitation ended. If his reaction was anything to go by, he hadn't had sex in nearly as long as I had.

The kiss that followed was long and wet and unbelievably thorough. He learned every inch of my mouth, as those clever, long-fingered artist's hands explored the curve of my waist, the slope of my breasts, the swell of my rear. The latter made me shudder with reaction as his hand met the bare skin of my thigh. I wanted to feel every inch of him naked against every inch of me.

His glasses tapped my nose, and I reached for them, but he swung me around, backing me against the wall. Though my eyes were closed, I sensed the room go dark, even as I heard the muted flick of the light switch.

I opened my eyes; the room was completely black, the curtains drawn so that not even a flicker of moonlight penetrated the darkness. His mouth left mine, caressing my chin, then the curve of my throat as he moved lower, his hands sliding higher, cupping my breasts, teasing my already hardened nipples through the thin layer of my tank top.

The press of his erection was just a little too high to be of any help so I grabbed his hips, went on my tiptoes and felt his gasp of both shock and excitement as everything came together just right.

Suddenly I was spinning out of control, twirled around, off balance, unable to see. My cheek met the wall, the chill of the smooth surface startling against my heated skin.

He nibbled my neck as he murmured words I didn't understand in Spanish, maybe Italian, even a little French, his breath icing the moist imprint of his mouth, making me shiver with cold, then shudder with the awareness of his body pressed tightly to mine.

I should have felt trapped, maybe a little scared. We were alone at Rising Moon; he was bigger than me, stronger, and possibly crazy. But we weren't doing anything I didn't want to do; arousal far outweighed any fear.

His teeth scraped my neck, and I caught my breath, the sound sharp and loud in the stillness that surrounded us. He froze, mouth hovering just above my skin, and I ached for him to—

"Do it again," I whispered, arching my back, offering my neck like a sacrifice.

He tensed, and the movement rode his erection along my backside in an enticingly intimate way. Muttering curses in several different languages, he grasped my hips and whirled me back around, lowering his lips to mine.

This wasn't what I'd meant, but I found it hard to complain with his tongue down my throat. Despite the voice in my head, which chattered that I was going to be sorry if I banged the boss, I didn't really *want* to complain. He tasted so good, this had to be right. With him kissing me, I couldn't be sorry about anything except that we were wearing too many clothes.

I slipped my hands under his shirt, ran my palms over the smooth, muscular expanse of his back. Though I would have liked to touch his chest, I still had the presence of mind to remember the thin, red slices he'd dismissed as mere scratches. Whatever they were, I had no doubt they hurt, so I did my best to keep my roving fingers away.

We both lost our heads; I'm not sure why. One minute my back was at the wall, and he was kissing me as I traced my palms over his shoulders. The next we were tumbling onto the bed in a tangle of limbs and clothing, buttons popping, elastic snapping, shoes flying, as we desperately attempted to get naked.

The attempt was mostly successful. I don't think I got his pants completely off; they might have been hanging from one ankle; my tank top ended up bunched over my left bicep. It didn't matter. I had to feel his skin against mine.

Warmth enveloped me; he gave off heat like an open flame; the hair on his legs brushed softly against my thighs as he settled between them. This time when I tugged on his sunglasses he let them go.

I resisted the urge to touch his eyelids, a greater intimacy than the one we would soon share. I didn't want to do anything that might make him stop. My body was humming with arousal, perched on the precipice of release. If I screwed this up, I'd never forgive myself.

He nudged my knees apart; I opened for him gladly and the next instant he was inside, the slick, hard beat of him pushing, pulsing, bringing me closer and closer to the edge.

I strained upward, searching for that final touch that would make everything right, and he stilled deep within. His arms trembled; his breathing became labored.

"John?" I murmured, and if possible he tensed even more.

Afraid he'd withdraw and leave us both undone, I locked my legs around his, tilting myself more intimately against him. With a sound that was part arousal and part surrender, he began to pump his hips, faster and faster, deeper and deeper, the thrusts almost rough, but I didn't mind. I wanted the friction; I needed the heat; I awaited the explosion with my eyes wide open to the night.

Lowering his lips to my breast, he scored the curve with his teeth. Pain and pleasure became one, and I urged him on with murmurs and moans. He laved my nipple with his tongue, drawing me into his mouth and suckling as his lower body continued to thrust.

My body tightened, milking him, yet still it wasn't enough. He lifted his head, rising above me, driving into me, grasping my waist with his once gentle hands and just holding on.

The orgasm went on and on, and when I thought I was done, when I was gasping, limp and languid, he reached between us, his thumb finding my clitoris, working it, riding it, making me come again, stronger this time, so hard I sobbed, and at last he cried out, emptying all of himself.

I drifted toward sleep before the heat between us had even cooled. The last thing I remember was Rodolfo tugging the covers up, even as he inched away.

I reached for him, and he took my hand, then kissed my knuckles. "Go to sleep, *chica*. I won't leave."

For some reason, I trusted him, and I relaxed. But as oblivion closed in I thought I heard him whisper, "What have I done?"

And I had to wonder the same thing myself.

W HEN I AWOKE he was gone. I shouldn't have been hurt. When he'd said he wouldn't leave, I doubted he'd meant forever.

What have I done?

The words flitted through my head. Had he said them, or had I only imagined he had because I'd been thinking them myself? In the bright light of day I had other concerns.

There'd been no mention or use of a condom.

I sat up. Though I was on the pill, had been since I was sixteen and got tired of missing two days of school every month with excruciating menstrual cramps, I didn't have to worry about an unwanted pregnancy. Just unwanted—

"Disgusting diseases," I muttered, and smacked myself in the forehead with the heel of my hand.

I'd heard stories of people so carried away by the moment they'd forgotten anything but that. I'd always scoffed.

Until today.

I glanced at my watch. Nine A.M. Far too early for nightwalkers like Rodolfo and me to be up. Where was he?

A door closed downstairs, and I leaped out of bed, crossed to the window, stepping over my scattered clothes as I went. Drawing back the curtains, I saw Rodolfo walking away with a man I didn't recognize.

"Must have an appointment."

The sound of my own voice, relieved, a little wistful, made me stiffen, then snatch my clothes and quickly put them back on.

I had no claims on him. What did I care if he wasn't here when I woke up? We had separate lives. This had been a one-night stand. It wasn't going to happen again.

Along with my unease over the missing condom, I felt a little guilty over the night's activities. Rodolfo had been hurt, and I'd jumped him. Not that he'd complained, but he was a guy. He'd no doubt have sex on his deathbed if possible. I should have put a stop to things before they went too far, except I'd been as out of control as he was.

My cheeks heated. What was wrong with me? I barely knew the man.

Or at least I'd barely known him last night. This morning, at least physically, I knew him pretty damn well.

Such behavior was unlike me. I was a plain, hometown girl, who spent her days and most of her nights working. I didn't have a boyfriend; I didn't go on dates; I only entered bars to check out leads on Katie.

Yet I'd come to the Crescent City and started slinging drinks, roaming the night, and sleeping with strangers. If I didn't know better I'd think I was under a spell.

Annoyed with myself, I stomped downstairs to my own room and pulled back the covers on my bed. "Just because they call this place the voodoo capital of America doesn't make it true."

I picked up my pillow and a small cloth bag tied with string fell to the floor. "What the—"

Tentatively I lifted the tiny sack to my nose, sniffed and then sneezed—once, twice, again. The scent was not unpleasant, kind of musty, dusty, but also pungent and sharp, like red peppers cooked over an open flame.

Probably just potpourri, though I'd never known anyone to stuff potpourri into a pillowcase. Maybe it was a Southern thing.

With a shrug, I tossed the bag into the trash. If there was one thing I didn't need it was an annoyance that might keep me awake when I should be asleep.

I managed to doze most of the day, rising with just enough time to shower, dress, and run down to the Central Grocery on Decatur for a muffuletta sandwich.

According to the propaganda, the muffuletta is a Sicilian creation. Though the Cajun and Creole cultures get the most press in New Orleans, Italians began coming to the city in the 1880s and formed a fairly large contingent.

I'd heard there might be a long line there, but I lucked out and only had to stand behind five people before I placed my order.

What appeared to be French bread was slathered with olive oil, olive salad, Italian cheeses, and salami. I wolfed mine down on the way back to Rising Moon, and considered going back for another. God, it was good!

If I ate like this for every meal, I'd put on ten pounds in a week. However, I was only managing one meal a day in between sleeping and my shift. At that rate, I might lose ten pounds, which wouldn't hurt me. Did losing ten pounds hurt anyone?

There was no sign of Rodolfo when I arrived at work, and as the night wore on, and he didn't show up, the crowd dwindled, and King got mad.

"Where in hell is he?" King smacked a tumbler onto the bar so hard I figured the glass would crack; instead Southern Comfort sloshed over the brim and onto his hand.

"I don't know." I set the glass on my tray. Not exactly a lie, I didn't know where he was. And what good would it do to tell King that Rodolfo had been with me last night? The information wasn't relevant.

Or was it? Had the man taken off because he couldn't face me?

I stifled a wince as I delivered the drink to an older woman who sat at the front window, staring at the crowd on Frenchmen. Was she waiting for someone too?

Annoyed with myself, I spun away and ran smack

into a massive chest sporting a tie shaped like an electric guitar.

"Oomph." I stumbled back, and Detective Sullivan caught me.

"Hey." He waited until I had my balance before releasing me. "You okay?"

"Yeah." I glanced around, but no one was paying us any mind, including King, who was once again engaged in the seemingly never-ending job of loading the dishwasher with dirty glasses. "What are you doing here? I thought we agreed that I shouldn't be seen with . . ." I waved my hand in his general direction.

"I didn't come to see you." He smiled. "Though that is a nice bonus."

I automatically smiled back. He was such a nice guy. Why didn't I want to rip his clothes off the way I wanted to rip off Rodolfo's? My smile faded and Sullivan's did as well.

"Something wrong?" he asked.

"Anne." King's voice made me turn. He frowned at Sullivan. "What the hell do you want?"

My brows lifted. "You know each other?"

"He's been hasslin' Johnny for months now."

Sullivan was unperturbed by King's hostility. "Is he here?"

"No," King said, and returned to the dishwasher.

Sullivan followed, pulling a photograph from his jacket and placing it on the bar. "Seen this guy?"

King stopped loading long enough to take a peek. "Nope."

"Never?"

"Sorry."

"This man, Harvey Klingman, was last seen at Rising Moon," Sullivan said, and my stomach dropped.

I inched closer, trying to see the photo, but the detective's big shoulders blocked it from view as he leaned over the counter to hear King's response.

"I suppose he disappeared like the rest." King didn't even glance up. "And just like those times, I don't know nothin' about it or him."

"You don't think it's a coincidence that people come in here and never make their way home again?"

"That's exactly what it is," King said slowly. "A coincidence."

Around us voices rose and fell, glasses clinked, someone laughed. Sullivan drew in a deep breath, then let it out again. He tapped the photo with one thick finger. "This guy didn't disappear. I know right where he is."

"Then why are you wastin' my time?" King snapped.

"Because he's in the morgue."

"Why?" I blurted.

"The usual reason," Sullivan said dryly.

I cleared my throat. "I meant, how did he die?"

"Hard to say for certain." The detective glanced over his shoulder at me, then back at King. "Someone set him on fire."

I started, remembering the barbecued bodies in the cemetery.

"Whether fire was the cause of death," Sullivan continued, "or a way to cover up the cause has yet to be determined."

"I don't know nothin' about that either," King said.

"Then you won't care if I look around."

"Go nuts."

The detective grabbed the photo and stuffed it into his pocket as he turned toward me. The movement tugged his jacket and cuff up just enough to expose a livid red scrape on his forearm.

"What happened?" I indicated the mark.

Sullivan's lips tightened; he glanced at King, then drew me toward the front of the bar. "The other night, after I left you on Decatur, some guy jumped me on the way home."

I frowned, remembering the weird canine shadows that had seemed to follow in Sullivan's wake.

"A guy?" I repeated. "You're sure?"

"Yeah." He gave me an odd look. "Must have been on something. He tried to bite me."

"What if he had rabies? You see a doctor?"

"I did. Luckily this"—he lifted his hand—"was from the pavement, or maybe his fingernails, which were pretty Fu Manchu. I never let his teeth get close enough to break the skin. According to the doctor, rabies is most often passed through saliva, although it can be transmitted through a scratch."

"What happened after he attacked you?"

"I shot him."

"You *shot* him?"

"I couldn't let the guy run off and bite someone else. Even though there's never been a documented case of human-to-human rabies infection, there's always a first time. Besides, just getting bit by a person is bad enough."

I nodded. Human mouths are filthy. Any bite usually gets infected and is a definite candidate for heavy-duty antibiotics.

"Did you hit him?" I asked.

Confusion washed over Sullivan's face. "I swore I did, in the leg, even found some blood, but he ran like a jackrabbit. There've been no reports of gunshot wounds in any of the ERs—or at least none matching this guy's description."

"Strange," I murmured.

"Yeah, although I've seen druggies do amazing things. If they're hopped up enough, they feel no pain."

"What if he *did* have rabies?" I asked.

"That would definitely show up on the ER reports."

"Unless he died on the street."

"I've been checking the John Does. So far I haven't found him."

"How long does it take a human being to die from rabies?"

"One to three months."

"Really?" I'd figured once bitten, the victim would turn into a slavering monster and die pretty quickly.

"Yes," Sullivan answered, "though once symptoms appear, death follows fast."

"What symptoms?"

"Extreme thirst but inability to drink, frothing at the mouth, confusion, convulsions."

Silence fell between us. A silence Sullivan finally broke. "Have you seen Rodolfo?"

"Last night." I conveniently left out how last night had extended into this morning.

"What about Harvey?" Sullivan tilted the photo toward me.

I stared at the face and tried to breathe. I shook my head and Sullivan strode toward the back door. I heard him stomping up the stairs, then across the second floor. I didn't even care that he might be going through my underwear drawer.

Go nuts, as King had said. I had more important things to worry about.

"You knew him, didn't you?" King stood at my elbow.

I shook my head again and retrieved my tray, performing a last call of the remaining customers as my mind spun.

I didn't know the man in the picture, but I *had* seen him.

Walking away from Rising Moon that morning with John Rodolfo.

12

B Y THE TIME Sullivan came downstairs empty-handed, I'd regained my composure.

"When did you find Klingman?" I asked. "Where?"

His dark brown eyes contemplated me with curiosity. "I thought you didn't know the man."

"I don't. But—" I glanced around for King, and when I didn't see him anywhere, leaned in to whisper. "You hired me to look into the disappearances. Shouldn't I know all there is to know about the latest one?"

"He didn't disappear," Sullivan reiterated.

"Just tell me, Conner."

His brows lifted at my use of his first name, then he shrugged. "He was found in Lake Pontchartrain."

"I thought he was on fire."

"Maybe that's why he wound up in the lake—either trying to put himself out or it could be whoever lit him up didn't want to attract too much attention."

"*When* was he found?"

"This afternoon. Although he could have been floating a while. We don't know yet."

I wasn't sure what to make of that bit of info. What had I been hoping he'd say?

If Harvey had been found dead last night, would that have let Rodolfo off the hook for killing him? Not even close, since he'd shown up beat to hell and gone. For all I knew, my boss had been struggling with Harvey instead of muggers.

The thought caused me to frown. I truly doubted a blind man could kill a healthy, sighted one, start him on fire, or vice versa, then dump him in the lake. Besides, I'd seen Klingman walking around after the sun came up. A fact that I should relate immediately to Detective Sullivan.

But I wasn't going to.

At least not until I'd talked to Rodolfo.

THAT PROVED HARDER to accomplish than I'd imagined. Rodolfo didn't show up that night, or the next, or the next. I started to get worried, and when King didn't share my concern, I got mad.

"If he turns up dead somewhere, I guess that'll let him off the hook with Sullivan," I snapped.

"He won't turn up dead." The big man's lips twitched, which only made me madder. "This isn't the first time he's gone AWOL."

"What does that mean?"

"Just what I said. Every so often Johnny needs to get away, so he does. He always comes back."

"Unless he's at the bottom of Lake Pontchartrain," I muttered.

"He isn't."

King seemed certain, and since he knew Rodolfo better than I did, I figured he was right. I also figured I knew why *Johnny* had needed some alone time. He'd wanted to get away from me.

So despite my unease, I didn't look for him. I didn't even check the third-floor room. If he ever came back, he knew exactly where to find me.

Still, I didn't sleep well. Each night I stared out my window as the moon shrank to gibbous, then a crescent, and finally disappeared altogether, leaving the sky dark but for the stars.

Downstairs, something went thud. Since King had left hours ago, the sound drew me away from my contemplation of the navy blue night. I'd taken one step toward my door when a squeal from outside made me return just in time to see a squat, somewhat roly-poly shadow dart away.

"There are no pigs in New Orleans," I murmured, though I didn't know if that was true.

I peered down the alley, but nothing, no one, was there. I decided to head to the tavern for a bottle of water. It was something to do.

I'd had no luck finding anyone who recognized Katie, though with the Mardi Gras festivities increasing daily, the crowds had also improved. I'd stay until Lent began, and tourism understandably fell off, then I'd return home.

According to the New Orleans *Times-Picayune* there'd been no more disappearances or murders—at least none without an explanation. I'd spoken to Sullivan a few times, and he confirmed the same. If there was a serial killer, perhaps he was waiting for the full moon, unless he'd skipped town, or been the victim of an untimely death himself.

I frowned, thinking of Harvey Klingman.

That thought flew right out of my head, as I let myself out of my room and immediately caught the scent of smoke. The same door was ajar as before, and when I opened it I discovered the altar had reappeared.

This time I knew better than to walk away and let the thing disappear. Instead, I strode in and scooped the tiny wooden animals into my hand. The candle went out as if blown by an invisible breath.

A chill trickled over me as complete darkness descended. My eyes were wide open, yet I could see nothing. How did Rodolfo stand it?

Another thud from downstairs had me slipping the icons into the pocket of my pajama bottoms and hurrying down the steps, silent on bare feet.

The tavern was also dark. I sensed movement in the room, though I wasn't sure where. My shin whacked into a chair; I stumbled over a table. Maybe all the movement was my own.

Still, I could have sworn I heard heavy breathing, so close my hair stirred. I paused, sweeping my arms in a circle, expecting to hit someone, maybe something, but there was nothing.

A footfall behind me, a tiny sigh ahead of me, the air swirled all around. I was disoriented, frightened, and I wished I'd stayed in my room.

The back door banged open suddenly, spilling in just enough light from the distant street lamp so I could see that no one was here but me. Except how had the door come to be open?

Most likely when the altar maker left.

I crossed the short distance and slammed it shut, flipping the lock, then returning to the tavern and flicking on the lights. I shrieked as a large, man-sized figure loomed in front of me.

Tanned, blond, and buff, he could have been a surfer in one of the Annette Funicello movies Katie and I had laughed at on Saturday afternoons. Despite the youth of his face, his hair and his clothes appeared to have escaped from the fifties.

He had a flattop, something I hadn't seen out and about in years. His shorts were shorter than his hair, exposing beefy, brawny thighs. He wore a white tank top, out of which his mountainous arms swelled. I didn't know what to make of him.

"Where is he?" the guy demanded.

"Who?"

"The alpha, the master, my lord."

Oh, great.

"Um, could you be a little more specific?" I inched toward the front door. The nutjob followed.

"He who is supreme. The one from whom all beasts spring." He leaped across the short space between us and grabbed the neck of my pajamas, then yanked my face close to his.

His breath was rank; I didn't want to know what he'd eaten last. His teeth were amazingly white and a little sharp. I leaned as far back as I could, but he only pulled me nearer and buried his nose in my hair, inhaling deeply.

He muttered something that sounded suspiciously like "Mother," and licked my collarbone. My skin crawled, and I brought my knee up fast and hard.

He was quicker than anyone I'd ever known and whirled away before my blow found its mark. At least he let me go. His growl caused the hair on my arms to lift. I'm not proud to admit it, but I ran.

I didn't get far before his fingers tangled in my hair, and he threw me to the floor. His eyes seemed to glow in the faint light, and his smile became feral. I was going to die, but probably not soon enough.

"Get away from her."

The words were spoken softly, but they held an undercurrent of command. I glanced up and so did my attacker.

John Rodolfo appeared no worse for wherever he'd been. He was dressed in black, his sunglasses firmly in place.

I saw no evidence of bruises on his face; the hand wrapped around his red-tipped white cane sported not a single scab. He certainly *did* heal fast. He moved with the innate grace I'd noticed the first time I'd seen him. Even blind he trod with more confidence than any man I'd ever known. If he'd broken a rib, I certainly couldn't tell.

"She yours?" the man asked.

Rodolfo set his cane against the nearest wall, took a final pull on the cigarette he held in his other hand, ground it out beneath his shoe and murmured, "Yes."

I opened my mouth to protest, then snapped it shut. I'd rather be Rodolfo's than this guy's.

"I want her."

"No."

Though I don't know how he carried anything in that small scrap of fabric he wore as shorts, the nut reached into his pocket and withdrew a long, thin metallic object. He flicked his wrist, and the distinctive swish of a switchblade followed.

"Are you worthy?" he asked.

Rodolfo's smile was equally feral. "Let's find out."

I scrambled to my feet, muttering what I meant to be a denial but must have been nothing more than gibberish since the two men ignored me and rushed each other.

Panic descended. How on earth could Rodolfo fight a sighted man, let alone a crazy person with a knife?

I dived for the phone behind the bar, figuring nine-one-one was my best bet, but before I'd taken two steps, I was only able to watch, fascinated.

Rodolfo ducked the first strike, jerking back from the second, which swished through the air centimeters from his nose.

Poised on the balls of his feet, head cocked as he listened intently, he became calmer as the other man became more agitated.

The beach bum thrust and parried, but he never came within an inch of Rodolfo again, though John seemed to be almost egging him on, letting him get near, then dodging away.

"You *fuck*," the stranger muttered, and John laughed.

The resulting howl of rage was inhuman. The man dropped to the ground on all fours, the knife skittering across the tile as he convulsed.

My inertia broke, and I dialed nine-one-one, requesting both the police and an ambulance. From the way the guy was twitching, he was going to need a pill, if not a straitjacket, and then, hopefully, a nice comfy padded cell.

As I hung up the phone, John felt around for the knife, which had slid to a stop near his feet. I didn't caution him against it, better he had the weapon than Mr. Insane-O. But as his fingers closed around the hilt, surfer dude gave a guttural cry and launched himself at Rodolfo.

Startled, John turned in his direction, and the blade sank into the man's chest to the hilt.

"Shit!" I blurted, then clapped my hands over my mouth.

I expected the wounded man to fall to the ground, or grab on to Rodolfo, maybe take him to the ground too. Instead he tore himself free and, with the knife still protruding grotesquely, raced for the door.

"Pas argent," John muttered like a curse, then moved forward.

I stayed him with a hand on his arm. "He won't get far."

Not with a knife in his chest.

Nevertheless, I started after him myself, reaching the gaping back door just as the guy passed beneath the streetlight.

In the garish glow, I caught one glimpse of his face.

It wasn't quite human.

13

I SHOOK MY head, and in that instant of movement, that tiny blink of an eye, the guy disappeared.

I stepped outside, but there was no sign of him anywhere.

Logically I knew the man couldn't just disappear. He'd probably ducked down an alley, maybe even collapsed in one.

The distant wail of a siren kept me from finding out. The police were coming, and it probably wasn't a good idea for John to be alone, with blood all over his hands, when they arrived.

I don't know why I felt so protective of him. Considering what had just happened, he certainly didn't need my help. Even blind, the man could take care of himself.

So what had happened the other night?

"Did he die?" Rodolfo asked as soon as I came back inside.

"Not anywhere that I could see."

He scowled and appeared as if he wanted to race off in pursuit. I stepped in front of him. "The police are coming."

His face jerked toward the front of the building. "You called them? What the hell for?"

"There was a guy with a knife trying to kill you."

"He didn't."

"Which is more than what you did for him."

"You said he wasn't dead."

"Not yet."

Which was just weird if you asked me. What kind of guy didn't fall down when you stabbed him in the chest?

The kind I never wanted to meet again.

"You really expected me not to call them?" I asked. "To let you race after a crazy man?"

"Who said he was crazy?"

"A sane man wouldn't run off with a knife embedded in his chest."

No, a sane man—or any *man* for that matter—would die.

I shook off the odd thought. Of course the intruder had been a man. What else could he be?

The true crazy person was the one in front of me who'd fought a knife-wielding assailant as if he did so every day.

I wondered sometimes if Rodolfo's blindness was so recent he forgot about it and just reacted. Why else would he begin to chase a madman when he had no hope of keeping up? For that matter, why had he fought the guy in the first place?

It couldn't have been for me.

"I'm not helpless," Rodolfo said softly. "I don't want you to think that I am."

His face was somber; his eyes as unreadable behind those damn sunglasses as ever. I moved toward him, intent on removing the barriers, seeing once and for all what lay beneath.

The door burst open. "Police! Let me see your hands."

Both Rodolfo and I lifted them; unfortunately John's were covered in blood. The cops took one look and tackled him.

Half an hour later, we'd ironed things out. I'd managed to convince the officers to uncuff my boss. They'd taken him into another room. Standard procedure for questioning.

Since there wasn't a scratch on me or on him, nor a bloody knife anywhere in the building, I think they believed our story. Problem was, the crazy guy had disappeared.

Oh, there was a blood trail, which helped, but no guy. Not anywhere in a reasonable vicinity.

"Had to have been hopped up on something to run off like that with a knife in his chest," one of the officers said. "He'll probably turn up in an ER."

"Or the morgue," answered another.

I'd had this conversation before, or one very similar to it. Sullivan had shot a guy and he'd run off like a jackrabbit, never to be seen or heard from again—as far as I knew.

"Can one of you call Detective Sullivan?" I asked.

"No need." Sullivan stepped into the bar. "I'm right here."

For the first time since I'd known him he wasn't

wearing a suit and tie but jeans with a light green button-down shirt. He appeared both comfortable and comforting. Strong, solid, sane. I wasn't attracted to him in the way he seemed to be attracted to me, but I was very glad to see him.

"I heard the call on my scanner," he continued.

Some cops were never off duty. It didn't surprise me at all that Sullivan was one of them.

"Got here as quick as I could," he said. "What's going on?"

I told him everything. Well, everything except the part where I swiped the altar icons. I'd left that out of my statement earlier as well. If I wanted to discover what they meant, I couldn't do so while they were locked up in the evidence locker at the NOPD.

The police had searched me, found the icons, and not even given them a second glance. For all they knew, the tiny wooden animals were my good-luck charms. I'd put them back in my pocket with no one the wiser.

They also hadn't mentioned the altar upstairs. Around here, the things were probably considered decoration.

Sullivan took my hand. "I'm glad you're okay."

"Me too." I squeezed his fingers.

A shuffle made me glance up; Rodolfo stood in the doorway. Though I knew he couldn't see us, nevertheless I snatched my hand away from Sullivan's guiltily.

"Detective," Rodolfo greeted.

My eyebrows shot up. How did he do that? Probably wasn't as big of a mystery as I thought. He'd no doubt heard Sullivan and me speaking even in the other room.

"Did anyone tell you I've been asking for you?" Sullivan glanced at me.

I shrugged. "He just got back."

"From where?"

Rodolfo tilted his head, staring slightly to the right of Sullivan's shoulder. "Am I under arrest?"

"Not yet."

Rodolfo smiled and the expression, without benefit of the eyes, was not a friendly one. "Then I don't believe I have to tell you where I've been."

Even *I* thought that sounded guilty.

"There have been disappearances," I began.

Rodolfo's mirrored gaze turned in my direction. "What do you know about them?"

Sullivan and I exchanged glances.

Whoops.

"Anne was here when I came in to ask about a man. Show his picture."

"And?"

"She didn't know him. Neither did your cohort."

"I'd like to help you, Detective, but I won't be any good with pictures."

"His name was Harvey Klingman."

"Was?"

Sullivan's sigh was impatient. "He was found in Lake Pontchartrain."

"People drown, Detective. I don't understand why Homicide is involved."

"Because the man didn't drown. There was the small matter of being set on fire before he wound up in the lake."

Rodolfo was good. If I hadn't been studying him,

I wouldn't have seen the flicker of emotion cross his face. I wasn't sure what it had been. Unease? Shock? Guilt? Whatever it was, I don't think Sullivan noticed.

"Set on fire," Rodolfo repeated. "Seems a little extreme."

"Not if you're trying to hide something."

"I'm an open book, Detective."

"Yeah, a regular fountain of helpful info, that's you," Sullivan muttered.

"If I knew anything that would help, I'd tell you."

"You didn't know Harvey?"

"No."

Well, that was a bald-faced lie. Or was it?

I'd seen them together, but who was to say Harvey hadn't given a false name, or perhaps not given his name at all? Maybe he'd merely been accompanying a blind man down the street, or telling John how much he enjoyed his music, then they'd parted company a few blocks over, and Harvey had gone on to meet his horrific and untimely demise.

If so, then telling Sullivan Rodolfo had been in the company of a dead man only hours before he became dead would ensure a trip to the slammer for my boss. I didn't want that.

I'd kept my counsel to give Rodolfo the benefit of the doubt. I planned to talk to him first, in private, about Harvey Klingman.

Time enough to tell Sullivan later, if there was anything to tell. Harvey wasn't going anywhere. Or at least I hoped he wasn't.

"I have several witnesses who saw Klingman at

Rising Moon the night before he disappeared," Sullivan said.

"This is the same tune, different verse, Detective, and just like those other times, with other people, I never saw them."

"You never see anyone. Which is damn convenient if you ask me."

I gasped at the rudeness. Sullivan gave me a glare; Rodolfo merely smiled.

"If you think this is convenient"—Rodolfo flicked a finger at his glasses—"you aren't as bright as I thought you were, Conner."

"And you aren't half as smart as you think you are, *John*. There's something about you that nags at me, and I'm going to find out what it is." With a nod in my direction, Sullivan left. The rest of the officers followed.

I waited until the door clicked shut behind them before I spoke. "I saw you with him."

Rodolfo didn't bother to pretend he didn't know which "him" I referred to. He crossed the short distance between us and grabbed me by the forearms, yanking me onto my toes. "You think I'm a murderer, *chica*?"

I meant to say no, but what came out instead was, "Are you?"

His fingers tightened to an almost painful degree, but I refused to glance away, even though I could read nothing from his hidden gaze. "I don't know any Harvey. I met a man leaving Rising Moon this morning and we walked together for a bit. He was pleasant. I enjoyed the conversation. I assume that was him."

"Why didn't you tell Sullivan?"

"I didn't know until you told me that the kind gentleman and the dead gentleman were one and the same."

Huh. He was right.

"How can you think I'm a murderer after we've been as close as two people can be?" he murmured.

"We had sex, John. We weren't close."

"And we never will be."

The despair in his voice made my throat thicken. Despite his darkness, his silence, his mystery, there was still an aura of need surrounding him that called to me. Was I using him to fill the empty place that was Katie? She'd needed me; I'd failed, so did I subconsciously hope to atone for my mistake with Rodolfo? I wasn't sure.

What I was sure of was that having him need me, wanting him to, was a very dangerous thing to want.

"I don't know how you can expect us to have anything other than an occasional bump in the night," I snapped, "when you lie at every opportunity."

He leaned into me, rubbing his cheek against my hair, brushing his lips across my temple, even as he continued to hold on to me so tightly I had no doubt I'd have a bruise come tomorrow. "And you don't?" he murmured.

I stiffened. "Me?"

"You say you're searching for your sister."

I pulled back, but he didn't let me go. "I am."

"You didn't mention that you're a private investigator."

"You checked me out?" I don't know why that annoyed me. Sullivan had done the same thing and I'd barely blinked.

"I may not be as smart as I think I am, but I'm definitely not as dumb as I look. You thought I'd let you work here, sleep here, and not make sure you aren't an extremely attractive escaped lunatic?"

"Are you—" I broke off before I said "blind." Instead I muttered, "I'm not attractive," horrified to discover I suddenly wanted to be.

"Pretty is as pretty does," he said, and I wasn't sure if that was an insult or a compliment. Lying wasn't very pretty.

"You're crazy."

Rodolfo smiled down at me. "Well, I never said *I* wasn't an escaped lunatic."

14

HIS HOLD GENTLED, his thumbs rubbing the insides of my arms so that I shivered. What was it about this man that made me behave completely out of character, had me doing things I knew were a bad idea, yet I couldn't bring myself to stop?

It couldn't just be his face, the body, that voice—which slid silkily from foreign endearments to guttural Anglo-Saxon curses, the accent here, there, gone again, never strong enough to figure out what, or even if, it was.

Couldn't be the sex either—though that had been spectacular—because I'd been fascinated with him long before he'd ever touched me.

I wasn't the kind of woman who fell in love at first sight—nor was I the kind to believe this *was* love. I was too practical for that.

What it was, was something that both scared and thrilled me, something I couldn't give up. At least not yet.

His palms cupped my hips. The pulse of his arousal pressed into my belly, and I shimmied against him.

He groaned and stepped back, putting out a hand to stop me when I followed. "We can't—"

"We can. Did. Will."

"Anne, I—" He shook his head. "I'm no good at this."

"I disagree. You're very good."

Most men would have been flattered. Of course, most men wouldn't be inching slowly away from a woman who wanted them.

He shoved a hand through his hair, then let it drop back to his side. "I meant you and I can't—"

"Can," I argued.

"Shouldn't. I'm not . . ." His voice trailed off.

"Not what, John?"

"Good for you. I'm not good for anyone."

"I disagree," I repeated.

"You don't know me."

"Then let me get to know you."

"No."

I don't know why that hurt. I didn't plan to stay; I doubted he'd go. This wasn't a love affair, and I didn't want it to be.

I'd made a promise—to myself, if not Katie—that I wouldn't move on with my life until I got hers back. I couldn't throw that promise to the wind and make a future with this man, even if he asked me to.

"Fine," I said, horrified when my voice shook. I stopped, cleared my throat and lifted my chin, staring straight into his . . . sunglasses. "We won't date. We'll just fuck."

The word tasted nasty on my tongue, but he'd hurt me and I wanted to hurt him back.

He muttered something in Spanish, but he didn't appear shocked or upset. All the anger went out of me.

"You don't have to worry about—" I broke off, uncertain how to broach the subject.

His head tilted. "What?"

"Me."

"But I do, *chica*, very much."

I didn't understand how he could say I was attractive, that he worried about me, then turn away the offer of my body. I knew I'd never model for *Vogue* or Victoria's Secret, but he didn't. Had I been that bad in bed?

"Never mind. I'm not accomplished like—"

"Who?" he asked warily.

"No one in particular. I'm sure the women you usually—" I waved my hand, then realized he couldn't see me. "Um, sleep with, I'm sure they're spectacular."

"You think I sleep with so many?"

"Why wouldn't you? The first night you thought I'd searched you out for sex."

"I don't sleep with just anyone."

My head came up. I wished for the hundredth time that I could see his eyes. "You don't?"

"No. I haven't been with a woman for a very long time."

"Why not?"

"I don't deserve happiness."

I wasn't sure what to say. How many times had I thought the same thing?

"Everyone deserves happiness," I lied.

"No," he said sharply. "They do not."

Since I agreed with him, I quit arguing and brought up the concern that had troubled me since we'd fallen all over each other. "You seemed upset the other night, after we— You know."

He smiled slightly. "I know."

"You don't have to worry," I repeated. His smile dissolved into confusion. "I'm, uh, on the pill," I finished quickly.

I *hated* this conversation.

"That wasn't what I was worried about."

"I don't have any weird diseases either." I bulldozed onward. "I've never . . ."

"Never?" he murmured, with a quirk of one dark eyebrow.

"Well, not never. I wasn't a virgin."

He muttered something I couldn't make out, and I decided I didn't want to.

"I've never been with anyone who hasn't used a condom," I blurted.

"Ah." Understanding dawned. "The modern plagues."

"What?"

"Haven't you heard the theory that the sexually transmitted diseases of this age are the Black Death of the old?"

" 'Fraid not."

"Well, you don't have to worry about me either. I was examined quite thoroughly when this"—he pointed to his eyes—"happened. Nothing wrong with me that a little eyesight couldn't cure. I haven't touched anyone since."

A tingle of unease began at the base of my spine. "How long?"

"Over a year now."

"You haven't had sex in a year," I repeated.

"That's right."

My shoulders sagged. No wonder he'd kissed me.

"What's the matter?" he murmured. "I'd think that news would make you happy."

"Sure. Of course." I laughed, the sound too loud in the sudden stillness. "I'm thrilled. But if you weren't worried about birth control or STDs then why were you so upset the other night?"

"I—" He lifted his hand as if he planned to touch my cheek, then lowered it and turned away. "I thought I hurt you."

"Did you hear me complaining?"

He remained silent.

"You didn't hurt me," I said. "If you had, I'd tell you. If you do, I'll tell you."

"My life, it hasn't been normal."

"Join the club."

"*Chica*, your life was so normal, it positively glowed." His sigh was long and sad and full of things I didn't understand. "Until three years ago."

Now I remained silent, because he was right.

"When are you going to give up?" he asked softly.

"Not until I know the truth."

"The truth can be an ugly thing."

"At least it's the truth."

"What if she's dead?"

"At least we'll know."

"What if she's worse than dead?"

"Worse?"

He turned, and the lights reflected off his sunglasses so brightly I flinched. For an instant the glowing white orbs had looked like eyes. In a horror flick.

"Believe me, there are things much worse than death."

"Is that why you talk to yourself? Why you have headaches? Nightmares? Why you won't let anyone close? Because of things that are worse than death?"

"Yes."

"Maybe if you talked about it—"

"No."

"I could—"

"What? Listen to my nightmares, kiss me and make them all go away? You can't. No one can."

"What happened to you?" I asked.

"Only what I deserved."

A sudden, shrill howling split the night. "What the hell is that?" I headed for the door.

His hand shot out, and he grabbed my arm—a pretty good catch for a blind man—then held on when I would have pulled away.

I opened my mouth to ask if he heard the howl, if he knew what it was, and he kissed me.

I tasted desperation on his lips, and I wasn't sure why. Was he as desperate for the taste of me as I was for a taste of him? I doubted it. He'd managed to convince me that the two of us together wasn't a good idea. I'd believed him when he'd said we couldn't do this.

So why were we?

I didn't know and, right now, I didn't care.

Mouth on mine, tongues at war, he walked me backward until my shoulders met the wall. An instant later, the lights went out.

I wondered momentarily what difference it made, then realized that with the lights glaring and the big window up front, anyone passing on the street would get a peep show worthy of Bourbon.

In truth, I liked the darkness. That glimpse of the lights reflected in Rodolfo's sunglasses had spooked me, and I didn't want to see it again. Especially now.

His body pressed the length of mine; he crowded me against the wall. I arched, moaning as his erection settled more firmly between my thighs.

Hands under my shirt, he filled them with my breasts, unfettered in the night. His fingers were so long and supple. With a musician's talent for coaxing music out of ivory and metal, he'd have no trouble coaxing everything out of me.

I could have sworn I heard that howl again, but when I broke the kiss, turning my attention toward the window, he swung me onto the bar in one swift movement, yanking my pajama bottoms to my ankles along with my panties, and I forgot about everything that wasn't in the room with me right now.

Perched on the edge of the cherrywood structure, I was several inches above where I needed to be. Or so I thought. When I tried to scoot off, to pull him upstairs, or maybe to the nearest table, he stopped me with a hand on my chest. "Lay back."

I resisted, but not for long, as his other hand dipped between my legs.

The bar was long and wide, not exactly comfortable on my spine, but I didn't care once his head descended.

His lips were as clever as his fingers; I felt like an instrument being persuaded to make music it had never before been capable of.

The tip of his tongue found the tight bud between my legs. How could a tongue be hard and soft, seductive and at the same time demanding?

My neck arched; I caught a glimpse of us in the mirrored wall behind the bar, his dark head framed by my thighs, pale in the slight drift of the distant streetlight through the window.

The picture as erotic as the sensations, I cried out, so near the edge I quivered with it. He pulled away, lifting me from the bar and depositing me on the nearest table. I had an instant where I felt like lunch as he gazed down at me, the black holes of his glasses familiar yet disturbing.

Then his loose trousers pooled at his ankles, and he pushed into me, stretching, filling, making what was empty full, what was two suddenly one, and the loneliness that lived inside of me receded.

I wrapped my legs around his hips, my arms around his neck. I was going to have a bruised backside in a few hours, but that seemed a small price to pay.

He slowed things down, his strokes deeper, longer, more deliberate. His clever hands traced my breasts, my belly, my nipples, as if memorizing their shape and texture.

When his fingers lifted to my face, I was tempted to deny him. Would he be able to tell I wasn't a pretty girl just by touch? Would it matter?

Except he whispered my name, and I couldn't tell

him no to that any more than I'd been able to tell him no to anything else.

He murmured words in several languages, his body moving in and out of mine as his fingertips traced my cheekbones, my jawline, the bridge of my nose. The latter made him smile and press his mouth to the crooked bone.

"Did someone hurt you?" he asked.

In that instant, I knew he was going to, worse than anyone else ever had.

I tried to shake off the weird premonition. I wasn't a woman who believed in such things.

"No," I said. "It was an accident, in a basketball game."

Speaking of how I'd broken my nose, taking an elbow on a rebound, made the last shiver of superstition die away.

"You're so . . ." His voice trailed off and I tensed. Did he know I was plain?

"Amazing," he finished, and an unladylike snort escaped.

"You don't think so?" he asked.

"People have called me many things," I said, "but 'amazing' doesn't happen to be one of them."

"Then most people are more blind than I am."

"I think you're seeing things that aren't there."

He tilted his head, seeming to look right at me, despite the barrier of the ever-present sunglasses. "I see better than you think."

I certainly hoped *that* wasn't true.

Unwilling to continue talking, I began to move against him, and his face tightened as did his body.

I came gasping his name, even as he gasped mine, the two words somehow more intimate than the actions that had preceded them.

The orgasm rolled through us both, his fueling mine and mine his, the sensations drawing out, seeming to become more intense rather than less.

When the final convulsion faded, he collapsed, his sweat-slicked skin sliding along my own.

I must have fallen asleep. That was the only explanation for what happened next. I sensed a shadow drift past the window, and I opened my eyes.

Staring through the glass was the biggest wolf I'd ever seen.

15

NOT THAT I'D ever seen one, except in a zoo. But those animals had always been scraggly, skinny, domesticated. This one wasn't.

The beast was big and pretty damn scary with its lips curled back and its fangs dripping saliva. The fur appeared light—white or perhaps gold—although I couldn't tell if that were the actual color or merely a reflection of the streetlight. I didn't remember ever seeing a white wolf.

That was my first clue that maybe the wolf wasn't real, even before I noticed the eyes. They were too damn human.

My own snapped open. How had they gotten shut?

I turned my head and stared at the gray light of dawn creeping through the suddenly empty front window. Rodolfo was nuzzling my neck, and my body ached everywhere.

I almost blurted, "Did you see it?" but managed to stop before I said something so foolish.

"Anne?" He straightened, bending to pull up his pants. "You okay?"

"Yeah." Mine had fallen off somewhere between the bar and the table. I retrieved them, yanking the pajama bottoms onto my legs as I continued to stare at the empty window.

"I—" He thrust his fingers through his hair. "I shouldn't have."

My mind, finally clearing of the last tendrils of sexual satisfaction, began to question, and my mouth followed suit. "Why did you?"

"Can't seem to help myself."

"No sex for a year will do that." I headed for the stairs.

He snatched my arm and held on. "That isn't the reason."

"No? It certainly isn't the way I look, the shape of my ass, the size of my breasts, or even my charming personality."

His lips twisted. "You don't know, do you?"

"Know what?"

"How truly beautiful you are."

"Oh, yeah. Prom queen material. That's me."

He stepped in close and ran his fingers lightly over my cheeks, my nose, my chin. I froze, unable to run away even though I should.

"This face has character. It's been lived in. Seen things, loved someone. That's more attractive than perfection could ever be."

A fingertip lingered on my lips. My body responded again to his, and I closed my eyes, fighting for a control that with this man seemed lost. Had he cast a spell on me?

I stepped away from his touch so I could think straight. Because to have been entertaining the idea of a love spell inside a building that was supposedly cursed, after I'd seen a wolf that couldn't exist, was definitely not clearheaded.

"Thank you," I managed, and I meant it. No one had ever told me I was beautiful before. Considering the first was a blind, self-admitted head case, I liked it more than I ought to.

"Maybe you should go home," he murmured. "To Philadelphia."

My heart gave one hard thud. "You want me gone?"

He took a deep breath, then let it out. "No. But it would be best if you were."

"Best for who?"

"You, *chica*."

"I'll think about it," I said, and I would. Though I doubted very much I would go.

"You need sleep," he said.

I did, so I headed for the stairs, hesitating when he didn't follow. "John?"

"Go ahead. I want to check on a few things."

I could understand that. The police had been everywhere.

I went to my room and lay down on the bed just as the door closed downstairs. I blinked a few times before vaulting up and racing across the floor to peer out the window.

The only thing I saw was a black cat darting across the street.

John must still be downstairs; maybe he'd put the cat out. That made sense.

But the sight of the animal reminded me of the carvings that were amazingly still in my pocket. I should show them to John, let him touch the wooden shapes, see if he noticed something I hadn't.

I went back into the tavern, but John was gone, which was just plain strange. How had he managed to disappear in the time it had taken me to get down there? For a blind man, he was unbelievably quick.

I checked the rest of the building. No John. No altar either. The thing had disappeared as if it had never been. Maybe that was why the police hadn't mentioned it. The altar hadn't been there by the time they arrived.

In my room I set the carvings on the nightstand. A cat. A pig. A chicken and a—

My eyes narrowed and I leaned in close. What I'd first thought to be a dog didn't look like a dog any longer. Was that only because I was paranoid, or was the carving actually that of a wolf?

THE NOTE TAPED to the front door of the voodoo shop informed all callers that the priestess was out of town until after Mardi Gras. There were business hours posted, but they were only for the retail establishment.

I couldn't say I blamed Cassandra for decamping. New Orleans was slowly going mad. With only a week left until Fat Tuesday, there were Mardi Gras parades galore. Hosted by private clubs known as "krewes," up to sixty-five extravaganzas might march through the city each season. Though none of them went through the French Quarter, the streets being too narrow, there was plenty going on there without them.

I stuck my hands in my pockets and jangled the icons. I didn't want to wait until after Mardi Gras to discover what they meant, so I headed from the voodoo shop on Royal Street to the café on Chartres. Maybe Maggie knew another voodoo priestess who could help.

Maggie's face brightened when she saw me. "I was going to call you when I got off. I did some research on those animal totems."

My stomach did a weird little dance, almost like déjà vu. "Quite the coincidence that I showed up."

"In voodoo we believe there are no accidents," Maggie said. "You came because you needed the information I can give you."

"And you just happened to be here?"

She rolled her eyes. "I'm always here. At least every morning at five."

"Last time I came, you said you'd never heard of icons on altars."

"That's because my studies were pretty general, and icons like the ones you described are quite specific."

"Do you have time for a break?" I asked.

Maggie checked her watch. "I'm about due."

She filled my order, then grabbed a cup of coffee for herself and led me to a table outside. The day was overcast, muggy, despite a lingering chill to the air.

I'd dug out the single pair of jeans my parents had sent, along with my favorite Philadelphia Eagles sweatshirt. I kept hoping that if I wore the shirt long enough, they wouldn't choke. However, I was starting to think the material would disintegrate from repeated washings long before the Eagles won a Super Bowl.

I pulled the icons out of my pocket and set them on

the table. She stared at them for several seconds, chewing her lip.

"This is such bad mojo," she muttered.

"What—who?"

Maggie lifted her gaze. "Mojo. Black magic. Which is why I didn't know about it."

My stomach did the dance again, and I doused the tickle with coffee. "You'd better explain."

"Voodoo is a religion of peace, understanding, inclusion. It's about gentleness and love, not violence and hate." Her smile became sad. "Which is why I like it."

"I can understand that. But why didn't you know about the black magic side?"

"Every houngan, or voodoo priest, has his own community, his own rules and rituals. But a houngan or a mambo, a priestess, only practices the light side. The dark side is known but never visited." She brushed her finger across the wolf icon, then yanked it back as if she'd been burned. "Only a bokor, an evil priest, would do this."

"Do *what*?"

"There's a legend in voodoo, of a shapeshifting sorcerer. This shapeshifter can take any form—horse, wolf, cat, pig."

"And what does the sorcerer do once he changes form?"

"The legend says he wanders the night, drinking the blood of children."

I flinched. "So he's both a werewolf and a vampire?"

"A were-something and a vampire."

"Does the legend have any theories as to why someone would want to do this?"

"Some say the sorcerer is cursed by the spirits. A bokor gains his power from the loas. He buys the magic at great cost, most often a life. If the bokor backs out of his promise, the loas might in turn curse him to become a shapeshifter. There are also those who feel such power is inherited and some who think it comes only after great illness."

"I still don't understand what a person would gain from being a shapeshifter."

Not that I was buying any of this. But I had a feeling someone was.

"Immortality?" Maggie suggested. "I think were-wolves are pretty hard to kill. I would assume were-cats, were-pigs, were-chickens aren't any easier."

"This is crazy," I said. "You're saying someone made an altar, set these icons on it, then changed into . . ." I waved my hand at the figures.

"I know it's hard to believe, and I'm not saying I do. I'm just telling you what I found out when I went searching for totemlike animals and a voodoo altar. I also found quite a bit of information on different Native American tribes who use totems to represent their spirit animal. Many believe their essence is contained in those icons, and they merge beneath the moon."

"I thought we were discussing voodoo; now you're bringing up Native Americans?"

"I'm just pointing out that many different cultures and religions have transformation legends. The Navajo believe certain shamans can don the skin of an animal and become one. They're known as skinwalkers, both witch and werewolf."

My head spun with all the information.

"I don't suppose you've noticed any strange animals lurking around under the moon?" Maggie smiled when she said it but I couldn't.

I'd thought the wolf in the window a dream, but what about the black cat in the stairwell and on the street—a cat I'd only seen at night, after first finding the altar?

My eyes flicked to the pig and I heard again the squeal, saw the potbellied shadow darting across the alley behind Rising Moon.

I shook my head; Maggie took that as an answer and continued. "Someone is probably just trying out a spell they read on the Internet."

"Right."

"That doesn't mean they turned into a lougaro."

"A what?" I managed.

"Technically, a voodoo werewolf."

Suddenly I was having a hard time breathing. Sullivan had intimated that someone who thought he was a werewolf was killing people.

But what if someone who actually *was* a werewolf was killing people?

16

MY LAUGHTER WAS slightly hysterical, which just wasn't like me. I forced myself to stop, take a sip of coffee and several deep breaths.

Just because there'd been an altar with icons that might or might not be a voodoo spell to transform a person into a wolf—or a cat, or a pig, or a chicken—didn't mean it had happened. I knew better.

"I have to go back to work," Maggie said.

I nodded, unable to speak.

"These are just legends," she continued. "There *is* magic in the world; I believe that, but not this kind of magic."

I cleared my throat. "You're right. I'm letting myself get spooked by this place."

"New Orleans will do that. Most haunted city in America, they say."

"Swell," I muttered, and she grinned.

"If you have any more questions, you know where to find me." She leaned over and wrote a www. address on one of the napkins. "Here's the Web site where I got most of the info. You can always try there first. There's even an e-mail address to ask questions. It's very helpful."

"Thanks."

"No problem." She left me alone in the courtyard.

Now what?

Someone with access to Rising Moon thought they were a lougaro, or at the least thought they could become one. People were disappearing or winding up dead after visiting the place. Were the two connected?

As Maggie said, "There are no accidents." I didn't think this was one either.

I should probably tell Sullivan, except what, exactly, would I tell him? He wasn't going to believe the shapeshifter theory any more than I did.

As I exited the coffee shop, I tossed the icons into the nearest trash bin. Maybe that would help.

Though, somehow, I doubted it.

A FEW DAYS later I was doing my best to catch some sleep before my shift and having very little luck. I tossed; I turned. My pillow felt all lumpy.

When I lifted it, another small bag of tangy-scented herbs rested beneath.

Who kept doing this? I didn't care for the idea that someone had been in my room and touched my pillow. What else had they touched?

I set the thing on my nightstand, determined to ask King about it. I'd also request a change of locks on both the club and my bedroom door. Seemed like any-one could waltz in here at any time and do just about anything. Yet no one ever saw them.

And why was that?

"Ghosts," I muttered, remembering Sullivan's admonition that this place, and many others in town, were haunted. However, I didn't believe in ghosts either.

Without the proverbial pea beneath the princess, I slept, waking at the first note of the piano downstairs. All around me the blue velvet darkness swirled.

I let the smooth tones soothe me. I didn't have to be downstairs for an hour and right now the appeal of just drifting was too strong to be denied. I hadn't liked jazz when I'd arrived, but the more I heard, the more I learned, the more it grew on me.

I slid away on the music, floating between the two worlds, not awake, not asleep, both hyper-aware and zoned out at the same time.

Suddenly my eyes snapped open. Had that been the door closing? Someone leaving, someone coming, or nothing at all?

"John?"

No one answered. Cold sweat tickled my pores. I wished, not for the first time, that I'd brought my gun to New Orleans.

Annoyed at my fear, sick and tired of cowering, I flicked on the lamp, leaving my hand around the base, prepared to throw the thing at someone's head if I had to.

But no one was there.

I gave a little laugh, which sounded more like a nervous cough. How did John stand the darkness? The uncertainty? The fear?

Except he never seemed uncertain or fearful. The longer I knew him, the more amazing he became.

It wasn't until I'd taken a shower, dressed for work,

then returned to the nightstand to grab the bag of herbs that I saw the white handkerchief. Since I didn't own a white handkerchief, I was understandably distressed.

Even more so when it became apparent the material was wrapped around something. I should probably call the police, but I'd never been very good at waiting.

I tugged on the handkerchief, wincing as it pulled free. I don't know what I expected—a severed finger, a toe, perhaps an eyeball. Too many horror movies during my teen years, no doubt.

However, what spilled out of the white cotton and thunked against the surface of the nightstand had me hyperventilating worse than any of those other horrific items would have.

Because the sterling silver bracelet was Katie's.

S HE'D BEEN WEARING it the night she disappeared. I remembered because we'd fought over the thing.

The last words she'd said to me had been, "You can wear this bracelet when I'm dead."

And being a sister, I'd said, "I'll look forward to it."

She'd flounced out of the house, and I hadn't seen her or the bracelet again.

Until now.

My fingers trembled as they reached out. I was centimeters away from picking up the silver band when I saw the blood, the dirt, and snatched them away.

"Oh, God," I whispered. Was that Katie's blood? If so, then who had brought the bracelet here?

I wrapped my arms around myself as a chill overtook me. Who had been in my room? When? Did it matter? I had another lead in a case that had been as cold as a January morning, even with the picture of Katie on the street outside this building. I'd take whatever clues I could get and run with them.

Wrapping the bracelet in the handkerchief, I glanced around the room for someplace to hide it until I could get the thing analyzed.

Maybe here wasn't the best idea. People seemed to come in and out at will. Instead, I sneaked into the hall, then into a spare bedroom, glancing about uneasily for another altar, thrilled when I didn't find one. I tucked the shrouded silver beneath the mattress, then returned to my room and dialed Sullivan.

I got voice mail. Never could find a cop when you needed one.

At the beep, I left a message. "I need something analyzed. Can you come to Rising Moon when you get a chance? I'm working tonight."

I ran down the steps and nearly slammed into a customer when I entered the tavern. From the size of the crowd, if not the skill of the music, I deduced John was at the piano, even before I glanced over and saw that I was right.

King scowled in my direction. I was late and we were busy. The next several hours passed in a blur of drink orders, laughter, and song.

Rodolfo was in rare form, playing continuously, seemingly inexhaustible, almost rabid in his intensity. I found myself anticipating the end of my shift. Would we climb the steps to my room and be together?

Thinking of him kept my mind off Katie and her bracelet, kept me from wondering, too often, what it meant. But it didn't keep me from watching the door, starting whenever it opened, then sighing in disappointment when Sullivan didn't walk through.

At last, long past midnight, John rose from the piano, and despite numerous urgings to the contrary, refused to go back, disappearing instead into the office and closing the door. The crowd began to thin immediately, giving me a chance to talk to King.

"Do you know what this is?" I laid the slightly crunchy bag of who knows what on the bar.

King glanced up in the middle of pouring Wild Turkey into a shot glass, and the liquor squirted wildly across the previously pristine bar.

I snatched the tiny bag out of harm's way. "Hey!"

He glanced furtively around. "You keep that thing out of sight," he snapped.

That wasn't quite the reaction I'd expected, but at least he appeared to know something. I tucked it into my pocket, then waited as patiently as I could for him to complete the order.

He motioned me to the end of the bar. "Where'd you get that?"

"Under my pillow—for the second time this week."

His perpetual frown deepened. "Makes no sense."

"I thought it was some New Orleans tradition. Like potpourri."

He snorted. "That's a gris-gris."

"Voodoo?" King nodded. "What's it for?"

"Could be protection, a curse, or even a love charm."

Love charm? Hell.

I removed the bag from my pocket and held it out. "What about this one?"

He stared at the gris-gris for an instant. "I told you before, I don't know nothin' about voodoo."

"Who would put this under my pillow?"

"Don't know nothin' 'bout that either."

"I think we need to change the locks on this place."

King's eyes narrowed. "I think you're right."

I turned, determined to finish my shift and hunt down Sullivan, then paused at the sight of John leaning in the doorway to the office. His dark glasses shone starkly against his overly pale face.

I started toward him, planning to ask him a few questions, but he backed away, lifting a shaking hand to his head. "Don't," he muttered.

I paused. "You have a migraine?"

He nodded, winced at the motion, then took several quick steps in retreat, before shutting the door in my face.

I was tempted to follow, but what could I do? From past experience with my mother, I'd learned a migraine sufferer was better left alone, in the dark.

"Anne," King called. "A little help here."

Rising Moon had started to fill up again. Some locals drifted in, started to play, and we got even busier. Mardi Gras was almost upon us.

I ended up running for another two hours and forgetting, for the most part, about magic charms *and* John Rodolfo. Around three A.M., Sullivan strode in.

"You got my message," I said.

That stopped him. "What message?"

"If you didn't get it, then why are you here?"

"I tried to call; no one answered."

I indicated the band, then the crowd. "I'm not surprised. What did you want?"

"Your boss has been arrested."

"But—" I glanced toward the rear of Rising Moon. "He's in the office. With a migraine."

"He was found standing over a murdered woman, and he says he doesn't remember how he got there."

"That's impossible."

"Why don't we take a look?"

I shrugged and led the way. Certainly Rodolfo could have left the office and slipped out the back door. But if he'd had a migraine, I doubted he'd gone far. Of course, he'd only *said* he had one. He could have been lying.

"What the hell you doin' here?" King demanded.

"Official business," Sullivan answered. "She says your boss is in the office; I say he's locked up for murder."

King moved swiftly, twisting the key on the register, then hurrying out from behind the bar, wiping his hands on a towel as he went. He paused at the microphone, yanking it rudely away from the young woman who was singing a very nice rendition of "Sentimental Journey."

"Everybody out," he ordered. "We closed."

People began to complain, but King drew himself up to his full height, flexed his impressive biceps beneath the smooth cotton of his white T-shirt, and scowled. Everybody got out.

"Did you see John leave?" I asked, following King toward the back of the club.

"No." King's gaze turned to Sullivan. "You see Johnny yourself?"

Sullivan's confidence wavered a bit. "No."

"Not him then. It's an easy thing to give another man's name."

The weight on my chest lightened. That was it. The man behind bars wasn't John, but someone who'd seen him play, remembered his name, then used it at an inopportune time. Sullivan had just jumped the gun.

I opened the door to the office. "John?" I murmured. "You here?"

Silence was my only answer. I hated to turn on the harsh overhead lights, though really, what would it matter? I didn't get a chance to decide. Sullivan flicked the switch.

I flinched in the glare, then stared at an empty room.

"So," Sullivan said, "which one of you wants to come with me?"

17

"WHY YOU NEED one of us?" King demanded. "You got your mind all made up."

"Rodolfo needs a lawyer, but he won't call one. Says he's innocent. Insisted that his one phone call be made here, and since no one answered . . ." Sullivan spread his hands.

"Such service," King murmured, eyes on me. "You'd think you had another reason for coming to Rising Moon altogether."

The detective's cheeks got a little red.

King gave a derisive laugh. "You go along, Anne. Talk some sense into Johnny while I finish up."

I continued to stare at the empty office. I was starting to wonder if Rising Moon had secret passageways I wasn't aware of.

"Sense?" I repeated. "How will I manage that?"

"Do your best." King shrugged. "If you need bail money, call me."

"There isn't going to be bail on a murder case," Sullivan stated.

King moved unbelievably fast for such a big man, crossing the short distance separating him from the detective in a fraction of time and pausing only centimeters away from bumping chests. "Johnny. Don't. Murder. People."

Each word was low, intense, clipped. Sullivan's fingers clenched, and I wondered what I'd do if they decided to go round and round. There was no way I'd be able to stop them. I doubted anyone could. Then I'd have to bail King out of jail, even if I couldn't do the same for Rodolfo.

Luckily, once he'd made his point, King went back to work without saying another word.

"He seems pretty certain," I said.

"He's going to have to be a lot more than certain to get your boss out of this."

I faced Sullivan. "You aren't very objective on the subject of John Rodolfo."

"I got a feeling." He shrugged. "There's something not right about the guy."

Far be it from me to argue with a cop's hunch. Besides, he'd need more than that to charge Rodolfo with murder and make it stick.

"Why did you call me?" At my puzzled look, he continued, "You said you left a message."

"Oh!" *Katie's bracelet.* "I'll be right back."

I ran upstairs, retrieved the item, then returned, beckoning Sullivan outside, where I placed the package in his hand. "Someone left this on my nightstand today."

He opened the white handkerchief, frowned and glanced up.

"It's Katie's," I said.

His eyes widened, before he nodded and pocketed the thing. "I'll take care of this."

"Thanks."

Sullivan had parked his car, a navy blue Crown Victoria, at the curb out front. We climbed in and buckled up. The car smelled almost new, not a whiff of old smoke or leftover food, not even spilled coffee. The floor mats were shiny, so was the console. I had a sneaking suspicion he'd recently used Windex on the rearview mirrors. Was the man human?

Frenchmen was a narrow two-way street trolled mostly by cabs. Sullivan glanced over his shoulder, then pulled a sharp U-turn and headed for the police station.

I still had hopes that the man in the cell would not be John. My hopes were dashed by the sound of a harmonica playing "When the Saints Go Marching In" even before I got close enough to recognize Rodolfo playing the thing.

A few other men were incarcerated nearby, but at this hour they were sleeping. Considering the city, and the imminence of Mardi Gras, maybe they were passed out.

"I'll leave you two alone," Sullivan murmured, and the music stopped.

John's chin went up. "Anne?"

He had a bruise on his forehead. "Who hit him?" I demanded, my fingers curling into fists.

Sullivan lifted his hands in surrender. "No one. He tripped when he was being booked." He shot a frown

Rodolfo's way. "Smacked his head right into the camera and broke the lens. I'll go see if they have another set up yet."

Sullivan left, quietly closing the door behind him.

"You need to call a lawyer, John."

"I didn't kill anyone."

"I never said you did."

"So there's no need for a lawyer."

"Obviously you aren't familiar with the U.S. legal system. There's always need for a lawyer."

He made his way carefully across the cement floor until he stood on the other side of the bars. "They'll have to let me out sooner or later."

"You really think so?"

He shrugged.

"Sullivan says you were found next to a dead woman."

"That's what they told me."

"You weren't?"

"I don't know where I was, and I couldn't exactly see what, or who, was next to me."

"Oh, that's right, you don't remember how you got there. Where *was* there?"

"Storyville."

My brow creased as I attempted to place the name. I'd heard it or read it somewhere.

Then it hit me. Up until about eighty years ago, Storyville had been the only legal red-light district in the country. To this day, the place retained the dangerous aura from times gone by—especially at night—though I doubted the area was referred to as Storyville anymore.

"Why on earth would you go there?" I demanded. "You want to die?"

He gave me that smile again, the one that could have meant anything—yes, no, have you even been listening?

"I don't know why I was there," he said patiently. "I didn't mean to be."

"Did you black out?"

"For want of a better word."

"You've lost time before? Woken up somewhere else?"

"Only when the headaches are very bad."

Which might account for the dead bodies turning up with disturbing regularity in the Crescent City. Until now I'd refused to believe John could be responsible for the killings; he didn't seem capable of it. But the more I got to know him, the more capable he became. And now that he'd admitted losing time . . .

"We definitely need a lawyer," I muttered.

"No you don't." Sullivan was back. He didn't look happy.

"Why not?"

"The doctor at the morgue examined the body." He broke off to glare at Rodolfo. John smirked as if he knew what Sullivan was about to say, except the detective didn't say it. He continued to stare at John, fury seeming to roll off him in waves.

Eventually, I couldn't stand it any longer. "What did the doctor say?"

Sullivan's gaze turned to me. "The rookie at the scene got a little spooked by all the blood. Throat wounds bleed like a bitch."

"I can imagine." And I could; what I wished was that I'd stop.

"The dead woman, a river of blood, Rodolfo standing over her, hands covered with it—"

"Perhaps I was trying to resuscitate her," Rodolfo interrupted.

"With a mortal throat wound, I doubt resuscitation would work," Sullivan pointed out.

"I didn't know she had a mortal throat wound."

"Do you know how to resuscitate anyone?" Sullivan pressed.

"No."

Triumph spread over the detective's face, but I put an end to it. "What did the doctor say that suddenly made you think John doesn't need a lawyer?

Sullivan's expression faded. "The throat was torn, not cut." His eyes met mine. "By an animal, not a knife."

"Another mysterious animal attack," I murmured.

"Yeah."

"What kind of animal?"

"Too soon to say."

I was starting to wonder about that werewolf; however, last night there had been a crescent moon and not a full one.

"You're free to go," Sullivan continued. "But don't leave town."

"He's still a suspect?" I asked.

"Not in this murder."

But there were so many others.

A uniformed officer escorted John away to be processed for release. I followed, but when we reached the main area, Sullivan put a hand to my elbow. "I dropped the bracelet off at the lab." His face was concerned. "I still wish you wouldn't stay at Rising Moon."

I glanced at John, who stood with the other officer near the front of the station. "I'll be fine. King's going to have the locks changed."

"There's something between you and Rodolfo," Sullivan said.

"Not really."

The only thing between us was sex, and really, that was nothing.

"I doubt you're going to catch him in the act," Sullivan continued. "He's pretty slick."

"Maybe he didn't do anything."

"He did something. I know it."

I shook my head and said, "You're obsessed by this, by him."

"I don't think I'm the one who's obsessed."

I didn't want to go there.

I knew Sullivan liked me, that he wanted more from me than friendship. I knew I should tell him I didn't feel the same way, but I wasn't sure how. I'd never once had to let someone down easy. And I didn't want to piss him off before I figured out what was going on around here. I needed his help and his goodwill.

"There's a connection between Rodolfo and the murderers," Sullivan continued, "and I *will* find it. I just wish I hadn't put you in danger."

"I'm not in danger," I said, but I wasn't so sure. "Katie was last seen at Rising Moon. I have to stay."

"I'm not so sure she was there."

"What?"

"You know, there are ways to alter photographs. It isn't hard."

"Why would anyone—"

"I don't know. Would you give me the photo? Let me have it examined by an expert?"

I hesitated. Though I hadn't been having any luck, I still wanted to show the photograph to people in the bar.

"I'll make a copy," Sullivan said.

I nodded and handed him the original. He was back a few minutes later with a very good reproduction.

"Thanks." I tucked the new photo into my back pocket.

"You have to consider that perhaps Katie wasn't here at all."

"But the bracelet—"

"Might have been left by the person who took Katie in the first place."

A shiver passed down my back. "Why?"

"I don't know, Anne." Sullivan stroked my cheek. His touch was nice—soft and sweet, despite the size and roughness of his hand. "You can't let anything go either."

"I guess we're two of a kind."

"Yeah." I could tell by the look in his eyes that he wanted to kiss me. I almost told him then that we could be nothing more than friends, but before I could someone cleared his or her throat and we jumped apart.

John stood only a few feet away. I knew he hadn't seen Sullivan touching me; he couldn't know how close we'd been to an embrace. Yet I felt as if, beyond the reflective sunglasses, his eyes were full of condemnation.

I stiffened. He had no claim on me, just as I had none on him. He'd made that clear.

"Are you ready to leave?" I asked, pleased that my voice sounded normal.

"Are you?" His voice dripped with sarcasm.

He hadn't seen Sullivan and me together, but he'd obviously heard what we'd said. Something about being two of a kind.

So what? We were.

"I'll be in touch," Sullivan murmured as I took John's arm and we headed for the door.

A squad car awaited us. I was tempted to say we'd walk, but between the police station and Frenchmen lay a lot of ground, and most of it was teeming with revelers in various states of inebriation. The music from Bourbon Street pulsed in the air; the multicolored lights pushed against the night sky like approaching dawn. We got in the car.

Only a few minutes later the silent officer deposited us in front of Rising Moon. The place was empty and dark. I'd figured King would be waiting to hear what had happened. Instead, a note lay on the bar.

Call me. K.

King had scribbled his number below the words.

Quickly I dialed and got voice mail. I guess he wasn't too worried.

"Everything is fine," I said. "There was a mistake. They released him."

I hung up and turned to John, who sat at the piano bench but didn't touch the keys.

"Do you want me to take you to your apartment?" I asked.

"I can find my own way home. I'm not a cripple."

My eyebrows shot up. How politically incorrect.

"Okay," I said slowly, uncertain what he *did* want from me. I sat in an overstuffed chair that faced the piano, and then I waited.

After a few more minutes of contemplation, John put his fingers to the keys and began to play. I didn't know the song, but I didn't need to. Closing my eyes, I let the emotions wash over me—pounding fury, a trill of longing that gave way to the pulse of desire. Music had never affected me like this before; I doubted it ever would again.

When the last note faded, I was breathless. I opened my eyes, and he stood right in front of me. How could he move so quickly and so quietly?

The bruise on his forehead didn't appear as dark in this light. I lifted my hand to touch it, and he spun toward the window. "You're awfully chummy with Sullivan."

Hmm. Could he be jealous? I couldn't get my mind around the idea that one man could be jealous of another over me. Such things didn't happen to plain PIs from Philly.

"I spoke to him about Katie."

"That's all?" He turned, and the black pit of his glasses seemed to bore into my brain. I found myself spilling things I should not.

"He hired me to help him."

"He hired you to watch me."

"Not exactly."

"He certainly didn't hire you to fuck me." His head tilted. "Or maybe he did."

I leaped to my feet, which only put us so close the heat of his body washed over mine.

"I'm not a whore," I snapped.

"No. Whores don't take money. Prostitutes do."

I slapped him. Or I would have if he hadn't caught my wrist before it reached his cheek. My eyes narrowed. "Have you been practicing the Force, Luke?"

Confusion flickered over his face. "What?"

"*Star Wars*. The movie?"

"I don't get to see many movies," he said sarcastically.

Considering this one had been made long before he'd lost his sight, I couldn't believe Rodolfo hadn't watched it. But I suppose everyone couldn't be a sci-fi action flick buff like me.

His fingers, which could coax such beauty from both a piano and a saxophone, were strong. They clenched, just short of brutal. "The thought that you were sent here by him, that you touched me because—"

"If you believe that, then you don't know me."

He released my arm as if my skin had suddenly become scalding hot. "But I *don't* know you, Anne. This is sex, not love. Right?"

Something in his voice made me ask, "Do you want it to be love?"

He didn't answer for so long, I gave up. "I'm tired. I'm going to bed."

I left him in the club alone, climbing the stairs, watchful for any black cats or potbellied pigs, maybe a stray chicken or two.

A thin shaft of silver from the fading crescent moon filtered through the window. I flicked on the lights, scoped the place out before I moved to shut the door, then I yelped.

John stood in the hall.

Before I could say anything, he wrapped his arms around my waist and kissed me.

The embrace was different from any we'd shared before. Gentler, sweeter, but for all of that it was also more intense—as if he were trying so hard to be something he was not.

He buried his face in my neck, took a deep breath and sighed. I sensed surrender in that sigh, but not surrender to the moment, to the rush and the need, but surrender to sanity, and I didn't want that. I wanted him.

Before he could withdraw, I sank to my knees, rubbing my mouth along the solid length of him. He wore only loose cotton trousers; I had no doubt there was nothing between them and him. When I tugged on the elastic waistband, I discovered I was right.

He leaned back, flicked off the lights, slammed, then locked the door. The darkness shrouded us, making me bold. My sexual experiences were minimal at best; they'd never included this, and suddenly I wanted them to. Before he could stop me, I took him in my mouth.

"Anne," he groaned, his hand cupping my head, thumb brushing my cheek.

I no longer craved the gentleness; I longed for something more. A scrape of my teeth against his tip, and his fingers tightened, tangling in my hair.

"Show me," I demanded.

The rhythm wasn't hard to pick up, especially when

he did as I asked, guiding my untutored mouth, encouraging me with low-voiced, slightly pornographic instructions. I'd never figured myself for someone who'd enjoy that, but tonight I did.

Was it because his talk of love had scared me, and I needed to put what was between us back on a plane I could live with? How could I fall for a man I knew nothing about? A man who, earlier, had been covered with the blood of a dead woman. A man whom I'd suspected of murder and more?

The heat of him, the scent and the taste, called to a wildness in me I hadn't known existed until I'd gone down on my knees. However, I wasn't the one begging; I was the one in control. I was more aroused than I could ever recall being and I still wore every stitch of my clothes.

My hands clutched his hips, slowed him down. I inched away, blowing a soft, warm breath across the wetness left by my mouth, and he shuddered. "Anne."

I took pity and led him to my bed. He sat on the edge and I drew his shirt over his head like a child, then gave him a little shove. He fell back, everything limp—except that one thing.

I wished that I could see him, admire him, but the darkness left him in shadow. So I took a page from his book and used my hands to "see" the rippling abdomen, the light dusting of curly, dark hair on his legs, the smooth, taut biceps.

Here and there I felt the ridge of a scar, with an especially thin, long one low on his belly. I paused, wondering if that was all that was left of the slashes he'd obtained during the mugging.

I drifted my palm over his cheek, his chin, his hair. "What color are your eyes?" I murmured, and he jerked as if I'd struck him.

"You mean, what color *were* they?"

I winced. Why had I ruined the mood?

He reached for the glasses. "You want to see them?"

"No," I said quickly, and his hand dropped back to his side.

I was still completely clothed, standing over him, completely naked. Crawling onto the bed, I indulged my fantasy, running my mouth across his warm, bronzed skin. Touching him, teasing him, causing him to beg all over again. I made up for my rude and foolish question; or at least I hoped I did.

Eons later, when he was gasping, straining, tugging at my clothes, I drew off my shirt, my pants, my underwear.

"Ride me," he urged, and I lowered myself onto the hard, hot bulk of him.

Perhaps it was the way he held my hips, his thumbs caressing even as his fingers gripped. Or maybe it was the way he said my name, a guttural moan that had the nuance of an endearment. Despite the intense nature of his movements, there was something tender about them too.

Regardless, when he arched, pressing upward with his body while pulling downward on mine, the orgasm was so strong I clenched my teeth to keep from screaming. As the waves of pleasure died away, we remained joined, bodies slick with sweat. I didn't have the energy to move. Thankfully I didn't have to.

His palm skimmed the length of my back, clever

fingers kneading my spine, drifting along my shoulder, down my arm, then hesitating for a fraction of a second before linking his fingers with mine.

"Doesn't everyone always want it to be love, *cher*?" he whispered.

18

His words weren't really a statement but a question. I wasn't sure how to answer them.

I didn't need to as, moments later, his steady, deep breaths revealed he'd fallen asleep, even before his fingers went lax in mine. I rolled to the side, staring at the ceiling as I rubbed my thumb across his palm.

Didn't everyone always want it to be love?

I had. But I'd never thought I'd meet a man who'd agree. Until I'd met him.

Everything had moved so fast, suspiciously so. I wasn't comfortable with my feelings for John Rodolfo, or his apparent feelings for me.

Slowly I inched from the bed and retrieved the gris-gris I'd tossed onto the bathroom sink before I'd headed to the police station. I remembered King's words. *Could be protection, a curse, or even a love charm.*

"Love charm," I murmured, squeezing it.

John moaned in his sleep; his head thrashed back and forth.

"Shh," I whispered, gazing at the gray light of dawn through the window.

I could really use some coffee.

W HAT DO YOU know about gris-gris?"
Maggie glanced up from the espresso machine where she was frothing milk for what appeared to be a cappuccino. The well-dressed businessman at the counter ignored both of us as he took the cup and tossed a dollar into the tip jar.

"Pretty much," she said cheerfully. "You want anything?"

I glanced at the chalkboard menu, brightening at what I saw there. "A large Jamaican Blue Mountain."

I loved that stuff. Might be expensive but worth every penny.

Maggie poured my coffee, then got some of her own—a cheaper blend—and joined me at the nearest table. "What do you want to know about gris-gris?"

"They're charms?"

"Right."

"What does 'gris-gris' mean?"

"The term itself comes from the French for 'gray' and refers to the black and white nature of the magic."

"They're magic?"

She smiled indulgently. "What is it about 'charm' that you don't understand?"

"The part where a bag of stuff is magic."

"It's not what's inside that counts so much as the

power of the one who prepares the gris-gris, combined with a strong belief in them."

"Do you know how to make one?" I asked.

"I know what goes into the most popular ones, but I can't make them. I'm not ordained."

"You *could* make one. You're not physically incapable."

"No. But like I said, the power comes from the belief and the magic, which comes from the houngan or mambo who makes it. I'm not one."

"Could a sorcerer—a . . ." I waved my hand for the word.

"Bokor?"

"Yes. Could he or she make a gris-gris?"

"Sure. Although bokors are more apt to make an *ouanga*."

"Which is?"

"A black-magic charm, sometimes a potion. The bokor will perform a travail—a ceremony to channel the negative supernatural forces of the loas directly into the charm."

I reached into my pocket and pulled out the small bag. "What's this?"

Maggie stared at it warily. "I doubt it's a *ouanga*."

"Because?"

"You only have to touch them to become ill."

I dropped the thing onto the table, and she laughed. "Relax. *Ouangas* aren't very powerful."

"Because?" I repeated.

"Because good is stronger than evil."

She was so young.

"Is it a gris-gris?" I asked.

"Yes." She reached for the bag, hesitating before touching it. "You mind?"

"Go ahead. I'd like to know what it's for."

She released the small string tied around the opening and poured the contents into her palm—a gray concoction spotted with particles of red and purple.

"Is it a love charm?" I asked.

"Oh, no. A love charm is made of sweetness—orange flower water, rose water, or sugar and the hair of the loved one."

I lifted my hand to my head and her eyes danced. "Underarm hair or pubic hair is most common."

I wrinkled my nose and she laughed at the expression before continuing. "This is . . ." Her voice trailed off as she leaned forward and took a sniff before I could warn her. She sneezed, violently, several times. "Pepper?"

"I thought so too, but not black pepper."

"No. Something red." Her face took on a faraway expression. "I know this."

Maggie got up and went behind the counter, snatching the register key, then a card for one of the computers. "Come on."

I followed her into the Internet section of the café, where she tapped at a keyboard, then began to surf.

I'd nearly finished my huge cup of coffee before she said, "Here we go. The combination of ashes from an outdoor flame and red pepper is a charm against beasts of the swamp."

"But I'm not in the swamp."

"Honey, this whole city is a swamp; you just showed up during the dry season."

"I see the ashes and the red pepper, but what made it purple?"

Maggie tapped at the computer a few more times then gave a low whistle. "Maybe I was wrong about this not being a *ounga*."

I moved closer, uneasy. "Why?"

"The texture of the purple bits, the slightly musty scent—I'm pretty sure it's monkshood." She glanced at me. "Wolfsbane."

"That's poisonous."

"Only if ingested."

"What does it do?"

"The addition of monkshood will fortify an everyday charm against earthbound beasts into a charm against a supernatural monster." She glanced over her shoulder. "A loup-garou."

My skin suddenly felt prickly, itchy, too small for my body. The word was far too familiar.

"Lougaro? Didn't we already go here?"

"No. A lougaro is a voodoo shapeshifter, a sorcerer who can shift into pretty much any animal he wants to. A loup-garou is a French werewolf."

"My head hurts," I muttered.

"There's a legend." She paused, then glanced around the café uneasily before continuing. "A legend of New Orleans, passed down only to those who believe."

"It's a secret?"

"An oral tradition."

After last night, I was thinking of starting my own oral tradition. I yanked my mind away from the image of John Rodolfo naked in my bed. I had work to do.

"This story isn't written down anywhere?" I asked.

"From what I was told, anyone who's tried to do so has wound up dead."

An involuntary bark of laughter escaped. "That's ridiculous."

"Tell it to the dead people."

"Maggie, you really believe that?"

"Well, let's just say *I'm* not going to write it down."

"But you are going to tell me about it?"

She glanced around again, then began. "Over a hundred years ago a man was cursed to run as a wolf beneath the crescent moon."

I started, remembering the thin, smiling crescent moon that had risen last night. Coincidence? Not if I believed Maggie's theory that there were none.

"Don't werewolves come out under the full moon?"

"A loup-garou is different. According to the legend, a loup-garou is cursed, not bitten."

"Then that whole thing about werewolves making other werewolves by biting them is true?" Or as true as a superstition gets.

"So I hear."

"Why was this man cursed?"

"Slave owner. One of his possessions placed a voodoo curse on him. Can't say that I blame her."

I couldn't either.

"How did she manage it?"

"Voodoo queen. They aren't anyone you want to screw with."

I'd take her word on it.

"So this voodoo queen cursed the man to become a werewolf under the crescent moon?"

I couldn't believe I was having this conversation, but I *had* asked.

"So the legend says."

"What's the difference between a werewolf and a loup-garou?"

"They can both be killed with silver, but werewolves are compelled to shift and to kill beneath the full moon—one night only—although I've heard they can transform any night if they choose. However, the loup-garou must shift and kill beneath the crescent moon, which arrives twice during a lunar cycle—both waning and waxing—and each crescent lasts several days."

Which meant a loup-garou would be under the control of the moon much longer than most. The curse was very clever, ensuring the former slave owner was subject to something he could not control, which was only what he deserved. Unfortunately, because of it, other people had suffered.

If I believed in curses, which I didn't any more than I believed in werewolves of any flavor. Still, I couldn't help but be curious.

"You said the woman who performed the curse was a voodoo queen."

"Right."

"But you called Cassandra a priestess. What's the difference?"

"New Orleans voodoo has always been more about the magic and the mystery than the religion, so most of the leaders have been referred to as queens or kings, with the queens being more powerful. In Haiti, the leaders are referred to as houngans and mambos, or priests and priestesses, to reflect their emphasis on voodoo as a religion."

Made sense.

"But if this voodoo queen performed a curse, doesn't that make her a bokor?"

Maggie smiled. "In a way. Every voodoo practitioner knows both the good and the bad. Voodoo is about balance—in the universe, the community, the soul. Only someone who knows and understands evil would have any hope of thwarting it. Each initiate to the priesthood studies black magic; they just swear never to use it."

"But she did."

"I'm sure she had a good reason."

I was sure she'd had plenty of them.

"How does one go about placing a curse?" I asked.

"The person doing the cursing would call on the loas for help. Each loa has a light and a dark side, *rada* and *petro*. To call the dark side requires blood, usually a large animal, maybe a pig."

My eyes widened. Why did pigs keep cropping up?

The question was shoved from my mind as I had another, much more unpleasant idea. "What about human sacrifice?"

Maggie shook her head. "The movies and books have demonized voodoo with the idea that we perform human sacrifice, but we don't. Voodoo is a religion of love and peace."

"I bet the sacrificial pig doesn't feel too loved."

"Neither does your pork chop, but that doesn't stop you from eating it."

Good point.

Still, what if someone was taking the Hollywood

version of voodoo for the truth and sacrificing people all over town? Maggie had said that voodoo rituals were best performed under the full moon. The idea was something to ponder, and perhaps share with Sullivan.

"You said there are many loas. Would a particular one be called on for cursing?"

Maggie tapped the computer again. "Baron Samedi is a Gede, a spirit of death. Neither a *rada* nor a *petro* spirit, the Gede are separate. They rule the realm of the dead. To curse someone to become a werewolf, you'd probably call on the Baron. He's the most powerful Gede and controls shapeshifting and the reanimation of corpses."

"Zombies?"

"Yes."

I wasn't sure what to say to that, so I moved on. "You think this voodoo queen called on Baron Samedi?"

"It would make the most sense. Although some might call on a loa they have a particular affinity with. Voodoo's kind of fluid. People make a lot up as they go along. Whatever works." Maggie fiddled with the computer again. "Here's Baron Samedi."

I moved in for a closer glimpse of the drawing that had sprung up on the screen. The man wore a frock coat, top hat, and sunglasses. He carried a walking stick in one hand and a long, thin, dark cigarette in the other.

Maggie tapped the cigarette. "The Gede are often pictured with tobacco, which is their particular favorite. They're the only loa completely indigenous to Haiti, with no corresponding African tribal spirit."

"I thought voodoo originated in Haiti."

"Not really. Slaves from every African society were brought there. Each one contributed pieces of their religion to a new one, which became voodoo. They also adopted some of the practices of Catholicism, which they were forced to accept right off the boat, along with the rest."

Something about the picture of Baron Samedi was so familiar. Which made no sense since the Gede wasn't real—or at least corporeal. Nevertheless . . .

If I took away the frock coat and the top hat, which were out of date anyway, that left sunglasses, a walking stick, and that foreign cigarette.

"Rodolfo," I muttered.

"Who?"

"My boss." I shrugged. "Never mind. It's just—" I pointed at the screen. "He kind of looks like that."

"Weird." Maggie glanced from the computer to me, and then back again, frowning.

"What's weird?"

"Rodolfo means 'wolf'."

19

"IT MEANS *WHAT*?" I asked, and my voice was far too loud for the silent, empty room.

"Wolf. In Spanish." She shrugged. "A lot of old names do. It was a common choice because wolves were seen as strong, independent, and loyal."

"Excuse me. Miss?"

A skeletal old man stood in the doorway, squinting as if the light were too bright, or perhaps his glasses weren't thick enough. His expression had drawn his eyebrows together until they resembled a bushy, white unibrow.

The guy kind of creeped me out. No one could be that skinny, or that pale, and live.

"Can I help you?" Maggie stood.

"I'd love something to drink, child. I'm parched."

"Sure." She smiled at me. "Playtime's over."

"Thanks," I said. "I appreciate the help."

She hurried from the Internet section into the café. The old man glanced at me as he followed, and the sun caught his eyes the way a camera flash sometimes does, turning them briefly red. I liked him even less than before.

Then the red disappeared and his eyes were just blue again; unfortunately, my paranoia remained.

So Rodolfo's name meant wolf. As Maggie had pointed out, it was a common enough derivation for very old surnames, and around here, I bet many of them were as old as the swamp.

However, since Maggie had left the computer card in the computer, I decided I'd make use of it. I typed in "loup-garou," got back nothing I didn't already have, but I did find a list of ways to determine if someone was a werewolf.

I hit PRINT, then started to read.

Hair on the palms.

"Not that I noticed."

Purple urine.

"I don't think I'll check that one."

Unnaturally long middle or ring finger.

I frowned. John had very long fingers, but none of them seemed any longer than the others.

Call the beast's human name while he's in wolf form, and he will revert to his human shape.

Which only worked if I happened upon a werewolf, and I really hoped that I didn't.

Pass iron over the head of the afflicted.

"Hmm. That's doable."

I felt kind of foolish as I read over the choices, but as my mom always said, better safe than sorry. Having the list would hurt no one, except maybe Rodolfo. If he was a werewolf.

I shoved the sheet of paper into my pocket and went to say good-bye to Maggie. Except she wasn't there. Behind the counter stood a young African-American man with skin the color of latte and impossibly tiny braids.

"I don't know where Maggie went," he said. "But I'm sure she'll be back soon."

"Thanks." I decided not to wait. I was certain I'd need coffee, if not information, again.

I considered returning to Rising Moon, but decided against it. I wasn't tired, thanks to the Jamaican Blue Mountain, and what would I do there anyway but brood?

Instead I made my way through the shops, tourist and antique, searching for something that would help me. I found it not long after lunchtime.

"Remember to hang the horseshoe open side up over your doorway," the saleslady said as she rang up my purchase, "otherwise all your luck will run out."

"I've heard that," I said.

"In Europe most horseshoes are hung open side down, so the luck runs into you." She frowned. "I'm not sure which way I'd hang mine, because in both traditions, if you do it wrong, bad luck follows."

Since I didn't believe in luck, good, bad, or otherwise, I wasn't worried. Although considering I was buying a horseshoe as a werewolf test, maybe I should reconsider.

"This is made of iron?" I asked.

"Of course, ever since iron was discovered that's what horseshoes have been made out of. Before, they used a kind of rawhide boot, which just wasn't the same."

Before she could launch into a treatise on the wonder of the Iron Age, I thanked her and made my escape.

By the time I returned to Rising Moon, afternoon waned. I was disturbed to realize that I'd left my anti-werewolf gris-gris at the coffee shop. I only hoped I wouldn't need it any more than I needed the horse-shoe.

King was already ensconced behind the bar. When I asked him for a hammer and nails he obliged.

"Somethin' wrong with your place? I'll fix it." I shook my head and pulled the horseshoe out of the bag. He grimaced. "What in hell is that?"

"What does it look like?"

"A smelly old horseshoe."

I took a whiff. "Doesn't smell like anything but metal."

"Thing spent years marinatin' in horse manure, girlie. That don't wash off as easily as you think."

"I'm going to hang it over my door for luck."

Who knows, maybe having it there would keep whoever waltzed in and out at their leisure from continuing to do so. Better even than a new lock and key—though I'd take the latter, as well.

"Did you get the locks changed yet?" I asked.

"Guy can't come until after Mardi Gras. He's an Indian."

"What does being Native American have to do with anything?"

King shook his head. "You don't know nothin' about New Orleans, do ya?"

"A little."

"If you're gonna be around for Fat Tuesday, you'd better know more. The Indians are groups of African-American men who parade on Mardi Gras, also Saint

Joseph's night and the Sunday closest to it, Super Sunday. Every year they make new suits."

"Suits," I repeated, as an image of a black man in a crisp summer suit, face painted like a Comanche, got stuck in my head.

"Costumes," King clarified. "Indian costumes, with beads and plumes and feathers."

"Why?"

"Tradition. Some say the Indians started when Buffalo Bill's Wild West Show came through town. Others believe they began because so many escaped slaves took refuge with the Indian tribes. No one really knows for certain. But the Mardi Gras Indians are a big deal, and the locksmith ain't comin' until the season is done."

I nodded. I'd just have to depend on the horseshoe, and maybe a chair under the doorknob, for added security.

I gathered everything into my hands. "Thanks, King."

As I left, he muttered, "Crazy white folks and their dumbass traditions."

He'd better watch it or I might really start to like him.

My bed was empty. I hadn't expected John to be there. Should be glad he wasn't since I was nailing the horseshoe up for him. Or was that against him?

I dragged a chair across the floor, climbed on top and went to work. I was pretty good with a hammer, and I finished a few minutes later.

"What's all the noise?"

Since I hadn't heard anyone come up the stairs or even down the hall, I started. The sudden movement caused the chair to teeter. I gasped, dropped the hammer, and pinwheeled my arms. I was going to fall and crack my head on the floor like a melon.

Then John was there, grabbing me around the waist. His save was a little clumsy—he socked me in the stomach first—but I didn't care. The chair fell backward and I tipped forward, sliding all the way down his body until my feet met solid ground.

My heart threatened to burst from my chest; I was dizzy with adrenaline. I could do nothing but hold on to him.

"You okay?"

I rested my cheek against his shoulder. I couldn't speak for several seconds. When my voice returned, along with my breath, I leaned back. My gaze lifted to the horseshoe, visible behind Rodolfo's head. When he'd grabbed me around the waist, he'd stepped into my room and directly beneath the iron.

I couldn't help myself. I kissed him—for quite a while. When I finished we were both breathless.

"How are *you* feeling?" I asked.

"Not too bad. Why?"

I made a noncommittal sound, continuing to peer at the horseshoe, uncertain. I wasn't sure *what* was supposed to happen if a werewolf walked beneath iron. Did John's being able to cross beneath it mean he wasn't a werewolf? Or did it just mean he wasn't one right now? Hell, maybe it meant the test didn't work at all.

I couldn't believe I was actually worrying about this. I'd seen John on the night of the full moon; for that matter, I'd seen him on the night of a crescent moon too. My behavior was nothing short of foolish, if not paranoid.

I inched out of his embrace, moving the chair against the wall before one of us tripped over it.

"What were you doing?" he asked.

"Hanging a horseshoe over my door."

His eyebrows lifted. "Need some luck?"

"Wouldn't hurt. I haven't found my sister yet."

His lighter expression faded. "I'm sorry."

"What do you have to be sorry for?"

He turned away. "I know it upsets you."

"Do you have any brothers or sisters?"

Rodolfo stilled. I'd gone too far, gotten too personal, which seemed an impossibility considering the amount of spit we'd swapped, but I guess there were lines between us I wasn't aware of.

"No," he murmured, and the word hung heavy in the air between us.

How could I have forgotten? All of his family were dead. What did it feel like to be both blind and alone in the world? I didn't want to know.

I laid my hand on his back, felt the slight tremble beneath his black cotton shirt. I wanted to take him in my arms and murmur to him like a child, but from the way he tensed, I doubted he'd let me.

John turned his face toward the door. King hovered in the hall. I hadn't heard him come up the stairs either, and I doubted the big man was very light on his feet.

"Problem?" John asked.

"Someone downstairs to see you." He was looking at me. From the curl of his lip, I knew who it was even before he said, "That detective."

"Thanks," I murmured, but King was already gone.

"I don't like him," Rodolfo muttered.

"Hey, he works for *you*."

"I meant Sullivan."

"No kidding?" I said. "I never would have gotten that from the way you two pal around."

His lips twitched. *Wow*. I'd almost made him laugh.

"What does he want?" John wondered.

"I won't know until he tells me." I stepped into the hall, glanced back. "You coming?"

"No. I've had enough of his company."

I guess I wouldn't be all that eager to talk to the man who'd tried to pin me with serial murder either.

Dusk approached as I entered Rising Moon. King bustled behind the bar; Sullivan stood at the front window; an older gentleman nursed a Bloody Mary near the rear. He must have been a friend of King's since we weren't technically open for business.

"Hi," I said, as I joined Sullivan.

Sunset cast multicolored shadows over Frenchmen Street, making both the people and the cars appear frozen in a bygone century. There were times since coming to New Orleans that I really wished I could paint.

Sullivan glanced at King, who must have been staring, maybe glaring, because the detective's expression hardened, and he took my elbow, turning me so that we both faced away from the bartender. "I have the results on the bracelet."

"That was fast." Excitement made my voice both too high and too loud. Sullivan scowled, and I lowered it. "What did you find out?"

"The blood was AB positive."

My heart lurched. "Katie's blood type."

His brown eyes flicked to mine, then away. "That doesn't mean the blood was hers."

True. Except—

"AB positive only occurs in about three percent of the population."

"Still—" He spread his hands.

I wasn't sure if I should be happy or sad that the blood on the bracelet might be Katie's. Blood was probably not a good thing, but at least it was *something*. After so many years of nothing, I couldn't help but be encouraged.

"We could do a DNA test," he continued, "but we'd have to have your sister's DNA as a comparison."

"That shouldn't be a problem. I'll have my parents drop off her hairbrush at the lab in Philadelphia."

"The test could take a while."

"They always do."

Sullivan glanced at his feet, shifted his shoulders, sighed.

"What else?" I asked.

"The photograph." He lifted his head. "It was altered."

"Altered how?"

"The picture of Katie was combined with a photo of Rising Moon."

My heart lurched. "She wasn't really here?"

"Doesn't look like it."

Which might explain why no one I'd shown the picture to had recognized her. Or it might just be that I hadn't found the right person yet.

"Why would someone do that?" I asked.

"To get you here."

"Me? No one cares about me."

Sullivan touched my elbow. "That's not true, Anne."

"You know what I mean. I'm just a PI from Philly. Why would anyone want me in New Orleans?"

"That's what I plan to find out."

The digitally combined photograph disturbed me. Not for the first time since coming to New Orleans, I felt stalked.

"I think you should stay with me," Sullivan said.

I tensed and a flicker passed over his face; it was there and then gone so fast I wasn't able to discern what the expression had meant.

"I can't," I said, and Sullivan's hand fell away from my arm.

I wished I could feel for him what he seemed to feel for me. Maybe if we'd met back in Philly, before Rodolfo and New Orleans had seeped into my blood and made me long for something more, things might have been different.

"I didn't think you would," he murmured, "but I had to try."

I wondered how much he knew about John and me, or how much he'd figured out.

Sullivan glanced away, then shuffled his feet and hunched his shoulders. I was starting to understand his shorthand.

"What else?"

Sullivan took a deep breath, then let it out before answering. "The dirt."

The tiny flutter of hope in my chest bloomed. "Were

you able to figure out where it was from?" That would be huge.

"Not exactly," he said, still not looking at me.

"*What* exactly?"

"The dirt had certain properties that made it different from run-of-the-mill dirt."

The science of forensics was so recent; new methods were being discovered every day and old ones were being refined. However, I couldn't recall anything about the analysis of dirt.

"You lost me," I admitted.

At last, Sullivan turned his face in my direction. I didn't like what I saw in his eyes. "The particles on the bracelet were graveyard dirt."

20

"I—I DON'T understand."

"The dirt came from a graveyard," Sullivan repeated softly. "An old one—back when people weren't so particular about how they buried their dead."

In other words, a place where bones and other body parts would mix in with the soil.

"That doesn't mean she's dead."

"Not conclusively, no."

"Even if we prove through DNA that the blood is Katie's, that might just mean she bled on the bracelet, then dropped it somewhere."

"In a graveyard?" he asked.

"It could happen."

Sullivan didn't comment, for which I was glad. I knew I was grasping at air, but right now, I needed to.

He put his hand on my shoulder and drew me closer. "I wanted to tell you in person."

I leaned on him, even though I shouldn't. I identified with Sullivan; I just plain liked him, but I didn't love him.

I rubbed my face against his shirt; my chest went tight with a longing to stay where I was safe, with a man who presented no mystery. But as his arms came around me, I knew that I couldn't.

I inched away, surprised to discover a slash of wet across his light green dress shirt. I flicked his tie—navy blue like his jacket and dotted with teeny-tiny shamrocks—with my index finger. "I messed up your shirt," I whispered.

He brushed my loose hair away from my face. "You can mess me up anytime, Anne."

I took his hand, squeezed his fingers. His gaze went past my shoulder, and his tender expression disappeared.

John Rodolfo had arrived. His face turned toward us, his sunglasses shaded his thoughts.

"John?" I began, and he went out the back door, into the approaching darkness.

King shot me a dirty look, and I opened my mouth to defend myself, then thought better of it. I hadn't done anything wrong.

So why did it feel as if I had?

Because I was the queen of guilt. I couldn't forgive myself for not protecting Katie, couldn't get over my inability to find her. I could find anyone, except the one person I really needed to.

And the one man I'd ever felt anything for was a man I kept hurting without even trying to.

"Thanks for coming to tell me." I released Sullivan's hand. "I'll call my parents about the DNA test."

"Good." He reached for his wallet. "I owe you money."

"No!"

Sullivan's golden eyebrows shot up.

"I mean—forget it. I never found out anything and—" I paused, then plunged ahead with the truth. "I told Rodolfo that you hired me."

The idea of taking money from Sullivan after I'd betrayed his trust, blown my cover, consorted with the enemy—take your pick—was an idea I couldn't stomach.

"What the hell did you do that for?" he demanded.

"He isn't who you think he is, Sullivan."

His eyes met mine and concern softened the dark depths. "He isn't who you think he is either."

AFTER PROMISING TO phone a colleague in the Philadelphia police department and ask for help expediting my sister's DNA test, Sullivan left. I watched him walk away, his tall, bulky form a shadow against the encroaching night.

I made a quick call to my parents, spent several minutes apologizing for not calling them earlier, then biting my tongue to keep from saying, "The phone works both ways." I loved them, but sometimes they drove me nuts.

"Have you found anything?" my mother asked.

I hesitated, unwilling to mention Katie's bracelet, the blood or the graveyard dirt until I absolutely had to.

"Not really," I answered. "But we might have a lead. I need you to take Katie's hairbrush to Detective Ransom."

"Why?"

"We need a DNA sample."

The line went silent. I could hear both of them breathing.

"Is she dead?" my father asked.

"No," I said firmly.

"Anne," he began.

"No," I said again. "Until I see her body, she isn't dead."

"Okay, Annie," my mother soothed. "We'll do it tomorrow."

"Thanks."

I said good-bye before they could ask any more questions and make me feel guiltier than I already did.

I turned away from the front window, where I'd gone to make my call, and stopped short at the sight of King's glower.

"Did John come back?" I asked.

"No."

King's Bloody Mary–drinking pal had left too, presumably by the back door since he hadn't passed me on his way out the front. I peered through the screen, hoping I'd catch the scent of Rodolfo's cigarette nearby.

The thought made me remember the sketch of Baron Samedi. Voodoo might be a legitimate religion, but there was too much magic in it for me to become a believer. That I'd even considered John might be masquerading as a Gede to become a werewolf, or help someone else do so, only proved how much this place was getting to me.

I should leave, ASAP, but I wouldn't.

I sniffed the air; I did smell smoke. Curious, I stepped through the door and caught sight of a shadow slinking past the garbage cans.

I leaned inside. "What's the name of your cat?"

King's head snapped up. "What cat?"

"The black one."

"There ain't no cat at Rising Moon, girlie. Never has been."

"But I—" I stopped. Maybe the cat was a stray. I wasn't going to argue.

Especially when I stepped onto the porch again and heard the distinct sounds of claws scrabbling nearby.

I rounded the heavy barrels and squinted into the darkness that loomed in the narrow passage between Rising Moon and the building next door. Keeping my eyes fixed on the other end of the alley, I followed, freezing when a distinctly canine silhouette appeared.

I tried to catch my breath and couldn't. I also couldn't tell in the faint light of the crescent moon if the apparition was a dog, a coyote, or a wolf. As it turned onto Frenchmen, I started to run.

The ancient pavement beneath my feet was slick with Lord knows what. I skidded and slipped, but eventually managed to burst out the other side of the narrow opening.

There wasn't an animal of any kind in sight.

I grabbed the nearest tourist. "Did you see a—a dog run by?"

The man, wearing so many Mardi Gras beads his shoulders slumped from the weight, snickered and spilled most of his cocktail down the front of my shirt. "You drunk?" he asked, which I thought incredibly ballsy considering the source.

I stared at the spreading bronze stain on my white blouse. "Shorry," he said, and began to brush it away, copping a feel in the process.

"Hey!" I snapped, and he lifted his hands in surrender so I didn't have to slug him. As I hurried past he announced, "With a face like that, the least you could do is have a decent set of jugs."

He and his friends burst into laughter. I reconsidered slugging him, but settled on the hope that they would come into Rising Moon later so I could spit into every one of their drinks.

I fought against the crowd; King was going to be overwhelmed if I didn't get back soon, but even that concern didn't stop me. I'd seen something, and I was going to find out what it was.

At last the crowd thinned. Ahead I caught sight of Sullivan's familiar silhouette. I opened my mouth to call out just as he ducked down a side street.

Should I follow him, or continue in the direction I'd been going? If there'd been a wolf, or anything else strange on Frenchmen, wouldn't someone have commented by now?

I was starting to believe I was seeing things, if not hearing them, when a long, low howl rose toward the sickle-shaped moon.

Only a few people milled on the street near me, but several of them stopped, frowned, and glanced at the sky.

"Did you hear that?" I asked the nearest woman.

"Coyote?" she said. "Sounded awful close."

That wasn't a coyote, and I figured it was closer than any of us realized. I sprinted for the opening between the buildings where Sullivan had disappeared, then froze at the sight.

Too big to be a dog, too solid for a coyote, in truth the thing was bigger than any wolf should be. The trickle of silver from above kept me from identifying any color beyond pale, the bright lights behind me and the dimness of the alley in front kept me from seeing its eyes. As I stood, paralyzed, the beast lifted its snout and howled again.

The sound was so loud, so wild, so shocking, I blinked, and in that instant the wolf disappeared.

The absence allowed me to move, if not to think; I shot forward, away from the bustle and relative safety of Decatur Street, from the streetlights, the music, the people, and into the solitary darkness of that forgotten alleyway.

I ran hell-bent for the opposite end and tripped over something in the middle.

Flying forward, my hands scraping the pavement, I sprawled on top of someone, and slipped when I tried to get up in what I really hoped wasn't blood, but probably was.

I opened my mouth to scream, but not a sound came out. My mind floundered as badly as my legs. It took me several seconds to think what to do.

I patted my pockets for the books of matches promoting Rising Moon, which I handed out at work whenever I was asked for a light, and struck one.

The snick was loud in the narrow alley that suddenly seemed so removed from the rest of the world. The glow was dim; yet enough to illuminate the victim's bloodstained face.

"Sullivan?" I whispered.

21

H IS EYES WERE closed; he didn't appear to be breathing. There was so much blood; I couldn't tell where it was coming from. Not in this light.

I leaned in, thought I felt the drift of his breath across my cheek, then the match burned down to my fingertips, and I dropped it, cursing.

Instead of lighting another, I scooted closer, ignoring the dampness of the ground beneath me and the metallic scent of blood all around me. Placing my palm on his chest, I closed my eyes.

I thought I detected a slight rise and fall, but I couldn't be sure. I strained to hear something, anything, and caught a faint whistle.

I lit another match, and with it started the whole book on fire. The resulting conflagration revealed what the single, tiny flame had not.

Sullivan's throat was a mess.

"Shit, shit, shit," I muttered as I tossed the matchbook into a damp corner where it hissed, smoldered, and went out. Then I punched nine-one-one into my cell phone.

The connection was fuzzy between the two buildings, but I didn't want to leave him. Instead, I shouted to be heard and held on to Sullivan's hand.

"Officer down!" That should bring them running.

I gave my name and our location, then agreed to wave them in as soon as I saw their sparkly red lights.

"Hang on, Conner." I squeezed his hand and nearly jumped out of my skin when he squeezed back.

His eyes opened, shining far too brightly considering the lack of light. The wheezing whistle became louder. I wanted to put my hand over the gap in his throat, and then again, I didn't. He tried to talk, coughed, and something gurgled.

"Don't," I urged. "The ambulance is on the way."

"See it?" he managed.

I opened my mouth to ask what, but I knew. "The wolf?"

He smiled and closed his eyes. I took that as a yes.

"Eyes." The word whispered out, low and desperate.

"Do they hurt?" My fingers fluttered over his face.

My knowledge of first aid was limited to CPR, which, from the size of the hole in his throat, was not going to do either of us any good. For all I knew, pain in the eyes signaled imminent death.

"No." His hand tightened almost painfully on mine, which encouraged me. He was still strong; he didn't seem to be fading. "The wolf's."

"What about them?"

"People eyes." Sullivan took a deep, uneven breath. "Werewolf."

"Sullivan," I began, though I'm not sure what I planned to say.

His own eyes flew open and once again they seemed lit by an inner flame. Reaching up, he grabbed me by the collar of my shirt and pulled.

"Knew them," he said, so softly I would never have heard the words if we hadn't been nose to nose.

"You knew the eyes?" I repeated.

He closed his in acknowledgment.

"Whose were they?"

Sullivan didn't answer.

"Sullivan? Conner!" I shook him a little, but he'd passed out.

Sirens wailed in the distance, coming closer, shrieking louder than the crowds, the music, any howling there might have been out there in the dark.

As if someone had thrown a switch, silver light splashed into the alley, and I lifted my face to the cheery crescent moon that had climbed high enough to peek past the buildings shielding us.

I should have been happy for the illumination; instead I began to shiver.

THE POLICE ARRIVED shortly thereafter; the ambulance right behind. The moon shone down like a beacon. Emergency services stopped right outside the alley and ran toward us without being hailed.

Then the lights were too bright, the voices too numerous. I wanted to go back to my room and hide. Especially since I was covered with blood, muck, and the remnants of that drunken guy's cocktail.

Looked like I wasn't going to get a chance to spit in his drink after all. Bummer.

I tried to call King, to tell him I wasn't going to be able to work, but no one answered the phone at Rising Moon. A little while later I caught sight of him lurking in the crowd. The noise and lights must have drawn him out, though I had to wonder who was minding the store.

I lifted my hand, and he acknowledged me with a sharp nod and a scowl at all the hoopla. He wasn't happy he'd be working solo, but he understood.

I scanned the crowd for John, but he wasn't there. Perhaps he could help King, though cocktail-waitressing was probably beyond even his spectacular abilities.

Emergency services whisked Sullivan away as quickly as they could. No one would tell me if he would live or die; everyone appeared grim, especially when I told them what I'd seen.

"A wolf?" The detective, who'd identified himself as Mueller, shook his head. "There haven't been any wolves in Louisiana for over two decades."

"So I hear. But you got one now. A freaking big one."

"How big?"

"About one seventy."

"What you're describing is impossible. A large male timber wolf would run about one twenty in Alaska. Lower forty-eight they don't get over eighty."

"You seem to know an awful lot about wolves for an officer in a town that doesn't have them."

"We've had sightings. Of course in New Orleans, we get reports of black panthers, leopards, wild boars, and dragons, which usually increase in number and frequency right around this time of year."

"I have no idea why," I murmured as I watched the crowd weave drunkenly past.

"We've never found any of them."

"I heard there was one rabid wolf in the swamp a year or so back."

His brow lifted. "You're awfully well informed for a newcomer."

"People don't become private investigators because they like the outfit." Whatever it was. "Most of the time it's because we're curious."

"Nosy," he muttered, and I didn't contradict him. "A wolf *was* reported. Powers that be brought in an outside hunter."

That jibed with what Sullivan had said. However, I was starting to wonder about that outside hunter. Who had he been? What, exactly, had he done? And where had he gone?

"My theory is that people see coyotes," Mueller continued. "City folk don't know the difference. Anything wild and canine—must be a wolf. Except for a coyote to come into town . . ." He shook his head. "Doesn't happen. Might have been a big dog or a hybrid."

"Even an oversized canine, or a wolf-dog mix wouldn't attack a man of Sullivan's size unless it was nuts," I agreed. "Or rabid."

Mueller started, then scribbled something on his notepad. Noticing my curiosity, he explained. "The detective will need shots if they can't find the animal."

One glance at Sullivan's throat and several of the officers had fanned out into the city. So far no one had reported finding anything—not a wolf, not a coyote, not a slavering naked man covered in blood.

I winced at the thought, but once I'd had it, several others followed.

A wolf that wasn't a wolf. A beast with human eyes. One that appeared beneath the crescent moon. In New Orleans that meant one thing.

Loup-garou.

I needed to talk to Maggie. Unfortunately I didn't know where she lived or even her last name.

I decided to head to the hospital instead. I'd already missed work. Mueller had kept me hanging around for hours. I doubted I'd sleep. I had to find out how Sullivan was doing. Sure, I could call, but I figured I'd have better results if I stood there until they answered me.

Mueller offered to give me a lift, but I could tell he was just being polite; he had a lot more to do at the crime scene.

I hailed a cab and shortly thereafter I was dropped off at the entrance to the ER. I should have known something was wrong even before I reached the chaos in the waiting room. An ambulance idled in the drive, but no one was inside; the rear cargo doors hung open as if someone had jumped out in one helluva hurry.

Maybe the patient had coded.

My steps increased in pace, wondering if perhaps that patient had been Sullivan.

I burst through the doors, causing the small huddle of people in the corner to jump; some of them gasped. They all stared at me with the pale faces and shocked eyes of accident victims.

Several chairs were upended. A table was smashed

into kindling. The reception desk loomed empty.

Beyond it, several nurses, doctors, and security personnel had their heads stuck together in deep discussion. From what I could see, there'd been a rampage back there too. Broken glass sparkled on the floor, shiny metal instruments had been tossed hither and yon, one of the white curtains separating the patient care areas appeared to have been shredded by a knife.

"Excuse me?" I called.

Every one of the hospital employees in the small group looked at me. Their faces were tense with shock. My nerves began to dance beneath my skin like Mexican jumping beans.

"I'd like to check on a friend."

One woman separated from the rest. Though her smile was strained, she still managed one. She'd no doubt perfected the expression from years in a very difficult job. I couldn't imagine how many hysterical people she dealt with each day in a place labeled "emergency."

"We've had a bit of trouble here," she said.

"Seems like more than a bit."

"Yeah." Her smile faded. "Who's your friend?"

"Sullivan. Detective Conner."

The nurse had been bending over her desk, peering at her admission sheet. Now she glanced up and her eyes widened.

"Uh—um. Doctor?" she called.

Uh-oh.

One of the white coats left the crowd and joined her. "She's asking about the detective."

"What's going on?" I demanded.

With a quick glance at the still-hovering ER waiting room crowd, the doctor murmured, "Come with me."

He strode through a second door marked HOSPITAL PERSONNEL ONLY. Just inside, he stopped. "I'm Dr. Haverough."

"Charmed," I snapped, my increasing nervousness making my borderline manners go south. "Where's Sullivan?"

"We're not sure."

"Excuse me?"

"He took off."

"With a mortal throat wound?"

The doctor, who appeared far too young and far too tired to be working here, rubbed his chin. "More mortal than you know."

I rubbed my forehead. "What the hell are you talking about?"

"The detective coded in the ambulance. We tried to resuscitate him, but we were unsuccessful. He was pronounced dead."

Tears scalded my eyes; my breath burned in my chest.

"Then he got up, trashed the place, and ran out the front door."

My tears receded as my lungs suddenly filled with air. "He wasn't dead?" ˉ

"Obviously."

"I guess it's a good thing you didn't send him for an immediate autopsy."

His lips tightened. "Mistakes are made, and miracles occur. Nevertheless, the detective's throat wound is severe. He won't survive without treatment."

"There was some concern about rabies."

"So I understand. However, that isn't a direct threat to life, given the incubation period of the disease; the blood loss is."

"If he was bleeding so badly, he ought to leave a trail even you could follow."

"You're right. He should have." The doctor's confused expression became even more so. "But he didn't."

22

THE CHAOS INCREASED when the police showed up. They were as unamused as I to discover their detective had disappeared. They concurred with Dr. Haverough's assessment.

No blood trail.

I left them to their search and rescue. I wouldn't be of much help. I didn't know the city. But I made Mueller promise to call me the instant they found Sullivan—dead or alive.

Nevertheless, I wandered up and down the streets of the French Quarter, hoping I'd find him, but I didn't. By the time I returned to Rising Moon, dawn wasn't too far away. The club was still lit from within, though no music spilled out. Inside several stragglers remained.

King glanced up. One look at my face and he ordered, "Everyone out."

The customers tossed money next to their half-empty glasses and left. I wondered if anyone ever argued, and if they did, what King would do.

"What happened?" he asked.

"Detective Sullivan was injured."

I didn't plan on sharing the whole wolf, rabies, throat-torn, blood-everywhere deal. I wasn't even sure if I was supposed to.

King frowned. "Is he okay?"

"He left the hospital before he was treated, and now they're combing the city for him. They don't think he'll survive the night without help."

"I didn't like him," King said, "but I don't wish him ill either."

I wasn't so sure about that, but I kept my opinion to myself.

"I'll just clean up and go," he said.

"You want help?"

"Always." He winked. "But you head up to bed. You look wrung out."

I was.

I didn't even think to ask if John had come back, left again, called, or anything in between, but as I passed the office on my way upstairs, the door opened. The man had ears like a—

I wasn't sure. Something with really good ears.

"Anne."

He leaned in the doorway, his shirt buttoned crookedly, the tail untucked, his short hair as mussed as hair that short could get. His slacks were zipped but wrinkled, and his feet were bare—pale and long, as elegant as his hands. The only thing neat about him was his well-trimmed goatee.

How did he keep that so nice anyway? I doubted King took care of it for him, but maybe I was wrong.

"Were you asleep?" I asked.

"No." He reached for me, and I went into his arms. I really needed a hug. He nuzzled my cheek, his mouth trailing softly to mine. He tasted dark, red, rich.

I pulled away. "Have you been drinking?"

He smiled, the expression both sweet and sexy.

"Un poco." His hand fumbled for mine, then found it. "Have a drink with me, *chica.*"

I wanted to say no, but in the next instant he seemed so sad, as if he'd lost his best friend—did he even have one?—and I couldn't deny him a moment's companionship. Especially since, right now, I didn't want to be alone either.

A bottle sat on the desk. Cabernet. A very expensive one too. I couldn't imagine Rodolfo drinking anything else.

John pulled a coffee cup out of a drawer and curled his long fingers around the rim before tipping the bottle to pour.

Glug. Glug. Glug.

"That's good," I said.

I certainly didn't need an entire coffee cup full of cabernet. I'd be on my ass before half of it was gone. Although, considering what I'd seen tonight, maybe getting sloshed wasn't a bad idea.

John handed me the cup, and I glanced into the depths. The swirling red liquid appeared far too much like blood. I swallowed thickly and set it aside.

"You don't like it?" he asked.

"I'm not much of a drinker."

"Me either," he said, then took a healthy swig.

I tilted my head. "Isn't red wine at the top of the 'to

be avoided like the plague' list for migraine sufferers?"

"There's a list?"

"Of course. Didn't your doctor—" I recalled his re-action after he'd been mugged to the idea of calling a doctor. "Did you even *see* a doctor?"

"Yes."

I narrowed my eyes. "Who?"

He took another large sip of wine. "You wouldn't know her."

A drop trembled on his bottom lip. His tongue swept out and captured it before it fell. I forgot what we'd been talking about.

My throat was suddenly dry, and I took a sip myself. When I swallowed, my stomach flared with heat.

"You had a difficult night," he said softly.

"Yeah."

I was upset and confused. Sullivan was out there, hurt, perhaps dead or dying, and I couldn't help. I didn't know who, or what, had hurt him.

He was my friend, perhaps more. I was as confused about what I felt for Sullivan as I was over what I felt for Rodolfo. How had things gotten so screwed up?

"This place—" I began. "It's—"

I couldn't articulate my thoughts. New Orleans was both mesmerizing and murderous, ancient yet modern, sometimes slow-moving and in the next instant fren-zied. There was something about it that was reflected in both of these men.

"When I was a child in New Orleans"—John took a deep breath, let it out again on a sigh—"she was so beautiful. This place was like no other."

"It still is." Of that much I was certain.

"The city is old. Older, I think than almost any. Some would say this makes her passé, but I think it makes her special. She has stood the test of time. She has weathered the plagues, the wars, the hurricanes, *oui*?"

I nodded, captivated by his voice. He didn't sound drunk any longer.

"Such ugliness has come and gone and come again. I love this place," he whispered. "She is a part of me, and I don't ever want to leave her again."

I found myself crossing the floor, taking his cup and setting it aside. "You don't have to."

His smile was sad with the melancholy that often follows the happiness brought on by too much drink. "We never know where fate may lead."

He had a point. I'd come to New Orleans looking for Katie, and I'd found him. What was supposed to have been a one-night stand, then a brief fling, had turned into something more. I wasn't sure if I'd be able to leave either when the time came.

I took his hand and turned it palm upward, tracing my thumb across the thin, white line. I never had asked him about it again.

"John," I began, and he pulled away.

"I have to go," he said.

"Where?"

"Home. My apartment."

"You can stay with me."

"I promised my landlord I'd give him the rent this morning, and—" He brushed a hand over my hair. "I think you need some rest."

I did. And while I wouldn't mind forgetting about last night in this man's arms, I also wouldn't mind just forgetting everything in some deep, undisturbed, solitary sleep. Besides, it seemed a little—rude? Insensitive? Disgusting?—to sleep with one man while mourning another.

I accompanied John to the door. All of the lights were off in the club. The place seemed deserted. "Maybe I should take you home."

"I'll do it." King loomed out of the shadows. I started. John did not. I suspect he'd known the bartender was there all along.

King stared at John for several seconds. Something passed between them, even though John could not know that King was staring. Nevertheless, he gave a nod, and the two of them left.

I stepped outside as they walked away. A strange haze swirled in from the river, thick enough, really, to be called fog. The two men went into it and were swallowed up almost immediately.

I stood for several minutes, letting the warm mist sift over my face. In the distance a horn sounded, one of the boats on the Mississippi calling out a warning.

I turned to go inside, and a voice drifted to me on the breeze. "Anne."

I hesitated. "John?"

"Don't go."

I was certain I knew the voice. But the night, my exhaustion, the weird, swirling grayness, distorted it just enough so I wasn't sure.

Then I heard the growl, low, vicious, close. The hair on the back of my neck tingled. The hot, moist evening turned cold.

I should have run into Rising Moon and slammed the

door. Instead, I remained on the back stoop, transfixed by the shadows flitting through the fog. Then one of them took shape, approaching from a different direction than the one in which John and King had disappeared.

A man, not a beast. One man, not two.

Someone I recognized, even before he stepped out of the mist.

23

SULLIVAN," I WHISPERED.

The streetlight several blocks down reflected off the shiny green shamrocks on his tie, which hung loose against his bloody shirt. He'd lost his jacket and one shoe. He'd also lost the hole in his throat.

I squeezed my eyes closed, then opened them again.

The gaping throat wound was still conspicuously missing. I couldn't say I was sorry to see it go, however—

"That's impossible."

Sullivan grinned and I cringed. Had his teeth always been that sharp?

"Conner," I began. "We need to get you to the hospital."

"I don't think so."

His voice was the same, except for the underlying gurgle that was more of a growl, which explained what I'd heard rumble from the fog. Had the injury damaged his vocal cords? Had there been an injury in the first place?

Yes. The blood on him had been real, and I wasn't the only one who'd seen him lying on the ground in a pool of it. He'd been in an ambulance. According to Dr. Haverough, he'd been dead.

"Anne." He came closer, weaving a bit as if dizzy or ill. I guess dying could do that to a person.

I giggled a bit hysterically, and Sullivan paused, his head tilting like a dog that had heard something far, far away.

"I feel so strange," he murmured, and fell to his knees.

I rushed forward without thought, leaning over, meaning to help him up, then get him inside while I dialed nine-one-one for the second time in twenty-four hours. However, when I touched him, he snarled at me.

Seriously. He emitted the deepest, meanest sound I'd ever heard. I snatched my hand back a millisecond before his teeth slashed the air where it had been.

His face was distorted. Foam flecked his lips. Were his teeth growing longer? If Sullivan himself hadn't told me rabies took one to three months to incubate, I'd have been calling him Old Yeller by now.

As it was, my mind traveled more along the lines of *An American Werewolf in New Orleans.*

I reversed my steps as fast as I could while keeping an eye on Sullivan. There was no way I was turning my back on him even to run. I wished like hell I hadn't been so cavalier about the gris-gris. What I wouldn't give to have the small bag clutched in my fist right now.

My heel had just smacked against the first step leading up to the porch and into Rising Moon when Sullivan turned his face to the night and howled. The sound both fury and joy, there was nothing human about it.

I couldn't move; I could only stare in both horror and amazement as he changed.

His teeth lengthened; his mouth erupted outward, merging with his nose. The forehead receded as the ears shot upward.

Bones crackled and popped. His shirt split; his pants tore; his single shoe seemed to explode. For an instant the streetlight reflected off glistening pale skin, then tawny fur sprouted from every pore.

His back arched; something rippled along his spine like an alien. Feet and hands metamorphosed into paws; nails became sharp, curved claws. The very last thing to burst forth was a tail. The appendage wagged, as the huge golden beast lifted its head.

Sullivan's eyes stared out of a frighteningly different face. The combination of the familiar and the foreign made me gasp, and his snout opened in a canine version of a grin. He was enjoying this.

He'd spoken of a wolf with "people eyes." The beast had bitten him, and now Sullivan was one too.

I'd been pooh-poohing the idea of werewolves, but seeing is believing, because I had no problem with it now. My big problem was how to make him turn back.

He snarled at me again. The difference between the previous sound, which had come from a still-human throat, and this one, which had come from the belly of the beast, was the difference between a thunderstorm and a hurricane—the first was disturbing, the second quite deadly.

I was captured by his eyes—chocolate brown surrounded by pure white—Sullivan's eyes in every way except one. Their expression.

I saw evil in those eyes—hatred, lust, though not for my body, more for my blood.

He stalked me, pacing closer and closer, seemingly unconcerned that I might run inside, then shut and lock every door.

My mind flashed on the front of the building—two huge windows through which the crowd on Frenchmen could view the lights, the music, the magic.

Mueller had said Alaskan timber wolves reached one hundred and twenty pounds. Sullivan in wolf form had to be close to his human weight of two hundred plus. He'd have no trouble crashing through either pane of glass. I doubted even a door would keep him out if he wanted to get in.

From the look in his eyes, he wanted to.

Regardless, I couldn't just stand around and let him kill me, so I continued to inch backward.

He lunged; I shrieked. Stumbling, falling, cracking my tailbone on the steps and whimpering.

The wolf nuzzled my crotch. My knee twitched, clipping him on the snout. He shook his head and sneezed.

"Get it over with," I muttered.

If he was going to kill me, then kill me. I was not going to be pawed, literally, by a werewolf. I had my limits.

His breath was warm on my arms, my chest, my

neck. I realized I had my eyes closed and forced them open. Sullivan's stared into mine, making me dizzy. The eyes were his, but behind them was someone, make that some*thing,* entirely different.

He seemed possessed.

I didn't have time to dwell on the whys and wherefores; I was a little busy saying my prayers before dying.

Then another growl split the night. Sullivan's hackles went up, and he swung his huge head around, tossing spittle into my face.

I couldn't see what was there until he clambered off me much faster than he'd clambered on. Slowly I sat up and stared at the second wolf emerging from the mist.

He was smaller than Sullivan and his coat was thick and black. The eyes were light blue or perhaps green, even light brown—but equally human. At this distance I didn't recognize them. And why should I? I wasn't acquainted with all the werewolves in town.

The two wolves stalked each other. I'd read somewhere that there were very few fights between wolves because of their pack nature. An alpha couple ruled the group, and all the rest were considered beta or subservient. However, it appeared as if wolves and werewolves didn't follow the same rules.

Another hysterical giggle threatened to break free, and I pressed my hand to my mouth to stop it. I didn't want either one of them to remember I was here. Although they seemed more interested in each other right now.

The black wolf rushed the golden one. They crashed together like battling deer, chests thumping instead of horns, teeth snapping, claws slashing.

Despite the difference in size, the black wolf landed the most blows. He appeared adept at the game, feinting, advancing, using his superior speed and agility to the best advantage. None of the blood flowing was his.

The fight was vicious; neither one showed any mercy.

The sounds were horrible—the snarling and the tearing of flesh. The sight was worse—teeth and claws, spittle and blood. I wanted to turn my head but was unable to. How many times in your life did you get to watch a werewolf fight?

I hoped only once.

The black wolf broke away and trotted a few feet toward the river. Though Sullivan was breathing hard, the second beast wasn't. He'd done this before. Many times.

Then the black wolf charged, rearing up on his hind legs, claws flashing. When the blond beast did the same, he lunged, getting his teeth around the throat and driving forward. They crashed to the pavement together.

"No!" I cried, recalling that the lighter werewolf was Sullivan. I didn't want him dead, did I? Could he ever be put back the way he had been? Could he even be killed without silver?

I zipped my lips, but the black wolf had heard me. He lifted his gaze, though he kept his jaw clamped warningly around Sullivan's throat. I might not recognize his eyes, but in them I didn't see the madness I'd recognized in Sullivan's—none of the anger, the hate, the bloodlust. This wolf seemed different.

He released Sullivan, though he stood over him until the larger wolf looked away in a gesture of submission. When Sullivan rolled to his feet, he kept his gaze down, his shoulders hunched. He was beaten and he knew it. One low, rumbling growl from the black wolf, and Sullivan raced into the fog, tail between his legs.

Now that he was gone, I was uneasy. Did I really want a crazed werewolf, a possessed former human, running loose in the Crescent City? Maybe I should have let the black wolf kill him. Except the idea of allowing Sullivan to die without at least trying to find a way to cure him was something I couldn't do.

The black wolf hovered at the edge of the fog. Despite the bizarre human eyes, he was a wolf in every way—wild, free, majestic.

"Who are you?" I murmured, and he tilted his head. "John?"

The name slipped out; I don't know why. The animal didn't howl in pain or morph back into a man. He continued to stare at me impassively.

"John Rodolfo," I tried again.

He turned slowly and melted into the waning darkness.

"Ooo-kay."

The list I'd found on the Internet wasn't working very well. Of course, what I should have done was call *Sullivan*'s name. I was certain the blond werewolf had been him.

I put a hand to my forehead where an ache had begun. In the space of a few hours my whole world had changed. Werewolves walked among the humans; the

dead rose, and I might just have to shoot one of my favorite people with a silver bullet.

If I could find one.

Sunrise sparkled through the fading fog. Time to
shower, change out of my bloody clothes, and have another talk with Maggie.

S HE HASN'T BEEN in."
       The kid with braids still worked the counter at
the café. I'd gotten the same answer when I'd come
and asked for Maggie yesterday. Today I wasn't leaving until I found out where she was.

"Has she been on vacation?"

"She hasn't shown up for her shift. Ain't like her."

Unease flickered in the pit of my empty belly. "Has
anyone gone over to her place?"

"Not my department, babe. You want coffee or no?"

I had when I walked in; now I doubted my stomach
would hold it.

"Where does she live?"

"Not—"

I held up my hand. "Your department. Got it. How
about her last name?"

He peered at me closely. "You like her or somethin'?"

"Excuse me?"

"Lesbo. Girl on girl. That why you wanna know?
'Cause I don't think Maggie swings that way, but—"
He shrugged. "To each his own, I guess."

My headache was back. Caffeine would probably
help, but I didn't have the time. I had a very bad feeling
about Maggie.

"Name," I gritted out between my teeth.

"Schwartz," he said. "Now that you ask, I think I heard her say once that she lived near Tulane."

"Thanks."

I paid for half an hour of computer time, which was the smallest amount I could get, and found her address in five minutes. A short cab ride later, I knocked on the door of Maggie's apartment, hoping she'd open it and be furious that I'd woken her.

No such luck.

I tried the door—locked. Then I moved on to her neighbors, who, understandably, weren't too happy to see me at this hour of the morning.

"Who the fuck are you?" greeted the bleary-eyed, unshaven young man in 1-C.

"I'm trying to find Maggie." At his blank look, I pointed toward her apartment. "Your neighbor?"

"Hot girl?"

I wasn't sure how to answer that. Maggie had turned out to be a sweet kid, but hot?

"Dark hair, light eyes, snake tattoo," I supplied.

"Yeah. Hottie. I'd like to get me some of that."

Too much info, I thought, but kept the words to myself. He seemed to know her, at least in passing.

"You seen her lately?"

"No." His expression went from slack-jawed lust to confusion. "That's weird."

"I don't suppose you have a key to her apartment, or know who does?"

"Landlady." He jerked a thumb at the apartment across the hall. "Mrs. Fitzhugh."

"Thanks," I said, already crossing the frayed, stained carpet to knock on 1-D.

I repeated my query to the tall, thin elderly woman in curlers. People still wore those?

"Haven't seen her." She punctuated the words with a loud pop of what appeared to be bright pink bubble gum. People still chewed that?

"She hasn't showed up for work in several days. I'm worried. Could you open her door?"

Mrs. Fitzhugh blew an impressive bubble, popping it and folding it back into her mouth with a creepily pale tongue. "You a cop?"

"Private." I whipped out my ID.

She sighed, long, drawn out, and annoyed, but she got the key and let me in. Then she hovered in the doorway as I moved through the apartment.

Maggie wasn't there.

I'd worked enough missing persons cases to know what to search for. No sign of a struggle. No blotch of blood on the carpet or the pillow. All good.

Her suitcase, backpack, purse, and toothbrush were all right where she'd left them. Her mailbox was full; her garbage pail didn't smell minty fresh. Those observations, not so good.

I hit the button on her message machine.

"Hey!" Mrs. Fitzhugh protested. "That's not your—"

She stopped when the messages began.

Three from the coffee shop wondering why Maggie hadn't come to work. One from her mother wondering why she hadn't called. Two hang-ups.

"When was the last time you saw her?" I asked.

Mrs. Fitzhugh had begun to look as nervous as I felt. "Two days ago when she left for work."

"You didn't see her come back?"

"No." She chewed her lip. "Should I call the police?"

I dropped Maggie's key into her hand. "I think you'd better."

24

I LEFT MY card with Mrs. Fitzhugh in case the police wanted to talk to me. I was certain they would. Right now, I was too disturbed to wait around for them to show up. I had a feeling most of New Orleans' finest were still out searching for Sullivan. Maggie would be another missing person in an increasingly long line of them. They might not rush right over.

Besides, I had a theory about her disappearance and a burning desire to check it out ASAP.

So I went to Rising Moon, retrieved the file Sullivan had given me on the murders and disappearances, then returned to the Internet café.

"Find her?" the kid behind the counter asked.

"No."

"Shit," he muttered. "I'll have to open again tomorrow."

I took the chai tea I'd ordered—my stomach was not up to coffee—and my computer card to the carrel that housed my favorite rental. I typed in the Web site address for the lunar calendar I'd used once before.

I entered the dates that did not match up with a full moon, including the last night anyone, including me, had seen Maggie. The information tumbled onto the screen.

"I hate it when I'm right," I muttered. The majority of the disappearances and deaths over the past six months had taken place under a crescent moon.

To be fair, that particular phase occurred twice a month and lasted several days. When it began and when it ended was fuzzy, unlike the single night of a truly full moon.

In addition, no one could be certain when some of the victims had last been seen or what day they'd been killed. Nevertheless, the coincidence was too strong to be ignored.

Too bad I couldn't tell anyone about it.

Maggie was gone, Sullivan too. I didn't think it wise to mention to Mueller that there might be a loup-garou loose in New Orleans.

I'd do best to keep my insane theories to myself. But I was starting to get disturbed by my diminishing roster of friends. Were they being killed because of me?

Nah.

Then again, someone *had* lured me here with a doctored picture of Katie.

Concern for Rodolfo flooded me. I was closer to him than I'd been to anyone else—at least physically. What if someone were stalking him even now?

I tapped at the computer and after a few cross-references found his address. The Internet was a private investigator's wet dream—and if most people knew how easy it was to be found with a few simple strokes of the keys, it would be their worst nightmare.

I tossed my empty cup into the trash, returned the computer card, and left my number with braid-boy, just in case Maggie showed up. I only hoped she didn't show up with a tail and fangs.

I took a cab to Rodolfo's. His apartment was typical of those in the area—business on the first floor, wrought-iron balcony with French doors on the second-floor apartment level. Some apartments had new windows, new paint around them, baskets of flowers cascading over the railings, droplets of water shivering on the blooms, then falling slowly to the ground.

Rodolfo's didn't. His windows were old, one was cracked, the paint was gray and peeling. There wasn't a flower to be had. Did the lack of home improvement mean he didn't plan to stay? Or that he just didn't care to waste time or money on something he couldn't even see?

I rang the bell. It took him so long to answer, I was tempted to break the small window in the door and let myself in, but I was terrified I'd find another empty house—all of his things right where he'd left them but no John.

So when he opened the door, sunglasses in place even though his shirt was unbuttoned to his waist, his feet bare and his beard more overgrown than I'd ever seen it, I murmured, "Thank God."

He winced, as if the sunlight were too bright, then shrank into the shadows. "God doesn't come here anymore, *chica*."

Turning sharply, he headed up the stairs, leaving the

door open, which I took as an invitation and stepped inside.

"That's a strange thing to say." I hurried after, nearly slamming into him when I reached the landing and walked into the biggest, emptiest living room I'd ever seen.

"Why?" he asked.

I wasn't much of a philosopher, but I still believed, as I always had, that God showed up now and again—usually when we weren't expecting him.

Which might be why I still hadn't felt his hand in my search for Katie. I expected God to help me. Why wouldn't he?

"You have to believe," I blurted. "In God."

"I didn't say I didn't believe."

"You do?"

"Of course."

Now it was my turn to ask, "Why?"

His lips curved. "First you insist I believe, then you ask why I do? What brought this on? Or maybe I should ask, what brought you here?"

I was uncertain what to say. I was all alone in this city. Did I trust Rodolfo enough to tell him what I knew? Or at least what I suspected?

"Are you a werewolf?" I blurted.

His dark eyebrows shot up from behind his sunglasses. I expected him to laugh, or at least be insulted. Instead he answered me with complete seriousness. "No, *chica*, I am not."

I wished I could see his eyes, gauge his sincerity, but all I had was his word. I decided to take it.

"I saw a man turn into a wolf last night."

"Your friend Sullivan?"

"How did you know?"

"I've lived here all of my life. I know people." He gave a Gallic shrug. "They tell me things. Sullivan was attacked by an animal. He seemingly died and rose again. His behavior at the hospital was rabid to say the least. I can put two and two together."

"You believe me," I said in wonder. I hadn't realized until that moment I'd been afraid he wouldn't, afraid he'd laugh, or worse, call the people with the big butterfly nets. Then again, I was talking about a man who frequently held conversations with himself in the dark.

"You asked why I believe in God," Rodolfo murmured. "I've seen great evil." His mouth twisted into a wry grimace. "Or at least I saw it once, and if there can be such evil, such utter lack of God, there must be God, no?"

He had a point.

"You aren't bitter because of—" I broke off, uncertain how to proceed.

"This?" He pointed to his eyes. "No." He smiled sadly. "Well, maybe a little. But I have no one to blame for God's wrath but myself."

"You believe you're blind because of God's wrath?" Seemed a little Old Testament to me.

"I believe God has every right to hate me, and that whatever punishment I receive is much less than what I deserve."

"John," I began, but he held up his hand to stop me.

"There are things I've done, Anne, for which there is no forgiveness."

Sunlight rained through a skylight and splashed bright light across his wrist, highlighting the thin, white line that marred his skin.

I crossed the short distance between us, took his hand and pressed my lips to the scar. He jerked, but I wouldn't let him go.

"Is that what this was about?"

"Yes," he whispered.

"Can't you tell me what happened?"

"No." He yanked his hand away and slid out of reach.

"Promise me you won't try to hurt yourself again."

"You don't have to worry. I can't seem to kill myself no matter how hard I try."

That wasn't a promise, but I suspected it was the best I was going to get.

"Besides." He turned his face upward, bathing in the light. "I have something to do first."

His words reminded me of my vow to find Katie. I wasn't doing a very good job. I'd been distracted by all that was going on around me. I couldn't blame myself too much. Things—I let my gaze wander over the long, broad line of Rodolfo's back—and people had been mighty distracting.

"Why did you come here today?" he repeated.

"I was worried." Quickly I told him about Maggie.

"You don't have to be concerned," he said. "I'll be around a long, long time."

He didn't sound happy about it.

I couldn't help myself. I went and wrapped my arms around his waist and laid my head on his shoulder. "You say God is punishing you."

"Someone is," he muttered.

"But God forgives, John. That's what he does."

"Not me."

"Why are you special?"

"I'm not." His muscles tensed, rippling beneath my cheek and hands. "I'm less than special. I'm—"

When he didn't finish, I prompted, "You're what?"

"Tired."

Despair radiated off him like a fever; his shoulders slumped. I knew only one way to make him forget, at least for a little while, all that haunted him.

Reaching around, I slipped the last two buttons from their holes and his shirt fluttered to the floor. I traced a thumb along the ridges of his abdomen, swirled a finger around his belly button, then traced my nails just beneath the waistband of his loose, cotton pants.

"Anne," he protested, and grasped my wrist.

I scraped my teeth across his shoulder, and he shuddered. I took encouragement from the fact that he wasn't pulling away. He could if he wanted to. I wasn't strong enough to hold him.

His skin smelled exquisite, like velvet midnight, summer wind, and man. He tasted even better when I opened my mouth and suckled the curve of his neck.

The grip on my wrist loosened; I took the opportunity to dip my hand lower and wrap my fingers around his erection.

My breasts pressed to his back; I wished I were naked too, but time enough for that later, when he'd forgotten his name, let alone his belief that he'd been marked by the wrath of God.

He swelled in my palm; his groan reverberated against my mouth still locked on his neck. I couldn't get enough of the taste of his skin. He began to pump his hips slowly forward and back, running his erection through the tight circle made by my hand.

"I can't," he muttered.

"You are."

He stilled, and I cursed my big mouth. Tightening my fingers, I increased the tempo. "You will."

"No."

"Yes," I insisted, and ran my thumb over his tip. Moisture swelled, and my lips curved against his neck. His body couldn't lie; he wanted me.

Maybe I should have felt bad about pushing him. Maybe I should have left him alone. But I believed he needed the connection to me as much as I needed the connection, right now, to him.

He turned in my arms, and suddenly we were face to face, my hand down his pants, his bare chest heaving enticingly close to my mouth. I leaned forward and licked him.

His sharply indrawn breath sounded like a droplet of water tossed onto a griddle. I carved a moist trail from just below his collarbone to just above his right nipple, then I lifted my head, my breath coming faster, harsher, sending puffs of air across his skin. As I watched, the nipple hardened to a tight, brown bud and I flicked it just once with my tongue.

John backed up so quickly, my hand came out of his pants with a thunk as the elastic waistband was stretched and released. For a minute I thought I'd gone too far, until he reached out with both hands and yanked my shirt open.

Buttons flew everywhere, pinging against the wall,

the floor, his chest. I should have been scared, at the least annoyed, instead I was aroused. No one had ever wanted me as much as this man did. I wasn't sure if anyone ever would.

Frantic now, we tossed clothes right and left. His erection brushed my stomach. I made a yummy noise and rubbed against him.

"I can't—" He began.

"Don't start that again."

He laughed, short and so very sweet. "I meant I can't wait."

"Where's your room?"

"First one on the left."

The place was shrouded in shadow—heavy, dark curtains covered every window. Day sleeper, like me.

As devoid of "stuff" as the rest of the house, the Spartan decor reminded me of a monk. His mattress lay on the floor; his clothes were folded in neat piles against the wall.

I tumbled onto the bed. He stood above me, silhouetted by the sunlight streaming down the hall. Even his outline was perfect—the honed biceps, wide shoulders, slim hips. I shouldn't be so fascinated by his appearance, but I was.

Plain girls didn't warrant the attention of men so beautiful they belonged on a magazine cover. We certainly didn't date them. We never got to sleep with them.

Unless they were blind.

Perhaps John was a rare breed—a man who cared more for the person beneath the package. Maybe he'd been that way even before he lost his sight. Maybe.

He moved away, fumbled a bit, found the door and

slammed it, effectively removing the last bit of light from the room. I could only see a dark outline as he continued to stand while I lay naked before him. What was he waiting for?

"John?"

At the sound of my voice, he tilted his head. He seemed to be staring at me from beyond the dark glasses, then he lifted his hand and removed them. A slight click split the silence as he set them on the nightstand.

I couldn't see his eyes—not a hint, not a glitter—because of the lack of light, the lack of eyes, or had he merely shielded the ruined orbs with his eyelids once more?

With a sigh of surrender, he covered my body with his. "This is such a mistake."

"Oh, yeah." I arched, and he slipped inside. "Huge. Mistake."

His hips flexed. "Huge?"

"Mmm. Definitely."

His laughter tumbled over me like warm rain. Something shifted in my chest, and I caught my breath in wonder. Reaching up, I touched his face, traced my fingertips through his short, soft beard until my nails brushed his skin, and he stilled.

"Don't, Anne. Don't make this more than it can be."

Deep inside, the first tremors of an orgasm built. His arms trembled, as he stilled.

Determined not to let what we had fall away, I began to move, slow, sure strokes, sliding my body up and down against his. His breath came in short, sharp pants, as did mine. He couldn't help himself; he couldn't stop and as one we came together.

His cheek against my breast, my hand still on his face, I whispered, "You're the one who said we always want it to be love."

He rolled until he was on one side of the bed, and I was on the other. "In my world, what we want the most is what we can never have."

25

I MADE A move to get up.

"Don't go," John murmured. "Please?"

The "please" got me, even though I didn't feel I should stay. How many ways did he have to tell me there could never be more than sex between us?

Where once the idea of being wanted for my body had been a novelty, it had fast worn thin. I wanted to be wanted for myself. Who didn't?

As he'd said—what we want most is what we can never have. Ain't that always the way?

The room was dark and cool. I fell asleep, awaking an indeterminate amount of time later with a start to an empty bed. My ears strained to catch the slightest sound.

Was John still in the apartment? Had the rush of the shower, the click of the door, the tread of a footstep drawn me from sleep?

I wrapped the sheet around me and walked through the house. He wasn't there.

Neither was very much else. I'd noticed the minimalist decorating in the living room, the monkish state of the bedroom, but there was nothing personal beyond clothes and toiletries here at all. Not a picture, not a book, not a letter. No driver's license, birth certificate, passport, not a single slip of paraphernalia for tax purposes.

It was as if John Rodolfo had popped up in New Orleans out of thin air.

Maybe he had another house in a different city or state. Maybe he kept everything important there. But why? What did he have to hide?

The lack of personality, the lack of a past revealed in his living quarters only brought home to me once more that I didn't know enough about the man to trust him with my cat—if I'd had a cat. Why in hell was I trusting him with my body, my heart, and perhaps my life?

I had no idea; but I should stop.

I returned to the bedroom, flipped on the overhead light and got dressed, becoming severely annoyed when I realized I was surreptitiously checking the floor, the pillow, the bathroom mirror for some kind of note.

"Pathetic," I muttered, then cursed when I tried to button a blouse that no longer had buttons.

What had been erotic earlier just pissed me off now. I stole what appeared to be a brand-new light blue T-shirt from Rodolfo's clothes pile, then let myself out of the house.

Night had fallen; the crescent moon hovered. The area around Rodolfo's apartment was not well lit or well populated at this time of the evening. I would have liked to take a cab back to Rising Moon, but there wasn't one to be had.

I hurried along, headed for the bright lights of Bourbon. I was probably paranoid, but I could have sworn someone followed me.

Whenever I moved, they moved with me. I only caught the pitter-patter of other feet interspersed with the thud of my own. If I stopped, so did the footsteps. If I turned, no one was there.

"Sullivan?" I murmured, then bit my lip. Did I really want to meet him again, out here alone in the dark?

Stupid question.

The creepy-crawly sensation of being followed continued and by the time I neared Bourbon I was running. I flew around the corner and nearly smacked into a wall of teeming humanity. The place was packed—curb to curb—with revelers.

I let out a sigh of relief and plunged into the mass of bodies. If someone, or something, was following, good luck catching me now.

The mounted police milling down the side streets, as well as making their way through the crowd, reassured me. From their exalted perch, they'd catch sight of a wolf long before I did, and they'd notice a crazy-eyed, rabid stranger even quicker.

I shook my head, laughing at myself. If this kept up, *I'd* be the crazy person.

Then the mass of humanity parted for just an instant, and I saw . . .

Katie.

Suddenly I was pushing people, shoving them aside, shouting her name, getting drinks spilled on me, some thrown at me. The crowd converged, blocking her out, and when it separated again, she was gone.

I stopped moving, staring at the place she'd been. I closed my eyes, tried to remember her face, then the face I'd seen. They'd been different somehow, though I couldn't put a finger on exactly how.

Had that been Katie? I wasn't so sure.

After she'd disappeared, there'd been a hundred times I thought I'd seen her—in places she couldn't possibly be. I'd heard that was common when you lost someone. The mind plays tricks; the heart tries to find a way to cope.

"Miss?"

I opened my eyes. A horse stared me in the face.

I took several steps back, caught my heel on a crack in the sidewalk and almost fell. I was caught and tossed in the other direction with a good-natured shove.

The horse blew his opinion of my clumsiness from loose lips, spraying me with equine spittle. It went very well with the alcohol, orange juice, and soda spotting Rodolfo's blue T-shirt.

"You okay?"

The mounted police officer peered at me. I guess I did look a little foolish, standing on Bourbon Street with my eyes closed.

"Yes, thanks. Do you see a blond woman"—I pointed—"that way?"

He rolled his eyes. "I see a million of 'em. Wanna be more specific?"

"Blue eyes. Small, but curvy. She was wearing . . . red. Her hair is longer. I mean long. Midway down her back."

The officer was already shaking his head. "About a thousand of those. You should scope out a meeting place ahead of time for when you lose your friends."

"Thanks," I repeated, but he was already making his way through the crowd in another direction.

And I was late for work.

Sure, I would have liked to search the bars, the restaurants, the hotels, interview each and every person on this street, but even if that were possible, I wouldn't have. If the face in the crowd had been Katie's, she would have run to me as I'd run to her. Instead she'd disappeared—just as she had three years ago.

I'd seen a dream, a wish, perhaps a ghost. I didn't want to believe the latter; nevertheless, I was beginning to wonder. If Katie were alive, why hadn't she contacted me?

Though I'd told myself I wouldn't worry about the bloody, dirty bracelet until we had solid evidence, in the back of my mind, I was more than worried. I was devastated.

Katie's blood type and graveyard dirt. I'd never been any good at math, but even I could add that much and come up with dead.

Leaving Bourbon Street behind, I went to work.

King was having a hard time meeting the demands of the sizable crowd, but one glance at my soaked T-shirt, and he jerked his head toward the stairs.

"Change," he ordered. "Then get your ass down here."

I did, but by then the police had shown up. Mueller again. I wasn't surprised.

"Did you find him?" I asked.

"Who?" Then understanding dawned. "Oh! Detective Sullivan. No. Nothing."

"How can there be nothing?"

"The city's pretty big, and he knew it as well as any of us."

"You think he's hiding?"

Mueller took a deep breath and wouldn't meet my eyes.

"You think he's dead."

"No one can live very long with a throat wound like that."

I bit my tongue to keep from mentioning that I'd seen Sullivan sans throat wound. I'd also seen him sans humanity, another tidbit I'd just keep to myself. I was going to have to look for him; and I was going to have to do it with something sharp and silver in hand.

"I'm here about Maggie Schwartz," Mueller said.

"Did you find *her*?"

"No."

"Shit."

His lips twitched, but he managed to keep a straight face. "What do you know about Maggie?"

"I met her at the café where she worked. We struck up a few conversations."

No way was I telling him what they were about. Luckily he didn't ask, which made me think he was new in the questioning biz. I certainly would have.

"How is it, then," he continued, "that you discovered she was missing?"

"I was the only one who cared enough to check. Her employer just assumed she was AWOL, even though she wasn't the type to miss work. I'm a PI, Mueller, I've done this before."

He nodded, seemingly satisfied, but then his gaze sharpened on something behind me. "Why is it that people around you have started to disappear, when before it was people around *him*?"

I turned to find Rodolfo only inches away. From the tightness of his lips, he didn't appear to care for Mueller any more than he'd cared for Sullivan.

"Why is it that New Orleans' finest can't find any of the missing," John countered, "or turn up the slightest clue to a single murder?"

"We will," Mueller snapped.

The detective left after admonishing me to, "Stay available for questioning." I couldn't blame him for being angry and frustrated. Lord knows I was.

"I had an appointment," John blurted. "And you were sleeping so soundly I didn't want to wake you."

"I didn't ask."

"No," he said quietly. "You didn't."

I wasn't certain if his words were a compliment or an insult. I wasn't certain of much where John Rodolfo was concerned.

He turned abruptly and headed toward the performance corner, where he picked up the saxophone and began to play. The song was achingly slow, bruisingly sweet. Without a word, with only music, he made me want and need and love.

I'd probably never get over him.

T HE REST OF the night passed in a haze. With Mardi Gras so close, we were incredibly busy. John played almost frantically, as if he didn't want to stop, to think, to exist anywhere else but in the music.

Later he passed me on his way to the office. His hair was damp with sweat, his face paler than I cared for.

"Are you all right?" I took his hand; he was shaking.

"I need a cigarette," he said, in a voice gone hoarse with exhaustion.

"You need to go to bed."

His lips twisted. "Been there, done dat."

I frowned as he slurred the last word. "Do you have a headache?"

"No, *chica*." He pronounced the words very clearly; he was trying too hard.

"Did you eat?"

"No." He laughed, and the sound was high-pitched, completely unlike the deep, sexy rumble I heard so infrequently. "But I'm sure I will."

He twisted out of my grip and disappeared into the office. I couldn't help but follow, and as I neared the door, I caught the familiar sound of him talking to himself.

Though he'd seemed better lately, with me, I wasn't a doctor or a psychiatrist. I had to realize that John might never be better, might never be normal—whatever that was.

"A little help here!" King shouted, and though I wanted nothing more than to go into that office and demand to know what had happened to make John the way he was, I also knew he wouldn't tell me.

I returned to work. Later, when things had at last died down so that I could breathe, I went back. By then he was gone.

Morning came and with it a new determination. I needed protection that worked on both man and beast. I found it at the same antique shop where I'd purchased the iron horseshoe.

"Yes, ma'am, that's real silver." The young woman manning the store today opened the glass case and removed the eighteenth-century letter opener. "They don't make them like this anymore."

I took the weapon—uh, opener—from her outstretched hand. The thing was needle sharp. I glanced at the price on the handle. And freaking expensive.

I pulled out my MasterCard. "I'll take it."

On the way back to Rising Moon, I stopped at the café to see if Maggie had miraculously reappeared. She hadn't.

I ordered coffee and a whole-wheat bagel, then sat outside for a few minutes. Someone had left a copy of the *New Orleans Times-Picayune*. I idly glanced at the front page, then grabbed the thing and stared at the picture of the man who'd run out of Rising Moon with a knife stuck in his chest.

Jorge Vanez was found in the Honey Island Swamp. Authorities had been looking for Vanez in connection with an attack in an establishment on Frenchmen Street where Vanez had sustained a knife wound. However, his body was so badly burned it might be impossible to determine the exact cause of death.

My hands clenched on the newspaper, creating a loud crackle that caused the businessman at the next table to toss a frown in my direction.

There appeared to be a lot of charred bodies turning up in remote places.

Coincidence? Hell, no.

Sullivan had told me about a missing corpse turning up barbecued in St. Louis No. 1. He'd thought voodoo was involved.

Damn, I missed Maggie.

No longer in the mood for a long, leisurely sipping of the coffee, I began to walk. When I reached Royal Street I turned down a path at the sign that read CASSANDRA'S.

This time the priestess was in.

26

I WAS GREETED by a tiny, dark-haired young woman with a startling white streak at her temple. She was wearing loose jeans washed nearly white and a red T-shirt that matched the polish on her bare toes. I figured she was hired help from Tulane.

"Welcome," she said, as a surly wail rose from beyond the cascade of beads that shrouded the open doorway behind her.

Her smile was one of pure joy even before a man stepped through with the baby in his arms. I couldn't help but stare. He was the most exotic-looking guy I'd ever seen.

His hair had once been brown, before the sun streaked it a hundred shades of gold. Tangled in the long, unruly strands were a few feathers and several beads, which clacked when the baby yanked on them. He laughed and the expression carved lines next to his misty gray eyes.

The hoop in his left ear brought to mind a pirate, as

did the golden bracelet around his bicep. I didn't know what to make of him.

The baby was adorable, with dark curls and light eyes the same shade as his father's.

"Ma!" he shouted, and reached for the girl.

"Excuse me," she said. "I've been summoned."

I blinked. "You're Cassandra?"

"Ma!" the baby reiterated.

"Yes. Cassandra Murphy." She smiled into the pirate's eyes. "Now."

"You were supposed to be unavailable until after Mardi Gras," I said.

"Close enough." She tucked the child onto her hip like a pro and tilted her head. "Have we met?"

"Sorry, no. I'm Anne Lockheart. I heard about you from Maggie."

"Maggie." Her smile deepened. "Great kid. I haven't seen her in a while. How is she?"

I tried to keep my face blank, but she knew. I don't know how, but she did. Her smile faded; her hands tightened on the baby, and he squawked.

"Devon, take him." She handed the child to his father, who stared at me consideringly.

Contrary to his laid-back, beach-bum appearance, his eyes were sharp. His lean body and honed muscles made me think he did more than work behind the counter of a trinket shop when he wasn't taking care of the baby.

"Come along then, Quinn, me man," he said with an Irish accent that sounded quite real. "You and your da will be havin' a bit of lunch."

"Schnake!" Quinn announced.

I jumped. "Did he say 'snake'?"

Cassandra's lips tilted, though her face remained strained and her eyes wary. "Lazarus." She indicated a chicken-wire enclosure in the corner.

I narrowed my eyes. "Is that a python?"

"Good call. My met tet is the loà Danbala, represented by the snake." At my confused frown, she elaborated. "A met tet is like a guardian angel. Snakes and I have an affinity."

"Like a voodoo familiar?" I asked.

"Yeah." She spread her hands. "Quinn is fascinated with Lazarus."

"I suppose any little boy would be."

"He can't seem to get his mouth around 'Mom' and 'Dad,' but 'snake' he can manage."

The child and his father disappeared through the beads and soon the clatter of dishes and silverware, the opening and shutting of the refrigerator, ensued.

"What happened to Maggie?"

Cassandra didn't waste any time. I liked that in a voodoo priestess.

"She disappeared."

"Seems to be going around."

"You have any idea why?" I asked.

She moved past me to the front door of the shop, locked it and flipped the sign on the window from OPEN to CLOSED. "Why don't we step into my garden?"

I followed her to a side door and through it into a lovely courtyard filled with plants and flowers. The faint sound of running water I traced to a fountain circled by a low stone wall.

Two chairs bordered the fountain. I could imagine

Cassandra and Devon sitting there at the end of the day, watching to make sure Quinn didn't tumble in headfirst.

"Have a seat," she offered, and took one herself. "Why did you come to me?"

I considered what to say and then didn't say anything.

Cassandra put a hand on mine. "Have you seen something that can't possibly be true?"

"How did you know?"

"I'm a voodoo priestess. Knowing things is what I do." She sat back. "Tell me. I promise not to call the men in the white coats."

After taking a deep breath, I began. "I came to New Orleans to find my sister. She went missing three years ago. Someone sent me a fake picture of her outside a jazz club called Rising Moon."

"Fake?"

"Digitally altered."

"They wanted you here."

"I guess. What I don't know is why. I came to New Orleans to check things out and was directed to Detective Sullivan—"

"Sullivan?" Cassandra snorted. "He's got his little paws in everything."

I jerked at the word "paws."

"What?" she asked.

I rubbed my forehead. "This is going to sound crazy, but the last time I saw him, he actually *had* paws."

Cassandra stilled. "Hell. I knew sooner or later his big nose was going to get him killed."

"But he wasn't dead, or at least he was walking around, talking—not like himself, but—"

"Let me ask you something. Did Sullivan have a little accident recently? Maybe get bitten by an animal of some sort?"

"He had a pretty huge hole in his throat. He said he saw a wolf and it had—" I stopped, unable to voice any further insanity.

"Human eyes?"

Our gazes met and in hers I saw everything I needed to. "Yes."

"You're not crazy, Anne."

"That's good to know. I keep wondering, even when I see things myself."

"Does anyone else know about this? Did Maggie?"

"No. I went to see her after Sullivan was hurt. She was already gone by then."

"How did you meet?"

"She'd been helping me research some things I'd found. An altar. Small icons of animals."

Cassandra frowned. "Where did you find those?"

"Rising Moon. Maggie thought someone was placing a curse, or maybe trying to remove one. She also brought up the term 'lougaro.'"

Cassandra's expression sharpened. "Voodoo werewolf."

"She said a lougaro could be anything."

"Yes. A lougaro becomes a shapeshifter by choice, not through a curse or a virus."

"What virus?"

"The lycanthropy virus is passed through the saliva when the victim is bitten, causing changes in the DNA. Within twenty-four hours a human will become a beast—day, night, full moon, new, it doesn't matter. The first time."

"And then?"

"Then the change can only occur between dusk and dawn."

"Under the full moon?"

"Under any moon. Though under the full moon, werewolves must shift and they will kill. They can't help themselves. The lycanthropy murders their humanity; they become demonic."

"Possessed?"

"Pretty much."

"You seem to know an awful lot about this."

"I've had occasion to learn more than I ever wanted to."

"What do you know about the legend of the loup-garou?"

Her eyes narrowed. "What do you know about it?"

"Only what Maggie said." Quickly I shared what that was. "Do you think she might have been killed because she told me? She did say anyone who'd tried to write it down had wound up dead or missing."

"Could be. Although she might have seen a werewolf or ten and decided to get the hell out of Dodge."

I hadn't thought of that. I liked Cassandra's explanation much better than my own.

"So there *is* a loup-garou in New Orleans?" I pressed.

"There was."

"What do you mean 'there was'?"

"Last I heard he, it, whatever was behind silver-plated bars."

"But—"

"But what?"

I told her about Sullivan's theory of a serial killer, his file, his notes, and what I'd discovered about the deaths and disappearances as they related to the phases of the moon.

"Sullivan thought your boss was a serial killer?"

"Yeah."

"What do you think?"

"I've been with him on the night of the full moon, the crescent moon too. Not a tail or a fang in sight." And I'd seen pretty much all of him.

"You were with him from dusk to dawn, every minute on those nights?"

I frowned. "No."

"Werewolves must only shift and kill under the full moon—or the crescent if you're talking loup-garou— once they do, they're free to turn back."

Rats.

"Anything else about him that's odd?"

"He's blind."

Her eyebrows shot up. "Well, that would preclude his being a member of the furry club of any flavor. Becoming a werewolf heals most ills, including the one that killed you."

I'd figured that out after my first glimpse of Sullivan's smooth, unmarred throat.

"Although scars obtained before the transformation remain." Her brow creased. "Don't ask me why."

"Could there be a second loup-garou? Or maybe just a werewolf who prefers the crescent moon to the full?"

"Damned if I know. We're talking about werewolves here. Anything could happen." She bit her lip, thinking. "Seen any other weird people who've behaved badly?"

"There was a man at Rising Moon; he attacked John, that's my boss. Long story short, the guy ended up running out of the place with a knife embedded in his chest."

"Werewolf," Cassandra muttered. "If the knife wasn't silver, it wouldn't even slow him down."

I fingered the package in my lap that contained the letter opener. At least I was on the right track.

"Of course, if it *was* silver, then we have another problem altogether."

"What?"

"Different monster."

"Monster," I repeated.

"There are more things on this earth than any of us realize, and some of them can't be killed with silver."

"Do I really want to know this?" I asked.

Her lips twitched. "Probably not. Did you ever see your 'should be dead' friend again?"

"In today's paper. His body was found in the swamp burned to a crisp."

"We're back to werewolf again. Silver causes them to burst into flames."

That didn't even surprise me. The question was—

"Who else knows about this?"

"You mean who knows enough about werewolves and silver to torch the guy in the swamp?"

"Yeah."

"I'll make some calls."

"To who?"

"That I can't tell you."

I narrowed my eyes. "Are you a secret agent or something?"

"Or something. Any more questions?"

"About a million, but I doubt you'll answer them."

"Try me."

"You said lycanthropy is a virus." She dipped her chin. "Is there a cure?"

"For some."

"You're beginning to get on my nerves."

"I have that effect on a lot of people." Cassandra leaned forward. "Like I said, I'll make a call. We might be able to help Sullivan, but we're going to have to catch him first."

"Catch him? As in trap, cage, get near his sharp, pointy teeth?"

"Uh-huh."

"We can't just slip some medicine into his Alpo?"

"No."

"Hell."

"Welcome to my world," Cassandra muttered. After a few seconds she continued. "You said Sullivan came to you after he was hurt. Is there something going on that I should know about? You sleeping with him?"

"No!"

Cassandra quirked a brow.

"I'm not. I wasn't. We didn't."

"But . . ."

I lifted one shoulder, then lowered it again. "I liked him. We have—or we *had*—a lot in common. He's a nice guy. Or at least he was before he grew a tail."

"He liked you too?"

I remembered the times Sullivan had touched me, when we'd kissed. "Yeah, he did."

"Which is probably why he came to you. The virus

may murder a person's humanity, snuff their soul, but there's always a little bit of their former self inside. Sullivan wanted you. Now that he has no scruples, he means to have you."

I frowned. "Have me?"

"Sexually."

My eyes widened. "But he's a wolf."

"Not all the time, though werewolves do like it kinky."

"Terrific."

"You probably shouldn't wander around alone. You definitely shouldn't be out alone at night."

"It's Fat Tuesday. Rising Moon is going to be so full of people I doubt even a wolf could squeeze in. I definitely won't be alone."

"Nevertheless, keep something sharp and silver nearby."

"Like this?" I withdrew the letter opener from its wrapping.

Cassandra's bright blue eyes met mine. "I like a woman who thinks ahead."

27

CASSANDRA PROMISED SHE'D get back to me as soon as she heard something from her mysterious contacts in regard to capturing and hopefully curing Sullivan. I agreed to call her immediately should the detective show up in any way, shape, or form.

The streets were already crowded as I made my way down Royal and headed toward Frenchmen. According to King, the best Mardi Gras started early and ended late. There would be dancing in the streets, food and music everywhere, public drunkenness, exhibitionism, and a general sense that the city had been taken over by the "degenerate of the day" club.

The tourists and the locals were adorned with rope after rope of plastic Mardi Gras beads in the traditional colors of green, purple, and gold. Many wore costumes. I passed a nun, a schoolgirl with very hairy legs, several Cleopatras, and two Charlie Chaplins. Quite a few wore masks—some funny, some demonic, most decorated with an array of sequins, glitter, and feathers in every imaginable color.

King had opened the doors early. A local band already played, and the sun hadn't even set.

He shot me a glare and I hurried upstairs, trying to figure out how I would conceal the letter opener so that I could get to the weapon quickly if necessary but not hamper my working like a wild thing all night.

I could either tape the opener to my calf beneath a pair of loose cotton pants, or tuck it into a fanny pack at my waist. I chose the latter, figuring I would be able to unzip the compartment and yank out the sharp implement more efficiently than I could pull up my pants leg and free the thing from a wad of tape.

Concealed weapons were a real pain in the ass.

There was no sign of John, but that was nothing new. He'd either show up or he wouldn't. Tonight we'd be busy regardless.

I could barely move between the bodies, had to pick and choose whom I listened to as drink orders were shouted whenever I went by.

I managed to introduce myself to the other waitresses and new bartender, who turned out to be imports from Biloxi. They came down for Mardi Gras every year, worked one night and went home several hundred dollars richer.

In order to stay as fresh as we could for the all-nighter we'd be pulling, those of us working the floor decided to rotate fifteen-minute breaks every hour, which would allow us a brief respite every three hours. Better than nothing.

When it came time for my break, I stepped out back.

Tonight even the alley was full of people moving from one bar to another, congregating in small groups, cocktails in hand, enjoying the cacophony of music spilling from the open doors and windows of all the clubs on the street.

People danced everywhere; they sang, they laughed. I couldn't help but smile as I allowed my gaze to wander over the teeming throng.

My smile froze at the sight of one woman standing apart from all the others. The mask covered most of her face, but even at the distance of several feet, I could see her eyes. They were both familiar and completely different.

"Katie?" I whispered.

My heart pounded too fast; I found it difficult to breathe. I didn't want to blink for fear she'd disappear in the space of an instant.

I didn't realize I'd descended the steps, begun to approach her, until she started to back away. I stopped; so did she.

Was it Katie? I couldn't be sure. My sister would never have worn a skirt so short, heels so high, or a blouse so low-cut. The dark circles of her nipples were plainly visible through the gauzy white material.

Her lips had been painted "do me" red, the shade a stark contrast to the paleness of her skin and the luscious violet of the mask.

If this was Katie, why didn't she speak to me? Why didn't she throw her arms around me? Why didn't she behave as a long-lost sister should?

The woman ran her tongue over her lips and smirked. That smile did not remind me of my little sister at all; it reminded me of some of the women who danced atop the bars on Bourbon Street.

I lunged forward, reaching out and snatching her wrist just as she whirled to run. Instead of jerking free, which was what I expected, she stilled, staring down at my fingers encircling her arm.

A wide scar ringed her wrist, as if she'd been shackled and tried for hours, days, weeks to pull free. Before I could question what had happened, where, how, why, or even to whom, she did jerk away, then darted into the crowd. Though breaktime was over, I followed.

She squirted through the melee with ease; whenever I tried it, any openings I'd seen closed, any agreeable people became suddenly disagreeable. My murmured "excuse me"s were pretty much ignored.

I wasn't going to give up. I couldn't—even when the crowd thinned as we left the arena of music and laughter and traveled to one much sadder, darker, and infinitely more dangerous.

At first I thought I'd entered an area where Katrina had done her worst. The washed-out buildings reeked of mold; despite the warm breeze, a damp chill permeated everything. The moon glistened off puddles scattered here and there. I trod carefully, afraid I'd trip over a piece of wood, a tin can, a body.

But as I moved along I decided that the place was just empty and had been for much longer than Katrina could be blamed for. I wasn't sure why, although the haunted yet somehow desperate air of the place might have something to do with it. I wouldn't want to live here, even if they did bulldoze everything and start over again. Some places are just like that.

I realized I was watching my feet and not watching the girl; I looked up. By then it was too late. She was gone.

"Fuck me," I muttered.

"Don't mind if I do."

With a shriek, I spun. Catching my toe in a crevice, I twisted my ankle and stumbled. Sullivan scooped me up in his arms and carried me away.

I struggled but I might as well have been a fly in a web for all the good it did me. He just tightened his grip and went on.

The moon glinted off his eyes, making them shine an unearthly silver-blue. His hair had grown in the few days since I'd seen him. No longer neatly military, it was now a shaggy mess. He didn't smell like sunshine anymore, but something darker, something that lurked in the shadows and only came out at night.

This was not the tidy man I'd once been attracted to, but then, he wasn't a man anymore at all, was he?

Sullivan ducked into an abandoned building, and I suddenly realized we were alone. How could the masked woman have disappeared so quickly and so completely?

"Did you see anyone?" I asked.

Sullivan grunted. I waited for words to follow, but they didn't, so I tried again.

"I thought I saw Katie. My sister? The one who's missing?"

"No," he said.

I wasn't sure if he meant no, he hadn't seen her, or no, he didn't remember who she was or even no, she wasn't missing. From the expression on his face—both dazed and slightly rabid—I wasn't sure if Sullivan knew what he meant either.

I had to get out of here. Preferably before he raped me, definitely before he killed me or made me like him.

Unfortunately Sullivan had been a very strong man; he'd be an even stronger non-man. I had a weapon, however, I wasn't ready, yet, to kill him.

He strode into one of the apartments at the back of the building. Moonlight streamed through a broken window; the glass on the concrete sparkled like diamonds. He moved into the silver stream, breathing in as if gaining strength from the light.

"Why don't we go over there?" I pointed to a section of the room not strewn with glass, nearer the great big stick I planned to use on his head.

His eyes shifted to mine. There wasn't a speck of Sullivan left in them. I bit my lip to keep from crying out or maybe just crying. His gaze lowered.

"I'll bite you till you bleed," he whispered, "then I'll lick you everywhere."

My resolve to keep him alive wavered. Sullivan wasn't in there anymore.

He kicked aside the glass, then lowered us both to our knees in the moonlight. His eyes continued to glitter with an unearthly sheen. Chill air feathered over me and I shivered.

Before I could inch my fingers to the zipper on my fanny pack and make a grab for the letter opener, he released the clasp at my tailbone and flung the thing against the wall. I was still gaping when he put his big hand into the neck of my T-shirt.

Screech.

He ripped it right down the middle, then yanked off

my bra too. Between him and Rodolfo, I'd be out of clothes in a few days.

"I wanted you from the first time I saw you, but all you saw was him," he muttered, his gaze fastened on my breasts.

"That's not true."

He backhanded me. "Liar," he whispered, and yanked me against him, pressing his mouth to mine and sucking the blood from my bottom lip.

I gagged, and he lifted his head and smiled. "I like it when they cry."

Reaching out, he cupped my breast and squeezed hard. I tried not to react, but from the deepening of his smile, I didn't succeed.

"Girls never liked me. I was too big, fat until I grew. They were always after the tall, dark, and broody types."

Well, that explained Sullivan's utter dislike of Rodolfo. Why did everything always go back to our childhood?

"But I'll have all the pussy I want now. That's what my friend said. Anyone, any way, all the time. Tonight I want you."

He shoved me onto my back. The glass crunched under my ass. I spent a wasted second being glad none of my bare skin had landed on the sharp shards, then he was yanking at my pants.

"I have to shift while I do you."

"Wh-why?"

"It'll be an orgasm like I've never had." He frowned. "I hope I don't kill you. At least not yet."

He glanced at the moonlight and his skin rippled, as

if there were something beneath just waiting to erupt. I began to struggle, disgusted and terrified.

He grabbed my hand and pressed it to his erection, which seemed larger than any human's should be. I cried out, and it leaped against my palm, growing bigger if that were possible.

Sure, I was frightened by the prospect of being raped; the idea of the act being performed by a man-beast didn't help any. But what really lent strength to my resistance was what I saw when I looked into Sullivan's face. He wasn't just insane; he was evil.

I'd never been very religious. I believed in God, but Satan? Not so much. Until he'd shown up in a gentle man's eyes.

Sullivan fell on me, his weight heavy, his penis hard, bruising against my pelvis. He hadn't managed to get my pants off or he probably would have rammed right into me. As it was, he kept trying, not seeming to understand the mechanics wouldn't work through two layers of clothes.

A low growl rumbled through the room. I gasped, afraid Sullivan had already begun to change. I didn't think he'd listen to reason then; I doubted he was capable of listening to reason even now.

Sullivan lifted his head from my neck where he'd been snuffling my skin like a kitten that had just discovered catnip. His eyes flared; so did his nostrils.

He rolled off me, and I didn't wait another instant before scrambling the other way. I came to my feet just in time to see a flash of black fur as the wolf in the doorway charged.

Sullivan was still a man; he hadn't had time to

shapeshift, although I could swear his teeth were protruding and his nose was too. As the beast flew through
the air, Sullivan swept out his arm and sent it crashing
into the wall.

I bit back a sound of dismay. The animal had helped
me once before; I had no doubt it was here to help me
again. Unless Sullivan killed him before he got the
chance.

But it wasn't easy to keep a good werewolf down.
The black wolf sprang to his feet, shaking his head as
if to clear it, then he began to stalk Sullivan, herding
him toward the door and away from me.

Unfortunately, that was also the only exit. My plan to
run away while the two wolves duked it out fell apart.

"Come on!" Sullivan shouted.

The wolf feinted to the right, then, when Sullivan's
weight was tipped in that direction to block the attack,
he suddenly shot forward and clamped his jaws into
Sullivan's thigh.

Sullivan howled and pounded on the wolf's head
with his fists. The blows didn't seem to bother the animal at all. He held on tight.

Blood splattered the cement floor, black beneath the
light of the moon. Sullivan fell to his knees, and the
wolf released him, backing away stiff legged, then
inching in for the kill.

Last time I'd kept him from finishing things. This
time I wasn't so sure.

The dark wolf's head tilted as if he'd heard something. He turned his back on Sullivan, who couldn't
seem to do more than curse and hold his leg, then approached me.

I retreated until my shoulders hit the wall. My eyes met those of the wolf—bright blue surrounded by white—human intelligence in a canine face. But what confused me the most was their expression. This wolf's eyes weren't evil, and how could that be?

Before I could wonder more than an instant, he'd spun away, racing toward Sullivan with a long, loping gait. The man cringed, trying to make himself as small as possible, which wasn't easy for someone of his size. The wolf leaped over him in a single bound, hit the ground once, and then crashed through what remained of the window.

Glass rained down, showering Sullivan with sparkling shards. He cursed and got to his feet, shook his head and sent the sharp crystals flying every which way.

Then he saw me, and the cloak of submission he'd worn in front of the black wolf disappeared. Sullivan seemed to grow taller, wider, stronger before my eyes.

"Where were we?" He reached for his zipper.

A muffled thunk split the night. Sullivan jerked. His roar of fury made me shrink back as if a gust of wind had rushed through the room, sweeping me along with its force.

His eyes rolled up, and he went down, with what appeared to be a tranquilizer dart buried between his shoulder blades.

28

I STARED AT Sullivan lying so still on the ground, surrounded by glass and speckles of drying blood, then
lifted my gaze to the shadow hovering in the hall.

I wasn't certain if things had just gotten better or
worse, until the shadow moved, and the moonlight
glinted off a pirate earring.

"You okay?" Devon Murphy knelt next to Sullivan
and checked his pulse.

Strangely enough, the first thing I noticed was that
he'd removed the beads from his hair, though the feathers remained.

"Anne?" Murphy snapped his fingers under my nose.
"You hurt?"

"Your beads," was all I could say.

"Shock," he muttered. "Happens every time."

"I liked those beads. Why'd you take them out?"

"Too hard to sneak up on werewolves when they're
clacking away."

"Oh. Makes sense. You sneak up on a lot of them, do you?"

"More than I'd like." He set the dart gun against the wall and pulled his dark T-shirt over his head. "Here."

He tossed the garment and it hit me in the face, then fell to the floor. He sighed. "Anne, put on the shirt. I'll attract less attention without one than you will."

I finally realized I stood topless in the moonlight. I flushed and dived for the shirt as Murphy turned to Sullivan.

"Is he—"

"Out for the count?" He yanked the dart from Sullivan's back. "Yes. And he should stay that way for several hours. Long enough for me to get him in a cage."

Sense was slowly seeping into my brain. "How did you know I was in trouble?"

"I've been following you since you left our place. Cassandra wouldn't let you just wander around unprotected." He flicked a thumb at the man on the floor. "You were wolf bait."

"Hey!"

"Sorry," he said. "We aren't the nicest people in the world when it comes to taking care of business."

"Who's we and what business?"

"Can't tell you that."

I frowned. "Who can? Considering I was wolf bait, I deserve some kind of answer."

"I agree, but I'm not in charge." Leaning down, he grabbed Sullivan's ankles and pulled him across the floor. "My truck's outside. Wanna give me a hand?"

I didn't plan to go near Sullivan ever again. He scared the living hell out of me. Which was so strange, since up until a few days ago I'd felt safe whenever I was near him.

Luckily Murphy didn't appear to actually need my help; he dragged Sullivan into the hall. I followed, stopping at the door, then hurrying over to dig through the garbage in the corner until I recovered my fanny pack. I didn't plan to let the sharp silver instrument it contained out of range again.

By the time I joined Murphy, he was lugging Sullivan's dead weight up a metal riser that reached from the ground to the back of his vehicle. Not a truck really, but a big white cargo van—the preferred mode of transportation for serial killers everywhere.

I narrowed my eyes. "What are you going to do with him?"

"Does it matter?" His voice was strained as he muscled Sullivan into the van, pulled up the riser, then closed the door.

The windows were tinted. He put a padlock through the handles and snapped it shut. I glanced in through the driver's side and discovered the back of the van was separated from the front by heavy fencing that appeared to be silver. Murphy didn't fool around.

I hesitated before answering his question. *Did it matter?* If we were talking about the thing I'd just encountered in the abandoned building, he couldn't die quickly enough for me. But the man? He was worth saving.

"He can be cured?" I asked.

"That's what Cassandra tells me."

"With voodoo?"

"He wasn't cursed; he was bitten. Voodoo won't help him."

"What will?"

"There's a woman who has the power to put them back the way they were before."

"What kind of power?"

"I don't know. Something spooky."

Once I would have classified Murphy with the crazies: now I wasn't so sure. I'd seen a werewolf. Hell, I'd seen two. Who was I to say some unknown woman didn't have the power to make things right?

"Where is she?" I asked.

"On her way. We'll keep Sullivan at the Ruelle place until she gets here. She had an emergency to deal with first."

"Is she a doctor?"

"Yes."

"Tell her he's got a pretty bad thigh wound."

"I doubt it."

"He was bleeding all over—"

"Werewolves heal, freakishly fast. By the time she sees him, he'll be fine." Devon tilted his head, and his earring gleamed. "How'd you get a lick in anyway?"

I grimaced, thinking of Sullivan's threat to lick me all over. "A lick?"

"How'd you wound him?" he clarified.

"I didn't. The other wolf—"

He tensed. "What other wolf?"

"Black, blue eyes. You didn't see—"

I stopped. The thing had taken off before Murphy arrived, probably because he'd heard Murphy coming.

Murphy's gaze swept the area. From the tension in his arms and chest, which I could see easily since I now wore his shirt, he was not only hyper-alert but nervous.

I followed his lead. The abandoned buildings were gray shadows against the indigo night. Nothing moved but us and the wind. If the black wolf was here, I couldn't see him. If the woman I'd followed was around, I couldn't see her either.

"I'll have to call someone to take a look," Murphy muttered. "I need to drop you at Rising Moon and get Sullivan to his cage."

"I can make it back on my own."

"You'll get there quicker and safer with me." He lifted a brow. "But try not to let any more masked women lead you toward a horrific and bloody death, would you?"

Well, at least he'd seen her too. I wasn't completely delusional.

"What do you mean, lead me?"

"She was playing you, Anne; I figured she had good reason."

"Sullivan."

"A lot of werewolves stick together. They follow the pack nature of real wolves—even have an alpha, who's usually the one who made them."

"You think Sullivan's the leader?"

"He's too new. There's a big dog." He grimaced at the terrible pun. "I mean head werewolf, around here somewhere. We just have to figure out where and who."

He opened the passenger door. "Get in."

From the set of Murphy's face and the firmness of his voice, I figured if I didn't obey, he'd toss me in and tie me down. It was easier to get in. Besides, I didn't want to walk back to Rising Moon any more than I wanted Sullivan to wake up before he was locked in a cage.

I glanced warily at his still form behind the grate. "Are you sure he's out for a good long while?" I asked as Murphy climbed behind the wheel.

"The dosage on the dart was created especially for him. He'll be unconscious for hours."

"You're sure he isn't dead?"

"Nothing will kill him but silver." He started the engine. "And another werewolf."

"What?"

"A werewolf can kill a werewolf, but it rarely happens. Some fail-safe in the virus."

"The black wolf tried to kill Sullivan."

Murphy frowned. "This black wolf is starting to make me nervous."

"You and me both."

M OMENTS LATER MURPHY rolled to a stop in the alley behind Rising Moon. The crowd had thinned markedly.

"Rodolfo must not be playing," I murmured.

"What did you say?"

"My boss. The owner. He's a jazz musician. A very good one from what I can tell. When he plays, the place is a lot busier."

"What did you *call* him?" Murphy snapped.

I jerked at his tone. "Rodolfo."

"Famous wolf," he said. "Rodolfo means 'famous wolf ' in Spanish."

"That's his name. John Rodolfo. Someone else mentioned that it meant 'wolf,' but isn't that common with older names?"

"More common than I care for." Murphy stared at

Rising Moon suspiciously. "What does your boss look like?"

"Why?"

His eyes met mine. "Humor me."

The seriousness of his tone, his face, made me do exactly that. "About six feet, hundred seventy-five pounds. Dark hair."

"Long?"

"Very short." I rubbed my chin. "Goatee."

"Eyes?"

"Blind."

He blinked. "What?"

"He's blind. Wears dark glasses. I've never seen his eyes."

"Huh," he muttered.

"You going to tell me what this is about?"

"You ever touched him with silver, just to see if he smokes?"

"Even though his name means 'wolf' in another language, that doesn't prove he's a werewolf. According to you and your wife, people get that way by being bitten. His name was Rodolfo from the day he was born, nothing werewolfy about it."

"You're sure that's his name?"

"Well, yeah. Sullivan checked him out. John's the last of a local family."

"They always are," Murphy said. "You know that not all werewolves are bitten."

I nodded. "The crescent moon curse."

"Among others."

"There are others?" My voice came out too loud and too high.

"I'm sure there are," Devon said calmly. "You need to be careful, Anne. This guy could be dangerous. He could be deadly."

"He could have killed me a hundred times, and he didn't."

I'd suspected John of being a werewolf too, which was why I'd bought the horseshoe.

"I didn't touch him with silver, but I passed iron over his head." At Murphy's confused expression, I elaborated. "That's supposed to reveal a werewolf."

"And?"

"Nothing."

"That doesn't mean he isn't one."

"Maybe not. But Sullivan was . . ." I shuddered at the memory. "Possessed. Even in human form, he wasn't right. John isn't like that."

"What's he like?"

"Sad. Sweet. Haunted."

Something shifted in the rear of the van, and we both spun toward the sound. I expected Sullivan to be awake and slavering at the fence, but he wasn't.

Nevertheless, I jumped out of the van lickety-split. "Thanks for the ride and the help."

"Any time." Devon reached under the seat and pulled out a gun. "Here."

I took the weapon without argument. I wasn't foolish.

"You know how to use that?" he asked.

I just gave him a look.

"Right. It's filled with silver. Should work on anything that breathes, and even some things that don't."

"Great."

"Anne?" I lifted my gaze. "Promise me you'll use it

if you feel threatened. There are beasts that roam the night . . ." A shadow passed over his face. "They frighten me."

After my encounter with Sullivan, I didn't have to be told twice.

"I promise." I shut the door, then tucked the gun into my shorts, pulled Murphy's extra-large T-shirt over the top, and went inside.

29

T HE BAND WASN'T very good, which might explain why the crowd was thin. Or it could just be that on Fat Tuesday, Bourbon Street was the place to be.

King saw me the instant I stepped inside. His glare told me I'd been missed. He made a sharp gesture that stopped just short of giving me the finger, but which I took to mean I'd better come over and quick.

"Where the hell were you?"

"I—I thought I saw Katie." The truth slipped past my lips and tears sparked behind my eyes.

His anger fled in an instant. "Hey." King put his big, hard hand over mine. "Take a breath."

I drew in a huge gulp of air and let it out again. With all that had happened tonight, I'd pushed from my mind what had started my mad dash in the first place. *Had* the masked woman been Katie?

I didn't think so, and that made me want to cry all the more.

"Go on upstairs." King began to wipe down his already pristine bar. "We're good here."

"You sure? I can take over for one of the others."

"Nah. They want to make as much money as they can before they go home. Besides, Johnny was lookin' for you. I think he's in the back."

I thanked King with a tired smile and headed for the office. But a quick glance inside, even after I'd turned on the lights, revealed an empty room, so I went up the stairs—first one flight, then two.

He wasn't in the attic room either. He'd no doubt gotten tired of waiting and left.

Disappointment flooded me. Maybe I'd just change clothes and follow.

I unlocked my door, snapped on the lights, and, removing Murphy's gun from the waistband of my shorts, shoved it into the nightstand drawer, then laid my fanny pack on top.

Turning around, I gasped. Rodolfo stood just inside the room. "Where did you come from?"

He didn't answer, just shut the door and flicked the lock.

"John," I began, but with his unerring sense of direction, he crossed the floor and took me into his arms.

He was shaking and my heart stuttered. "What's wrong?"

"Anne," he murmured against my hair. "Anne."

He didn't seem capable of saying anything else. In truth, I didn't mind. I hadn't realized how much I needed to be held. The violent encounter with Sullivan had confused, frightened, and exhausted me. I started to shake too.

John lifted his head, brushed his lips across my brow, touched my cheek. "You're freezing. Come on."

He led me toward the bathroom, one hand around my wrist, the other stretched in front of him. Once there, he released me to turn on the hot water. After testing it, he put in the stopper and straightened. "Get in."

Despite the heat of the night, the lingering shock had chilled me. I was also beginning to ache from being thrown around like a rag doll by a lust-crazed werewolf. I wanted to sink into the warm water, but—

"You won't leave?"

"No." He stepped into the bedroom and closed the door.

I stripped and jumped into the tub, nearly groaning at how good it felt. I lay back and closed my eyes, but as soon as I did, I saw Sullivan as he'd been tonight, heard the echo of his words, felt again his bruising hands.

My eyes snapped open. "John?"

The door opened an inch. "You all right?"

"Could you . . . come in? Talk to me?"

The door opened wider. "You're not all right."

"No," I whispered.

I was mortified at how not all right I was. I didn't want to be alone, which was not a good thing for a single woman to want. What would I do if I suddenly became afraid of the dark?

John sat on the edge of the tub. If it had been anyone else, I might have been embarrassed to be naked in the water, but he couldn't see me. He'd never see me. There was a comfort in that.

"You scared me to death, *querida*."

Querida? My Spanish wasn't good, but I thought the word an endearment. I didn't want to ask, just in case it wasn't.

"What did I do?"

"One of the waitresses said you ran into the crowd. Then you didn't come back and I couldn't—" He broke off, tilting his head until the lights bounced off his sunglasses like a flare. "I couldn't go after you, Anne. I couldn't protect you."

"I don't need anyone to protect me."

Big, fat liar. If Murphy hadn't been there—

I didn't want to think about that now; though I had no doubt I'd be thinking about it a lot in the nights to come.

But I wasn't going to share the experience with John. Sometimes a lie was the best policy. He was already upset enough; telling him I'd almost been raped by a werewolf . . . What good would it do?

His head lowered, and he seemed to be looking at me, although the lights still reflected in the dark lenses like sunbursts.

He trailed his long, supple fingers through the water, creating a current that swirled against my neck, down my breasts, over my stomach, and across my thighs. I caught my breath as my body came alive.

What was it about this man that made me feel things I never had before? Things I was afraid I'd never feel again, with anyone else but him?

"Relax, *querida*." The way he murmured the word was itself a caress. I didn't care if he was calling me "pig face," as long as he said it like that. "Lay back, close your eyes. No one will hurt you when I'm here."

I heard the contradiction, even as my eyes fluttered closed. In one breath he said he couldn't protect me, in the next he said no one would hurt me.

But I'd seen John in action; he'd fought a crazy guy with a knife and won. Though the sense of safety Sullivan's presence had once brought was gone, and I doubted I'd ever get it back, I felt safe now, with John.

He continued to draw his fingers along the surface of the water, just enough to make the liquid swirl. I was both relaxed and aroused. The heat made me languid; the water made me moist. His presence made me hot, as usual.

His fingers trailed lower and lower. My breasts ached for the touch long before it came. Skin against skin, I needed it like I needed my next breath. Finally I arched, and his palm cupped the fullness, his thumb stroked my nipple beneath the surface of the water. I sighed and let my legs drift open, relishing the lap of the current between them.

"I can't seem to stop myself from touching you," he whispered, "even though I know I shouldn't."

I opened my eyes, startled at the sight of myself reflected in his lenses. I looked so erotic in the water, my skin pale, his fingers dark against my thigh.

"Touch me," I said, and watched the tendons in his hand flexing and releasing as he stroked.

I reveled in combination of the gently flowing water, the eddies swirling past my breasts, my belly, the press of his thumb against me as one finger slid in and out of my body. My eyes wide open, I watched myself in his sunglasses, feeling, not for the first time, as if he were watching me too.

I rose from the water like a serpent, a nymph, a goddess—I don't know, something magical. I was prepared to yank off his clothes and do him on the slippery tile floor of the bathroom, but he wasn't so crass. He evaded my grasp, tossing me a towel, then leading me into the bedroom, as he dropped his own clothes like the proverbial trail of bread crumbs.

I could see nothing. He'd shut off the lights; the curtains were drawn, this hour the darkest in every twenty-four, when the moon falls and the sun has not yet risen.

The bed creaked with his weight, the sound drawing me onto the mattress.

I'd been perched on the edge of orgasm, but the slight chill of the room, the few minutes it had taken to get from there to here, had cooled me. One touch of his tongue to my breast and everything came back, stronger than before.

I could smell him, hear him, but I couldn't see him, and the not-seeing increased the anticipation, made the intimacy more compelling. No wonder he was so good at sex. With only touch, scent, taste but no sight, the senses left behind were almost painful in their intensity.

In every brush of his hand lay the gentleness of an artist; with every nudge of his mouth, I relished the slight scrape of his goatee that surrounded the incredible softness of his lips, the sharp nip of his teeth.

His hair but a whisper, the slide of his glasses was both hard and smooth. He rubbed his face against the underside of my breast, breathing in as if memorizing the essence of me before taking my nipple into his mouth and suckling as if he'd draw me into his very soul.

I tangled my fingers in his hair and urged him on,

the pull of his lips, the press of his tongue, seeming to start an answering contraction within so that when he rose above me the first thrust of his hips, the weight of his body over mine, had me both opening to him and closing in on myself, savoring the pleasure, the wonder, the blessed gift of this moment when it was just the two of us together in a way we could never be with anyone else.

I had to feel him closer, deeper. My legs over his hips wasn't enough, I lifted them higher, locking my ankles behind his neck as he gripped my buttocks and found a rhythm that had me moaning in both surprise and shock as sensations I'd never experienced before washed over me.

"I'm sorry," he said, and then he was pulsing, coming, causing an answering wave in me.

My legs slid bonelessly down his shoulders as we held each other, shuddering together until it was done.

"Don't be." I ran my hand from the crown of his head, along the slope of his back, my fingers coming to rest at the base of his spine. "I couldn't wait either."

He began to roll away and I held on. "Stay. Please."

I thought he'd argue, at least shift to the side, remove his weight, at the most get up, get dressed, walk away. Instead he remained buried inside me, toe to toe, hip to hip, cheek to cheek, the drift of his breath stirring my hair, tickling my ear, making my lips curve and my heart flutter.

I must have fallen asleep because I woke alone, though the bed was still warm next to me. A knock sounded on the door. John must have gone downstairs for—I don't know what—and now he couldn't get back in.

The clothes I'd worn the night before were folded on my dresser; the fanny pack lay on top. Weird. How long had I been sleeping for John to have tidied the place before stepping out?

I grabbed some clean underwear, threw on a T-shirt and shorts, then picked up the fanny pack, carrying it with me as I opened the zipper and checked to make sure the silver letter opener remained inside. It did.

I opened the door, blinking in the sudden flare of light from the hall.

At first I thought the man was John, except he had long hair, a clean-shaven face, and very familiar blue eyes.

I blinked, staring into his face, unable at first to remember why I knew him, or at least why I knew those eyes.

And then it hit me.

I'd seen them on several occasions—staring back at me from the face of a great black wolf.

I cried out, stumbling back, somehow having the presence of mind to yank the letter opener free of the fanny pack and hold it in front of me like the weapon it was.

Sure, the black wolf had saved me from Sullivan on two occasions, but that didn't mean he wasn't here to kill me. According to anyone who knew anything about werewolves, they were evil, murdering machines—and there was one of them in front of me now.

He stepped inside, flicked on the light, then shut the

door behind him. My gaze lifted, then lowered. He'd walked right under the horseshoe and hadn't even noticed it was there. What a waste of money.

His mouth twisted wryly at the sight of the letter opener clutched in my hand. "De silver doesn't work on me."

He had a pronounced Cajun accent. The last time I'd heard one that sexy I'd been drooling over Dennis Quaid in *The Big Easy*. I never had stopped lusting after the man, throughout countless less wondrous movies.

I shook my head. Now was not the time for an Ebert & Roeper flashback.

"You're a—a—" I couldn't get the word out of my mouth.

"Loup-garou?" he supplied, inching nearer with every passing second.

He was close enough to touch, so I pressed the flat of the silver opener against his arm.

Nothing happened—until he snatched it right out of my hand.

"Shit," I muttered.

The man flipped the opener end over end, catching it by the handle. I shuddered when those too familiar blue eyes met mine. The sharp silver implement would work on humans as well as werewolves. All he had to do was shove it into a vital organ and twist. I began to back toward the nightstand where Murphy's gun was hidden.

"I'm not here to hurt you."

"Then why are you here?"

"I'm looking for de loup-garou."

"But I thought you were—"

He shook his head. "I'm as human as you are."

"If you're not a loup-garou, then who is?"

The bathroom door opened and I whirled in that direction. John Rodolfo stood in the doorway.

"Hello, Grandpère," said the blue-eyed man.

30

G RANDPA?" I REPEATED, glancing at the guy behind me, who kept his eyes fixed on John.

"Tell her," he ordered.

My gaze went to Rodolfo. He continued to lean in the doorway, his slumped shoulders projecting exhaustion, even as the tilt of his head broadcast awareness of every movement and word.

There was something familiar about him. I looked at the other man. With shorter hair, a goatee, and sunglasses, he would be John's twin. What was going on?

"First things first." I jabbed a finger at the intruder. "Who the hell are you?"

His bright blue eyes flicked to John, then back to me. "Adam Ruelle."

I frowned. I'd heard that name recently.

"Your friend Sullivan is a guest of my dungeon," he continued.

"Dungeon?" My voice squeaked.

"I mean cage. Big one. Silver bars."

That explained why I knew the name but not much else. "How did you get in here and, more importantly, why?"

His lips tilted. Not a smile, but close. I wondered if the man ever truly smiled, which gave him a lot in common with John.

"I was once in de army," he said. "I did a lot of breaking and entering in places where, if they caught me, I'd wish I were dead long before I was."

Translation: hush-hush, Special Forces stuff. The locks on Rising Moon, and on my bedroom door for that matter, would have been child's play to a guy like him.

"Once I spoke with Murphy," he continued, "and I heard de name Rodolfo, I had to come."

"Why?"

"Rodolfo means 'famous wolf' in Spanish."

"That seems to be the consensus," I said.

"Ruelle means 'famous wolf' in French."

Uh-oh.

"It's at de heart of our curse. The reason man turns into wolf and not alligator, snake, hedgehog. Names have power."

I must have been staring at him blankly—could you blame me?—because he continued to explain. "You've heard of de loup-garou? Our crescent moon curse?"

"I got the highlights."

He swept out his hand. "Meet de cursed one."

I glanced at John. He continued to stand immobile, everything he felt and thought hidden behind those damnable glasses.

"That's impossible," I said.

"You've seen a man turn into a wolf. Nothing's impossible."

Memories flickered—of John telling me he'd been touched by God's wrath. If that wasn't a curse, I don't know what was. I still couldn't believe it.

"I asked you if you were a werewolf," I pointed out. "You said you weren't."

"I'm a loup-garou."

My eyes narrowed. "You're a liar."

"Of course he is," Adam snapped. "You think if he murders de innocent night after night, year after year, century after century, he'd balk at lying?"

I rounded on Adam. "Why do you know so damned much?"

"I'm cursed too. Or I will be if Grandpère ever dies. I become a loup-garou and my son after me and so on until de end of time, or we break this curse." He sighed. "My money's on de end of time."

"You're telling me John is your grandfather"—I glanced back and forth between the two of them—"even though he looks young enough to be your brother."

"Looks deceive. He was born in eighteen thirty, died de first time in eighteen fifty-eight."

"His name isn't even Ruelle." I grasped any excuse to refute this claim. "It's Rodolfo."

"No," Adam said, "it isn't. He took another name when he came back here. What I don't understand is why?" His gaze went to John—or whatever his name was. "Why would you come to New Orleans, Grandpère?"

"Quit calling him that!" I snapped.

Hearing a man who appeared thirty years old calling

another who appeared of equal age "Grandpa" made me want to shriek mindlessly until my mind snapped, if it hadn't already.

"Should I call him by de name he was born with?" Adam asked. "Henri," he said, pronouncing the name in the French manner, dropping the *h*, putting the accent on the second syllable. "Why did you come here?"

"He can't be who you say he is," I put in desperately. "Cassandra told me any afflictions heal once a person becomes a werewolf. He's blind."

"No," Adam murmured. "He isn't."

Slowly John straightened away from the doorjamb, lifting his hand to his sunglasses, then removing them. I'd wished countless times that I could see the color or the expression of his eyes. Now I could.

They were blue; they were agonized, and they were no more blind than mine were.

"Why?" I turned away. "Why pretend?"

"I'm sure he didn't want anyone to recognize him, or me as de case may be," Adam said. "No one would suspect him either. A blind man can't be a murderer."

I flinched. I'd said as much to Sullivan.

"I'm not a murderer." John's voice was low and furious.

Adam snorted. "Grandpère, you're one of de most vicious beasts in history. Angelus has nothing on you."

"Angelus?" John asked.

"Buffy the Vampire Slayer," I murmured absently. "Television show—hot guy, vicious vampire."

"I'm *not* a vampire."

"Werewolf. Vampire. What's the difference?" I threw up my hands. "You kill people, don't you?"

John's eyes met mine. "Not anymore."

"People are dying all over de place," Adam interjected. "You expect me to believe you aren't involved?"

John rubbed his forehead. I kept getting distracted by the blue of his eyes. Hell, just *seeing* his eyes was such a novelty I couldn't get past it.

"I didn't say that." He dropped his hand and leaned back against the wall. "I'm not killing *people*."

"I don't understand," I said.

"I'm killing werewolves. They aren't people anymore."

"And neither are you," Adam murmured.

Suddenly the room was hot; I was dizzy. I'd had sex with this man, only he wasn't a man. Not really.

I ran into the bathroom and threw up.

It didn't take long. I couldn't remember the last time I'd eaten. When I was done with the dry heaves, I levered myself to my feet and saw John hovering.

"Back off." I doused my head with cold water, then brushed my teeth.

My mind raced, trying to remember all that had happened in New Orleans, all that I'd heard and learned.

I came out of the bathroom to discover Adam and John on opposite sides of the room. Adam appeared contrite. "This is a lot to take in."

I just glared at him, then I turned the evil eye on his *grandpère*. "Sullivan said he recognized the eyes of the wolf that attacked him; from the very beginning something about you bothered him."

I paused, considering that John might have killed Sullivan because of me. How many times had he come in the room when the detective had been touching me, whispering to me, had John even seen us kiss? He'd never seemed jealous; but then, he hadn't seemed evil either.

I pulled my attention back to the big question. "Was that why you killed him?"

"I haven't been making new wolves," John insisted. "I've been killing the old ones."

"And I should believe you because you've been so truthful up to this point?"

"Why are you here, Henri?" Adam repeated.

"My name is John now."

"You can call yourself by any name you like, but it doesn't change who you are."

"You think I don't know that?" John's voice broke on the last word. "I hear them shrieking. Hundreds upon hundreds haunt me. It doesn't matter that I'm different now, they won't let me rest."

I remembered his headaches, his nightmares, the times I'd heard him talking to himself in the dark.

"What do you mean by different?" I asked.

The two men exchanged glances, and John dipped his chin. Adam turned to me. "Once bitten, or cursed, humans are possessed by a demon."

"I know." Or at least that was what I'd been told, and my firsthand observations of the changes in Sullivan had made me believe.

I stared into John's eyes. I saw many things, some of them frightening but none of them evil.

"What happened to you?" I asked him.

"There's a cure."

"Which is why we captured Sullivan," I murmured, turning to Adam. "So why isn't John cured?"

I couldn't call him Henri; I just couldn't.

"Because he was cursed and not bitten de demon was removed, but de need to shift and to kill remained."

"Killing werewolves takes care of the hunger," John said.

"What about the fail-safe in the virus?"

"What do you know about it?" Adam demanded.

"Murphy was chatty."

Adam rolled his eyes. "He always is. As near as we can figure, being cursed or cured or having de normal process of being a werewolf screwed up in some way throws de fail-safe out of whack. It's happened before."

"Again I have to ask why you know so freaking much about this and just who the hell is 'we'?"

Adam shook his head. "I can't tell you."

"Or what, you'd have to kill me? Get in line."

"No one will hurt you, Anne—" John began.

"Except you?"

"I wouldn't."

"How do you know what you'll do when you've got fangs and a tail?"

"I know," John said tightly. "One of the special talents of a werewolf—wolf body, people brain."

"No wonder they're so dangerous."

"Got that right," Adam muttered.

The idea of a beast with teeth, claws, the remarkable abilities of a wolf, and the intelligence of a human, it boggled the mind.

"I still can't believe this is real."

My eye caught on a shiny silver object atop my nightstand. Adam had discarded the letter opener. I scooped it up and swooped it toward John's arm.

The scent of burning hair and flesh made me drop the weapon. As it clattered to the ground between us, smoke curled upward.

He stared at me impassively. "You believe me now?"

I couldn't speak, could only stare at the white scar on his forearm. "I thought all wounds healed once you were a werewolf?"

"Unless they're made with silver."

Reaching out, I turned John's palm over and stared at the thin white line across his wrist.

31

"WHAT DE HELL?" Adam demanded, and grabbed John's arm himself. "You didn't have that when you went to Montana."

John pulled out of Adam's grasp and moved to the window without answering.

"Did someone tie you with silver wire?" I asked.

"No." John still faced in the other direction.

"You tried to kill yourself with a silver knife," I blurted.

"Are you insane?" Adam pulled at his hair. "Stupid question." He took a deep breath, let it out, seemed to be working on calming down and failing. "What if you'd succeeded? You would pass your curse to me? To Luc? Don't tell me you've changed, old man, you're de exact same selfish prick you were a hundred and fifty years ago."

Hearing Adam call John "old man" would have been funny, except nothing seemed funny anymore.

"I wasn't thinking clearly at the time," John said. "It was right after—" He rubbed a thumb along the thin white line. "When the voices were the loudest. You don't know what it's like."

"You could have plunged de thing into your heart if you wanted to do de job right."

I winced at the thought of what would have happened then—an explosion of fire, the resulting conflagration that would have left John Rodolfo nothing but ashes.

"They stopped me before I got that far," John said.

Adam went silent; he appeared uncertain. "You won't try anything like that again?"

"No."

I wasn't sure I believed him; from Adam's expression, he didn't either, but he chose to let the matter drop. For now.

"I'm still not clear on how the curse would pass from John to you."

"If Grandpère dies," Adam said, "I am cursed."

"Out of the blue one night, bam—suddenly you're a werewolf?"

"That's what happened to me," John said softly.

"Except it wasn't out of de blue." Adam's lip curled. "You deserved it."

"I never said I didn't."

"Seems a little far-fetched," I murmured.

"It's magic," Adam snapped. "Not logic."

"You can't be certain the curse will pass to you."

"I don't plan on killing him just to see." He glared at John. "Although I have been tempted on more than one occasion. You never told me why you came back to New Orleans, Grandpère."

"I told him to."

The voice from the hall made me jump a foot, but I recognized the large, wide form of King, even before he stepped into the light.

"Who are you?" Adam demanded.

"This is King," John said. "He's my friend."

"But he's . . . black," Adam pointed out.

"I am?" King murmured dryly.

"He was—is—" Adam didn't seem able to continue, which was probably for the best. How did you explain that the man in front of you had once been a slave owner a century and a half after slavery had ended?

"You want to tell me of his slave-owning past?" King asked. "That he was one of the more brutal owners my ancestors ever knew?"

"Who is this guy?" Adam murmured.

"I'm the great-great-several-times-great-grandson of Mawu."

Adam's eyes widened. "The voodoo queen who cursed Grandpère?"

"The very same," King agreed. "That's how I got my name. My mother wanted to keep the family connection alive."

I remembered Maggie explaining that New Orleans voodoo priests and priestesses were more often referred to as kings and queens. *Hell.*

"You said you were named after Elvis," I muttered.

"I lied."

My gaze went to the sharp silver implement on the floor at my feet. I wondered if it would work on him.

"Why didn't you kill him when you had the chance?" Adam asked. "Not that I want you to, but—" He spread his hands. "I would have."

"He isn't the same man."

"He isn't a man," Adam murmured.

"We got that," I said, sick of hearing it myself.

John cast me a curious, almost hopeful glance, and I looked away. I couldn't bear to gaze into those eyes. Just seeing them reminded me of each and every lie. Had anyone told the truth about anything around here? Including me?

"I didn't want to live with the knowledge of all I'd done," John explained. "I was haunted by the faces, driven mad by the voices. But after the first time I tried to die and failed, I realized I couldn't do that to you." He shifted his gaze to Adam, who made a derisive sound.

"None of the cures worked," John continued. "Not magic, not potions, not science, not medicine."

"There's still Mawu's method," Adam said.

"Mawu the voodoo queen who cursed him over a century ago is still walking around?" If so, I didn't want to meet her.

"No," Adam answered. "Cassandra raised her from de dead."

My eyebrows shot up. "Wow. She is good."

John's lips curved. "Mawu said I could only be cured by committing the ultimate sacrifice. However, I can't give my life, or others suffer."

I frowned. "What if in giving your life, the curse is broken?"

"We wouldn't know if it worked until too late. And

to be honest, *chica,* my life isn't that big of a sacrifice. I no longer relish it."

I felt a twinge in the region of my heart. Hadn't his life been a little better with me in it?

Idiot. He was a formerly psychotic werewolf, with the "formerly" still out for votes. He'd probably been using me all along, trying to make me love him just so he could break my heart and laugh maniacally. Isn't that what sadists did?

"We're going to have to figure something out," Adam said.

"I did." John indicated King. "He's a lougaro."

Adam tensed. "A what?"

"Voodoo werewolf," I supplied.

"No." King held up a hand. "I'm a shapeshifting sorcerer. There's a difference."

"So you don't wander the night, drinking the blood of children?" I felt rather than saw Adam inch closer.

"Old wives' tale." King made a face. "You shouldn't believe everything you hear."

"You told me you didn't hold with voodoo."

"I—"

"Lied," I interrupted. "That was your altar?"

"Yes. The spell allowed me to shift into other forms and roam the night."

"You were the black cat." He nodded. "The pig?" Another nod. "Were you a wolf?"

"At times."

Adam suddenly had a gun in his hand and I hadn't even seen him move. I hadn't detected the telltale bulge of his carrying one either. Impressive.

"He isn't evil," John said. "He's magic."

Adam didn't look convinced, and he didn't lower the gun. "Magic didn't work before, what makes you think it'll work now?"

"In the form of a beast I commune with the loas," King explained, "and from them I learned what John must do to be cured. He must kill them all."

"Kill what?" Adam asked. "Who?"

"The werewolves."

"He has to kill every werewolf before he's healed?" Adam rubbed his forehead. "Grandpère, that'll take another hundred and fifty years."

I opened my mouth, shut it again. There were that many of them?

"Not all the werewolves, *petit-fils,* merely the ones I made."

Adam hesitated. "That might also take a really long time."

"Not as long as you think." John glanced my way. "There is only one more."

"*One* more? How can you be sure? You've been killing and maiming and having a grand old time for a century and a half."

"The hunters have taken care of many."

"Hunters?" I asked.

"Later," they said as one.

"The ones left I called to this place, and they came."

"Called?" Adam appeared confused.

"I am the alpha; their leader."

"The master," I murmured.

John's eyes met mine. "Yes."

The crazy guy who'd come to Rising Moon had been one of his protégés.

"What does *pas argent* mean?" I asked, remembering what he'd muttered after the knife had gone into the man's chest.

"Not silver," he said.

I should have taken French in high school. Two years of German wasn't doing me a damn bit of good.

John hadn't been able to kill the man without silver, or without becoming a wolf himself—and how could he with me standing right there—but I had no doubt he'd been the one to take care of the problem later, then dump it in the swamp.

"Your evil spawn was spread across de country," Adam said. "How could you call them here from all over? How do you even know who they are?"

"I remember every single one," John murmured. "It's my cross to bear."

"And nothing less than you deserve," Adam said. "But how did you do it?"

"I had help."

Before he could elaborate a cell phone rang. Adam reached into a voluminous pocket of his khaki pants. *"Oui?"* he answered, then listened, his frown deepening. "Yes, it's Grandpère. I will."

He flipped the phone closed and glanced at John. "Our presence is requested at de mansion."

"What if I don't wish to go to the mansion?"

"Then I'm supposed to drug you and drag you anyway."

John's lips tightened. "Edward's here."

Adam dipped his head.

"Who the hell is Edward?" I demanded.

"My boss," Adam said, at the same time John murmured, "My fate."

"Well, that's informative."

Adam shrugged. "You'll meet him soon enough."

"No." John stepped between us. "She isn't going."

"Edward says she is. Cassandra told him that Anne knows just about everything. Besides, they're going to cure Sullivan, and if they do, he's going to be confused. He'll need someone there he trusts."

Over my better judgment, I was intrigued. "I'll go."

"Me too," King said.

"No," John ordered. "Edward can smell a shapeshifter a mile away, and when he does, he kills them."

"You're still breathing."

"I'm a guinea pig. When I cease to be useful, my days of breathing will end."

"Fine," King snapped. "I'll stay."

"Good choice." Adam led the way out the door.

As I passed beneath the horseshoe I wondered aloud, "Why were you able to walk under iron?"

"Doesn't work." John glanced back. "Most of the old myths don't."

"Which is why calling your human name when you were in wolf form was a bust too."

"John Rodolfo isn't my name."

"Crap."

"I doubt it would have worked anyway."

We reached the ground floor and slipped onto Frenchmen as dawn turned the sky a pale peach.

"Does anything work?" I asked.

An ancient, rusted Chevy was parked at the curb.

The thing must have been thirty years old; the paint had been sanded off, leaving a body with no true color to speak of.

Adam went around the front and opened the driver's side door. "I stick with silver." His eyes met John's. "Works every time."

32

J OHN OPENED THE passenger door, but before I could climb in Adam spoke. "I don't want him sitting behind me."

John did as Adam indicated without comment, opening the back door for me, then climbing in next to his several times great-grandson. I still couldn't get my mind around that.

Adam used one hand to drive, leaving the other free to hold a gun on John. I didn't have to ask if the thing was loaded with silver bullets. Adam didn't mess around.

Casting a sidelong glance at John, Adam made a U-turn and headed for the road that would take us over Lake Pontchartrain toward the swamp.

"What happened to your accent?" Adam asked.

"I couldn't keep talking like you and expect people not to connect the dots. Especially with Sullivan snooping around."

"True enough. Still, it can't be easy to put aside over a century of habit."

"I had plenty of time behind silver bars to practice."

There were a lot of dots I was connecting myself as I listened to them talk. John had been incarcerated somewhere in Montana. There were hunters out there, of which Adam seemed to be one. And someone named Edward, whom I would meet very soon, was in charge of it all.

"You had a Cajun accent?" I guessed.

"Oui," John said.

I recalled the few instances he'd slipped into French, an occasion or two when he'd called me *cher.* The one time he'd used "de" for "the" I'd merely thought him overtired.

For the most part he'd been very convincing, speaking with no discernible accent and interspersing his dialogue with Spanish now and again. Calling me *chica* had helped. He wouldn't have to bother anymore.

"You said your whole family was dead."

"I said a lot of things."

"Did you tell her how they died?" Adam asked.

"You didn't kill them, did you?"

"Not directly, no."

"Men in our family often choose to eat a shotgun barrel rather than become like him."

"How many?" I asked.

"Too many," John said in a voice that was both haunted and detached.

"Sullivan checked out John Rodolfo," I continued. "He exists."

Adam glanced over, then back at the road. "How'd you swing that? Eat de guy, then assume his identity?"

"Not this time."

"How did you do it?" Adam pressed. "You aren't exactly a computer-hacking genius."

I bet not. The thought of all that had happened in the world since John had been alive made my head spin. I started to wonder how much of a gift immortality might be.

"I had help with that too," John explained.

"Edward's lost his fucking mind," Adam muttered.

We were silent for the rest of the drive to the Honey Island Swamp—at least half an hour, maybe more, I lost track. Out here, away from the Quarter, the damage from Katrina was still visible. Sure, they were working on putting some places back together again, but others appeared as if they'd never been touched—except by a hurricane.

Miles upon miles of abandoned apartments and houses, collapsed walls, broken windows. Hundreds of cars beneath the overpasses, filled with silt, white with dust and corrosion. Empty strip malls, Wal-Marts, McDonald's. Ghostly parking lots, deserted streets without a single moving vehicle. As we rolled past, all I could do was stare and try not to cry. I'd seen it on the news, but nothing could have prepared me for this.

At last, Adam turned off the main road and we sped down a two-lane highway, before turning into a long dirt path shrouded by huge cypress trees, which should have been dripping Spanish moss but weren't. Instead, new growths had sprouted where the old had been torn away, spiky tendrils that resembled melted steel wool.

The sun burst over the horizon, causing the dew to sparkle like fireflies on every blade of grass.

I'd read the swamp had been devastated by Katrina,

with hundred-year-old trees being ripped from the ground and tossed about like matchsticks, houseboats driven into the mud up to their decks; a lot of the wildlife had died. For quite a while the only living things in abundance were the vultures. But I could see the swamp was coming back much more quickly than the strip malls ever would.

Around a tight bend a house appeared. More than a house, really, a mansion, as they'd said.

"How on earth is that still standing?" The structure appeared to have been built before the Civil War.

"Cypress wood." Adam stopped next to several other cars. "Doesn't rot."

"What about the hurricane?"

"We were very lucky," was all he said.

I saw evidence of recent improvements, or perhaps repairs. The porch was new, the windows and roof as well. A coat of paint was in order, but first things first, I suppose.

A light mist shrouded everything, making the place appear spooky, even in the sunlight. There might have been a yard once, maybe even some crops somewhere, but the swamp had spread nearly to the front door, the only solid area a small circle around the house and the slightly higher hard-packed dirt driveway.

The gentle, peaceful lapping of water filled the air, broken occasionally by a splash as fish jumped. Larger, heavier splashes made me wonder how close to a house an alligator might roam.

"The gris-gris," I murmured.

Adam turned with a lift of his brow. "What gris-gris?"

"There was one under my pillow—actually two. Someone familiar with voodoo said it was meant to repel werewolves."

"Who would have done that?" Adam kept the gun trained on John.

"I did." John continued to stare at the house.

"Why?" I asked.

"From the minute I heard your voice, I was—" He broke off. "Never mind."

King had said my voice called to him. I'd relished the idea that he couldn't see my plain face, my average body, that all he knew was the essence of me. But John had been able to see me all along. I wasn't sure what to make of that.

"You tried to keep yourself away from me," I guessed. "But why?"

"Why do you think?" John said tightly. "I'm a werewolf, Anne. I don't know if that will ever change. And even if it does . . ." He rubbed his forehead with one beautiful hand. "I'll always be haunted by what I've done. I'll never deserve a life after all the lives I've taken. I can't give you anything you should have. I can't be a husband, or a father. I wasn't much of a human being even before I became an animal."

"Why did you hire her if she was so irresistible?" Adam asked.

"I didn't."

"King did," I said slowly. "He said I'd be useful. I thought because of Mardi Gras."

John glanced away. "He had the crazy idea that if I fell for you it might help."

"How?"

"We need to go inside," Adam murmured.

I followed his gaze. A tall, voluptuous redhead wearing jeans and a tank top stood on the porch. She was flanked by an ancient, skeletal old man dressed from head to toe in camouflage. He had a bandolier of bullets across his scrawny chest, a pistol at his hip and a shotgun in one gnarled hand.

On the other side a gorgeous willowy blonde in black jeans and a red tank top stared intently at John. I didn't like that look at all.

"Who the hell is that?" I demanded.

"My wife, Diana," Adam said.

"The redhead or the ice queen?"

His lips twitched. "Redhead. The other one is Dr. Elise Hanover. She's here to cure Sullivan."

Blond, gorgeous, *and* a doctor. Didn't that just figure?

John opened the door and got out. So did Adam and I.

"Where's de boy?" Adam called.

"I sent him with Devon," Diana answered. "He doesn't need to see—" Her gaze flicked to John; wariness filtered over her face.

John dipped his head politely. Diana merely narrowed her eyes.

"Henri." Elise came down two of the steps, then paused as if she didn't want to get too close. "Have you found what you were searching for?"

"Not yet. And I'm John now. Thanks to Edward."

He glanced at the old man, who kept his shotgun pointed at the ground, but angled in John's direction. Edward stared at me. "Anne Lockheart?"

"Yes."

"Edward Mandenauer." He bowed and clicked his heels, his heavy German accent complementing his Old World mannerisms.

"According to Cassandra, you are aware of the world that exists parallel to your own?"

"The werewolves? Yes."

"You are searching for someone you have lost?"

"My sister." What did one have to do with the other?

"Let's get on with this," John interrupted. "Poor Sullivan doesn't need to be psychotic any longer than he has to be."

"Poor Sullivan?" I echoed. "You didn't like him much before."

"I don't like him now, but I don't want anyone to be tormented when they can be cured."

"Except it isn't a torment," Elise murmured, "and you know that as well as I do."

The two of them stared at each other and something passed between them, something I liked even less than the smell of rotting vegetation in the swamp.

"Why did you give him a new identity?" Adam demanded. "Why didn't you tell me you'd let him loose?"

"So you could stick your nose in things and mess them up?" Elise turned her attention from John to Adam. "The only way to cure him is to find a way out of his curse. He couldn't do that in Montana."

"He was a sadistic werewolf for over a century, then he went crazy—or crazier. You just let him come back to de scene of most of his crimes and start killing people?"

"I wasn't killing *people*," John said tightly.

"So you say. But you've lied before."

Adam had a point.

"The *Jäger-Sucher* society is supposed to be some all-powerful Special Forces agency with tentacles everywhere," Adam said.

Diana glanced at me and shrugged as if to say, he's on a roll, there's no stopping him now.

I could translate *Jäger-Sucher* to "Hunter-searcher" as well as the next mid-level German student, but the word didn't tell me any more than I already knew. However, Adam didn't give me a chance to ask any questions.

"Yet Grandpère can just walk out of an impenetrable compound and trot into New Orleans, then set up shop with none of us de wiser?"

" 'Impenetrable' means no one can get *in*." Edward leaned his shotgun against the porch rail.

"Lately," Elise muttered.

Edward ignored her. "It does not mean someone cannot leave if they are allowed to."

"You took him there to fix him," Adam said.

"I couldn't." Elise spread her hands. One palm sported a tattoo in the shape of a pentagram. She didn't seem the tattoo type.

"He might have been doing anything down here."

"He wasn't," she said.

"How do you know?"

"You think I would let one such as he wander about?" Edward shook his head and made a tsking noise. "I am not stupid. There was an agent close to him at all times. One with orders to contact me should anything go awry."

"Who?" Adam asked.

"King."

"But I found him," John said.

"That is true." Edward spread his hands. "However, I found him first. It occurred to me that you might try and contact the last remaining ancestor of the woman who cursed you. King has been on my payroll for months."

"You'll find out soon enough," Elise murmured, "that Edward has his bony fingers in everything."

"Then King hasn't truly forgiven me." John sounded lost. "He was just following orders."

"His orders were to blow out your brains with silver if you did anything you shouldn't."

"Killing Grandpère makes me a loup-garou," Adam said. "We're trying to avoid that."

"My duty is to protect humankind from the beasts. If that involves killing one, but making another to be killed at a later date . . ." Edward lifted one shoulder. "So be it."

Adam scowled, and turned toward John. "You actually thought de man whose grandmother you *owned* could be your friend?"

"You need to back off." I stepped forward. "He's trying to make things right, and you aren't helping."

Adam's eyes narrowed. "You have no idea what he's done, *chica*." The emphasis on the last word was insulting.

"Never mind," John said in a voice that was infinitely weary. "Let's get on with this."

"Yes," Edward agreed. "Let's."

33

WHEN ADAM HAD said he was keeping Sullivan in his dungeon, he'd been exaggerating. Slightly.

The six of us tramped into the swamp. I wasn't wild about the idea, but then again I wasn't going to let John out of my sight. The way Adam kept glaring at him and Diana kept flinching whenever he came near, combined with Edward's habit of pointing a gun in his direction, made me worry he wouldn't come out of the swamp at all.

Why did I care? I wasn't quite sure.

What I *was* certain of was that I wanted to see Sullivan cured and not just because I missed the man who'd been my friend; I wanted to see magic done. Who wouldn't?

A cool breeze brushed the long grass, causing the tiny tendrils of moss hanging from the cypress trees to sway. The damage was more visible deeper within the swamp. One tree had been yanked from the earth by the wind, then driven back into the muck branches first, the roots reaching like emaciated arms toward the sky.

A heavy splash to the right made me skitter in the other direction, and my tennis shoe sank ankle deep in ooze. I tugged, but my leg was stuck.

"Was that an alligator?" Panic made my voice wobble.

"Most likely." Diana paused to help me out.

"I—I thought a lot of the wildlife died in Katrina."

"Some did. But there were plenty of alligators to go around." She gave my leg a good yank and my foot came free with a wet, gloppy squelch. "Don't worry; they won't come near us."

"You have a gris-gris?" I shook my foot, and globs of mud flew.

"No." She glanced at John. "They don't like wolves."

She turned on her heel and hurried to catch up to her husband.

After half an hour of hoofing it through the swamp, we topped a slight rise and stared down at a dilapidated cabin that seemed to have sprung from the earth.

"Sullivan's here?" I asked.

"You don't think I'd keep him near my family, do you?" Adam headed down the hill.

Man, the guy was cranky. I guess I wouldn't be too cheery either with the prospect of the crescent moon curse hanging over my head, and that of my young son; but he was starting to get on my nerves.

We filed into the cabin. The main room was dominated by a cage, and in that cage resided Conner Sullivan.

"Where are his clothes?" I whispered, staring in

spite of myself at the thick muscled legs, the bulging arms, and flat, rippling belly.

"He shifted, which makes clothes garbage," Diana explained. "There wasn't any point in getting new ones until he was cured."

"That's kind of inhumane, isn't it?"

"He isn't human," Diana answered.

Sullivan had been eyeing all of us with a sardonic smile. When his gaze reached me he licked his lips and his eyes flared. "Glad you're here, Anne. That'll save me time once I've killed them all."

Why had I come again? Oh, yeah, to get my friend back. But I was starting to wonder if I'd ever be able to look at him and not remember what he'd done. I couldn't stop remembering it now.

My thoughts must have shown on my face, because Sullivan laughed, the sound causing the hair on my arms to dance.

"I knew you couldn't stay away," he murmured. "Rodolfo's cock isn't big enough for you." Reaching down, he began to stroke himself. "Mine will be. I promise."

"If you're going to fix him, do it," John snapped.

"Hit a nerve?" Sullivan stopped masturbating— thank God. "Although now that I see you, *really* see you and him"—he jerked his head in Adam's direction—"I don't think your name is Rodolfo. It's Ruelle, isn't it?"

His lips pulled back in a sneer. "I always knew you were killing people. How many was it? Twenty? Thirty? Do you like to fuck them as they die? Doesn't the blood taste better when they're scared? You must know all sorts of ways to make the experience better. Can we talk?"

The contrast between the previously proper and polite Sullivan and the disgusting animal before us now was astounding. If this was the way John had been when he was Henri, I could understand why no one in the room could stand to be near him. Even I inched farther away.

Sullivan grinned. "She knows you for what you are now. You'll never get into her pants again. I'm surprised you managed it in the first place. But then, she doesn't know what you did, does she?"

"Shut up," John said. "It wasn't me."

"No? I bet your victims could pick you out of any lineup. But then, once they're victims, they'd never betray you. They're part of your pack. Under your control." His eyes, darker than John's with much scarier shadows beneath the surface, shifted to mine. "You know, I remembered where I saw the eyes of the wolf that bit me."

"No," John whispered.

"It took me a while to place them because I'd never seen them up close."

Elise had moved nearer to the cage while Sullivan rambled on. He didn't appear to be paying any attention to her, but with a movement so fast it blurred before my eyes Sullivan yanked her against the bars.

He roared and slapped his hands to his face. Elise doubled over and did the same.

I started forward, but John pulled me back. "Don't go near him."

"But she's hurt. What happened?"

"Elise is a werewolf too."

I didn't know what to say to that except, "Huh?"

"When we touch skin to skin, we know," he murmured.

Elise straightened, dropping her arms to her sides. "Extreme ice cream headache on contact."

"But how can she . . . ?" I trailed off, uncertain how, or even what, to ask.

"Elise is different." John let go of my arm, his gaze on Elise. "She was born a werewolf, although she was never evil."

"Born?" I echoed, as horror rolled through me. "Is that possible?"

He caught my expression, immediately understood my concern. "Not the way you think. We can't—" He took a deep breath. "Impregnate."

I couldn't help but wince at the word, and a flicker of sadness shone in John's eyes before he continued. "Elise is a special case. Her mother was Edward's daughter."

"She's his grandchild?" I whispered, glancing back and forth between them.

"The werewolves turned his only child into a monster in vengeance for his killing so many of their kind."

"What happened to her?"

"I did what had to be done," Edward murmured.

"You killed your own child?"

"She wasn't my child anymore."

I couldn't help but stare at the man. How could he have done such a thing? Then again—

My gaze went to Sullivan. Maybe it was understandable.

Sullivan dropped his hands and snarled at Elise. "That hurt, bitch."

"Sticks and stones," she murmured.

He bellowed with fury and she reached out, smacking her tattooed palm against his forehead. Sullivan stilled, his face gone slack, his eyes unfocused.

Elise closed her eyes; an expression of complete peace flickered over her face.

"What's she doing?" I asked.

"Curing him."

John stared at Elise with such longing, a shaft of unwelcome jealousy burned in me. Something was between them, but what?

"She was given the gift to make us whole again in the Land of Souls," he continued.

"Voodoo?"

"No. Ojibwe heaven."

My eyebrows lifted. "She doesn't look Ojibwe."

"She isn't."

A tiny smile curved his lips, though it didn't reach his eyes. "I know it doesn't make any sense."

"There you are," Elise said, and dropped her hand.

Sullivan's eyes opened. He blinked, staring at Elise in confusion. "Who are you?"

"Dr. Hanover. You've been unwell, Detective. But you'll be all right now."

"I was sick? I don't remember."

"Some things are better forgotten." She glanced at Edward, then took Sullivan's hand. I braced for the outcry, but this time nothing happened.

Smiling, she released him. "He's good."

"I'm naked," Sullivan said in shock.

"Here you go." Elise handed him what appeared to be sweatpants and a T-shirt, socks and underwear, some shoes.

Sullivan frowned when he saw the rest of us. "What the hell?" He used the pile of clothes to cover his nether region. "What kind of hospital is this?"

"Private," Elise said, unperturbed. "You needed special care. What you had was . . . contagious."

A mild way of putting it.

Sullivan got dressed in a hurry. Elise glanced at the rest of us. "If you could step outside for a bit? I have a few tests to do."

"Anne?" Sullivan called. "Why are you here?"

I glanced at Elise, uncertain, and she took over. "I asked Anne to come and take you home."

"Oh. Great. Thanks."

He seemed lost, almost childlike. I should feel sorry for him, maybe even protective of him. But I didn't. Every time he spoke, I heard him saying other, more hateful things. When he stared at me I had to fight not to run away.

John and I followed Adam and Diana outside. Edward remained with Elise.

The Ruelles moved off, heads together as they whispered. John stared after them. He knew they were talking about him as well as I did.

"Sullivan doesn't remember anything about being a werewolf?" I asked.

"No," John said. "When she touches them, everything that happened from right before they're bitten until the moment they're cured is gone. Otherwise we'd have a lot of screaming, crying, insane people instead of just confused ones."

"You remembered," I murmured, "and it drove you mad."

"Yes," he said simply.

"What are they going to tell Sullivan about the time he lost?"

"They'll be able to convince him he was sick."

"How are they going to explain away a mortal throat wound that disappeared without a trace to all the people, besides me, who saw it?"

"I'm not sure, but they always do. Most choose to believe a logical explanation, however illogical it might be, rather than believe the unbelievable."

Strangely enough, that made sense. I know *I* wanted to forget about Sullivan's gaping throat and pretty much everything that had happened after it.

"The tough ones are those who've been around for several hundred years. How do you tell someone it's the twenty-first century when their last memory is from seventeen fifty?"

"How do you?"

"That's Edward's job—or at least that of the *Jäger-Suchers*."

Here was my opening. "What's a *Jäger-Sucher*?"

"Hunter-searcher."

That much I knew, and perhaps a little bit more.

"They hunt monsters, don't they?"

"Yes."

"And Edward is their leader."

"He formed the group after World War Two. He was a spy, his mission to discover what Mengele was up to in his secret lab in the Black Forest."

"Wasn't Mengele the one who performed all those sick experiments on the Jews?"

"And anyone else Hitler didn't care for. The Fuehrer

ordered a werewolf army. Mengele made him one."

"But—" I broke off. "History might not have been my best subject, still . . . I'd have remembered a werewolf army."

"The Allies landed; Mengele panicked and released what he'd made into the world. Edward got there too late to stop him."

"So he formed the *Jäger-Suchers* to remedy that."

"Exactly."

The thought was disturbing on many levels. That such a group existed, and no one knew about them, that there were monsters everywhere, and no one knew about them either. Most of all—

"If he's been hunting for over fifty years, why aren't they all dead yet?"

"Monsters multiply, and from what I've gathered, the werewolves have been using magic, mysticism, drugs, to create new and better monsters."

"You weren't one of Mengele's werewolves."

"Obviously."

"There were werewolves before he invented them."

"Definitely. There are legends of humans becoming wolves as far back as the Bible and then some."

"I guess that explains why the *Jäger-Suchers* are still in business."

"Things that have been around since the beginning of time are hard to exterminate."

"Henri," Diana called.

John's lips thinned. "My name is John."

Diana stopped several feet away and eyed him warily. "Adam and I think you should stay with us."

"No," he said shortly, biting off the word with that snooty twist only the French seem capable of.

"But—"

"I have a place of my own. I have it for a reason."

"What reason?" Her face creased. "To play jazz?"

"While that's always enjoyable, and soothing to the savage beast"—his voice took on a sarcastic twist—"that's not why I do it."

"You're not making any sense, Grandpère." Adam came up behind his wife and laid his hands on her shoulders. I was distracted momentarily by his long and elegant fingers, which looked exactly like John's. They were so alike it was downright creepy.

"He's calling in his wolves." Edward stood in the doorway. "The music is an extension of him—the human equivalent of a howl—although I'm sure he howls on the nights of the crescent moon as well."

John spread his hands in a gesture that said, *Of course*.

"A jazz club is busy," Edward continued. "No one will notice people coming and going."

"Except Sullivan," I muttered.

Edward's sharp blue eyes flicked to mine, and he dipped his head in acknowledgment.

"When he plays the saxophone, the wolves come to him," Diana murmured, "but how did you get them to New Orleans in the first place?"

"That was my doing," Edward said. "We recorded his howl, then I used new satellite technology to embed the sound in various satellite products."

For a minute we were all silent, no doubt thinking of

all the things satellites were used for in this day and age.

"Each wolf's howl is distinct," Edward explained, "and they howl for many reasons. For instance, to assemble a pack."

"My wolves knew the sound, and they were compelled to come to me."

"But how would they know where to come?" I pressed.

"You've heard legends of dogs traveling hundreds of miles to return home? Wolves are no different. My home is New Orleans, which makes it theirs too."

"Didn't they notice they were being picked off one by one?"

"I fought most of them in wolf form, then dumped the bodies in the swamp."

"Sullivan is ready to leave." Edward was staring at me.

Suddenly I was hyperventilating. I'd thought I could face Sullivan once he was "himself" again, but I couldn't.

"I don't want to see him," I blurted.

Sympathy crossed the old man's face. "Then you don't have to."

34

I WAS GRATEFUL to be spared an encounter with Sullivan before I was ready. I wasn't sure I'd ever be.

What I'd love to do was hightail it out of New Orleans and never come back, but I still hadn't found Katie. I was starting to think I wouldn't.

Adam drove us into town. Diana remained behind to deal with Sullivan. "I'll take him home, get him settled, talk to his boss."

"I will take care of the rest," Edward murmured.

I took "the rest" to mean the hospital, the doctors, the EMTs, the police who'd handled his case. Edward would be busy for a while.

Late afternoon sunshine slanted over the roof of Rising Moon as Adam pulled to a stop at the curb. Through the big front windows, King was visible behind the bar.

"Don't leave town, Grandpère. I wouldn't like having to come after you."

"He's hardly going to leave town before he finds that last werewolf and ends the curse," I said sharply.

"What she said." John climbed out of the car and headed inside.

Adam watched him go with a concerned expression. "Be careful."

I got out of the car too. "He isn't Henri Ruelle. Not anymore."

"I hope to God you're right." Adam drove away.

As I stepped into the club, King came out from behind the bar and trailed in John's wake. I shut the door, flipped the sign to CLOSED, and engaged the lock just as King snagged John's arm.

Expecting an outcry as pain erupted in both of their heads, I was surprised when John merely stopped and stared pointedly at King's hand.

King withdrew it with a wary gaze. He seemed almost scared, and while that was ludicrous considering King had a good six inches and probably a hundred pounds on Rodolfo, with the strength of a werewolf, John could no doubt toss King across the room without even trying.

"How can he touch you?" I murmured.

"He isn't the boss of me," King snapped.

"No, I didn't mean—" I gestured vaguely. "The headache. When werewolves touch skin to skin."

Understanding spread across King's face.

"He's not a werewolf." John's voice was weary. "He's a lougaro. Sometimes a wolf, sometimes a cat, a pig—anything he desires he can become by performing the spell. He's not infected by a virus that alters his genetic makeup."

"You were cursed," I said. "Not bitten. Your DNA should be the same as mine."

"The curse made me a lycanthrope in every way.

I'm merely compelled to shift on the nights of the crescent moon."

"How can you be certain your DNA is different?"

"When I bite people, they become like me."

A horrible thought came to mind. If lycanthropy was a virus passed through bodily fluids . . . Well, I'd been exchanging a lot of fluids with John Rodolfo.

My fears must have shown on my face. I'd never been very good at hiding things. "Only through the bite in wolf form, *chica*. There's no other way." He stared at me for a long minute, then whispered, "You can't think I'd make you like me."

"No. Of course not."

But what if he didn't want to be alone? What if he wanted someone to share eternity with? What would I say if he asked me?

I'd say no. Because if John bit me I wouldn't be like him, I'd be like Henri. And while I hadn't met the man, not really, I'd heard enough to know I'd rather be dead than a werewolf like that.

"Where are your sunglasses, Johnny?" King asked.

John patted his shirt pocket and withdrew them.

"You need to keep wearing those," King said. "Folks might get a little freaked out by your sudden ability to see."

John slipped the glasses over his eyes and turned away.

"We need to talk," King said.

"You're one of Edward's men. You've orders to kill me if I start eating the customers."

"Johnny," King said softly, and John sighed, then faced him. "I want to help you. That hasn't changed."

"Why would you help me?"

Confusion flickered over King's face. "Because I can."

"I owned your grandmother. Hell, I did a lot more than own her. Just because it sickens me now doesn't take away the truth of it."

"That wasn't you." King put a hand on John's shoulder. "I believe that, and you should too."

"If it wasn't me, then why do I remember it as if it were yesterday? I don't even have to be asleep to see her face. To see all their faces."

"John," I began, and he cut me off.

"Don't, Anne. Of all the people in this world, you shouldn't—" His voice broke.

I glanced at King, worried, but he had no time for me. "Voodoo is about balance. Good and evil. Happy and sad. Life and death. You asked why I helped you? That's why. You've done a lot of evil; time to do some good. The only way you can, is if you're cured. I've seen your pain. You've paid your debt."

"I never can. The debt's too great."

"You were possessed by evil," King said quietly.

"I was evil before that."

"The only way to atone is to help others. Love someone. Create life instead of spreading death."

My heart began to pound faster. If John were cured, he'd be a normal man. What would that mean to me?

I was afraid to hope. Because there was a big "if" on the other end of that wish.

King grabbed John's hand, turned it over and pressed his thumb to the white scar that marred John's wrist. "Your death won't change a goddamned thing."

"There are people who'd be glad of it."

"To hell with them. They need to forgive."

John lifted his head. "Did you forgive me?"

"You didn't own *me*, Johnny."

"That doesn't matter."

"True. But what good is forgiving someone for a minor offense? I'll pave my way to heaven by forgiving the incredibly huge fuckups."

"Thanks," John muttered.

Silence descended, lingering heavily until King spoke again. "If I can forgive you, then so can she."

John stilled. I did too.

"She who?" I asked.

The men ignored me.

"No," John said. "She won't."

"Tell her," King insisted.

"Tell her what?" I asked.

The three of us were so intent on our conversation, we didn't notice someone had come in the back door until a shadow fell over the floor. I glanced up.

A woman stood framed in the doorway, the setting sun flaring red all around her. I couldn't see her face.

"I think you're supposed to tell Anne about me," she said.

A wave of dizziness made me sway. I knew that voice.

35

K ATIE?" I WHISPERED.
     John grabbed me around the waist before I
could rush forward. I kicked and fought; he lifted me
right off the ground as Katie laughed.

It was the laugh that made me stop fighting. That
laugh didn't sound like Katie at all.

"Is that her?" My voice shook.

She stepped closer, out of the fading sunshine and
into the light. Someone else stared out of my little sister's eyes.

"Oh, God," I whispered, because I knew, even before the woman who was my sister, and yet not my sister, spoke.

"Hey, John. Long time no bite me."

Her teeth were whiter, sharper and seemingly more
numerous than I remembered. She was dressed differ-
ently than the Katie I'd known would have been—
black leather miniskirt and a lacy black blouse, which
was unbuttoned far too low, plus four-inch sling-back

heels. Her hair was longer, wilder, and her eyes appeared bluer with the insanity burning from within.

"Put me down." My voice was calm and very, very cold.

"Don't go near her," John murmured before he set me on my feet.

I didn't want to. This Katie frightened me.

"He brought me here to kill me," she said, though she seemed more amused than afraid.

"I know."

"And you fucked him."

I winced. Katie laughed that horrible un-Katie-like laugh.

"Don't sweat it, sis. You didn't know."

"Anne," John began.

"Let her finish."

Katie's smile became more of a smirk. "I waited for you at the Caradaro Club, remember?"

I nodded, unable to speak past my guilt. I'd said I would meet her, then I hadn't. I'd been annoyed over a bracelet, like a three-year-old child. Well, I had the bracelet back, but where was my sister? Staring into Katie's eyes, I couldn't find her anywhere.

"Look at him." She flicked her fingers in John's direction. "Who wouldn't want to go home with a guy like that? He was even hotter then. No goatee. Long hair." She made a sound of pure lust.

I found my voice. "You didn't—"

"Sleep with him? Never got a chance when I was human. And once we're werewolves"—she lifted her hands, then lowered them—"we've got touching issues."

The movement fixed my attention on her wrist, which was horribly scarred. "The bracelet," I murmured.

She glanced at the ridged tissue. "I should have let you wear it. When I changed the first time, it nearly fried me alive."

Well, the thing *was* pure silver.

"Graveyard dirt," I blurted. "The bracelet was covered in graveyard dirt."

"Lover boy buried me in an old cemetery. He knew I'd come back to life and heal all wounds." She held up her wrist. "Except this one."

I glanced at John, who'd removed his glasses. In his eyes I didn't see the evil she described. He'd been different then, but I was having a hard time remembering that. Right now, I wanted to kill him.

"Why did you leave the bracelet?" I asked Katie.

"To mess with you. This is a game, sis, and you were the bait. He brought you here to get to me."

"But John told me to leave. King—" I glanced around. King had disappeared. My eyes met John's, and in them I saw the truth. "The photograph was King's idea."

"Yes," John said.

"Sullivan told me it was doctored."

"Ah, Sullivan." Katie licked her lips and closed her eyes in mock ecstasy. "He was a very good year."

Sullivan *had* said he knew the eyes of the wolf that had bitten him. He hadn't recognized them right away because he'd only seen them before in a snapshot.

"John was having a helluva time finding me," Katie continued. "I always was the best at hide-and-seek."

She had been. Whenever we'd played as kids Katie always won.

"What I don't understand"—Katie frowned—"is how he compelled me to come here in the first place."

That I knew, but I didn't think it was relevant at this time.

"I can't say I minded since I love Mardi Gras season. It's like a buffet." Katie winked. "But once I got here, and I saw you, I figured out my maker was up to no good."

"Why didn't you leave?"

She glared at John. "What good is being a werewolf, with the power over life and death, if I have to come whenever he calls me? I wasn't leaving until one of us was dead. Preferably him."

"What about the fail-safe in the virus?" I asked. "Werewolves can't kill werewolves—unless they're different, like John."

"You've been busy." Katie contemplated me with a lifted brow. "But you always were nosy as hell. I can't kill him, you're right. But I can get someone else to do it."

"Who?"

"A familiar," John murmured.

"Like a witch's familiar?"

"In a way," Katie said. "Except a werewolf familiar is a witch."

"You have a witch helping you," I repeated.

"I sent Lydia after him, but he's strong and clever; she couldn't kill him. Although she did manage to beat the crap out of him once."

The night John said he'd been mugged I hadn't understood how anyone could do such a thing. Of course I hadn't considered the culprit might be a werewolf familiar. And why would I have?

"He killed her." Katie scowled. "Gypsy witches aren't that easy to come by."

King suddenly appeared between Katie and me holding Murphy's gun. I guess that explained where he'd gone.

"Be careful." I laid my hand on his arm. "The thing's loaded with silver."

"It wouldn't be any good with lead, girlie." He shouldered me back, his gaze on Katie.

Katie growled, her lips pulling away from lengthening canines. John cursed and I glanced at the window. The sun was almost down, and the moon would soon be on the rise.

"Let's get this over with," King murmured.

"Don't kill her," I blurted. "Elise can fix her."

"I don't want to be fixed." Katie's voice was a low rumbling growl emanating from a still human throat. "I like what I am."

"You aren't you," I pointed out.

"I'm more me than I ever was before. The inner Katie is free."

"You weren't a killer."

"I am now. I've been making my own little pack. Sullivan would have been a wonderful addition. As it is, your little friend Maggie has been fun."

"Maggie?" My voice was faint.

"She was so easy. I sent one of my wolves to the café, and she came away with him like a lost lamb."

The old man. I'd known there was something weird about him.

"Why?" I whispered.

"I thought you'd like to have a friend who could

show you the ropes." Her lips curved. "When I make
you like me."

The night was warm, but I shivered anyway. "Call
Elise," I said.

King and John didn't move.

"You guys got a hearing problem? Get Elise over
here."

"Fixing her won't fix him, girlie. If John doesn't kill
her, he won't be cured."

My heart sped up until it was pounding thickly at
the base of my throat. "How do you know that for
sure?"

"The loas told me over and over again the way to
break his curse," King said. "They've never lied to me."

"Hell," I muttered.

"Ain't it though?" Katie asked in her strange dual
voice.

King held out the gun to John, and he took it. Katie
glanced at me as if waiting for a protest, but I hesitated.
Katie wasn't here anymore; in her place was a woman
I didn't recognize. One who enjoyed killing, one who
had killed, countless times, one who planned to make
me a monster just like her.

She must have sensed my indecision because she
seemed to gather herself, forcing back the call of the
rising moon so that when she spoke again, her voice
was the one I remembered, although it said things my
sister never would have.

"You think a guy like Rodolfo would want you? He
only fucked you to get to me."

"Nice," King murmured.

Katie shrugged. "Truth is truth, and she's not special."

I'd been happy while I'd resided in the fantasyland where John cared about me because he "saw" the extraordinary Anne who lived inside the plain wrapper. His being unable to see had freed me in ways I'd never been free before.

Except John *could* see me, had *always* seen me, just as he'd always known who I was, even though I hadn't.

I'd been a means to this end; I'd been bait for the werewolf who was my sister, or who'd at least been my sister before Henri Ruelle came to town.

While I could understand John's reasoning, I couldn't go along with his plan.

"Don't." My eyes met his. "Please."

He didn't hesitate. He lowered the gun.

King cursed. Katie smiled. John went to the phone and dialed.

"Elise? There's someone at Rising Moon who needs to be cured."

Though King was visibly furious over John's refusal to kill my sister, he put himself between Katie and the back door, leaving John between Katie and the front door.

I relaxed. By tomorrow I should be able to call my parents and tell them I was bringing Katie home.

A sudden blur of motion and an outcry from King made me turn. Katie streaked toward the front door. John moved in front of her, and she changed direction in the blink of an eye, leaping at the front window, crashing through the glass, hitting the pavement on both feet, and disappearing into the shocked crowd on Frenchmen Street.

• • •

W HAT DO YOU mean she got away?"
Adam, Elise, and Edward had arrived less than an hour after Katie had made her escape. Adam was understandably angry. When I'd begged for Katie's life, I'd conveniently pushed aside all of the other people who would be affected by my need to get my sister back. I guess selfishness wasn't limited to werewolves.

"I couldn't find a trace of her," John said.

He'd gone after Katie immediately, but the moon was gibbous and his curse did not allow him to shapeshift until the shiny silver orb waned to a crescent. With the power of her wolf, Katie had evaded him with ease.

"I'll find her," Edward muttered, and pumped his shotgun.

"No!" I cried. "She can be cured." I put my hand on Elise's arm. "Right?"

"I don't know if I've ever tried to cure a wolf made by one who was cursed." Elise bit her lip. "The cure didn't work with Henri."

"We have to try. She didn't ask to be a werewolf."

"Maybe she did," Adam said. "Grandpère always liked to make them choose."

"Choose?"

"Life or death. You may be a werewolf or no." Adam glared at his ancestor.

John rubbed his forehead and turned away.

King reached out and smacked Adam in the chest with the flat of his great big hand. Adam fell back. "You will stop tormenting him," King ground out. "He has been tormented enough."

"It will never be enough." Adam walked out, and he didn't return.

"He's right," John murmured.

"No," King said. "He isn't."

Edward lowered his gun. "I will begin searching for your sister. If I find her, I will call Elise. She may attempt the cure, but if it doesn't work, I must kill her."

"No," I said, then hurried on when Edward sighed impatiently. "If it doesn't work, let *John* kill her."

Edward's faded blond brows shot up, but after peering into my face for several seconds he gave a sharp nod.

Elise stood behind John. He didn't look at her, but continued to stare through the unbroken window at the moon. She reached out to touch his shoulder, then snatched her hand back before she did so. "I'll keep trying to find a cure. There has to be something."

"Perhaps," John said, but he didn't sound any more convinced of it than she did.

Edward left, and when Elise followed him, I followed her. The old man got into the car. Adam waited behind the wheel. I murmured her name and she paused

"There's something between you," I said.

Elise tilted her head, studying me. "I understand what he's going through. I've been there."

"You weren't evil," I pointed out.

"No, but I've killed. I have to live with that. So does he."

"He killed my sister."

"Yes," she agreed. "I've never been possessed as

Henri was, so I can't say what it's like. But I've studied hundreds of werewolves, and they aren't the same as they were when they were human."

I thought of Sullivan and agreed. Except—

"Henri was horrible before he was a werewolf."

"So I hear. But as he said, he's John now. He *is* different. A century and a half can change a man." Her lips twisted wryly. "And you have to remember, he was made a werewolf against his will too. A curse is just as much of a coercion as being bitten."

"From what I've gathered of Henri, he probably would have welcomed what happened to him."

"We'll never know, because Henri died a long time ago."

Elise got into the car, and they drove away. When I went inside Rising Moon, King had disappeared, leaving John and me alone.

The CLOSED sign on the door would remain there until the glass company replaced the hastily constructed barricade over the broken window. All I knew was that I wasn't going to stay here tonight. Maybe John would let me stay with him.

I blinked at the thought, one I hadn't realized I entertained until that moment.

Though Elise and Edward were struggling to see John as anyone other than Henri, and Adam couldn't see past his evil Grandpère, I'd always seen John as John. Discovering his secret, his past, his former identity, didn't change that. The man I'd met and fallen in love with was a different person from the one who'd been born, died, and then born again a Ruelle.

"Take me home with you," I murmured.

Shock widened John's eyes. "How can you even look at me when you know I killed your sister?"

"You didn't. Henri did."

John held out his lovely, gifted hands. "These become paws under the crescent moon, just as they did for Henri." One shot out and curled around my neck. "How do you know I won't rip out your throat?"

I lifted my own hand, which held the silver letter opener. "I won't let you."

He released me with a little shove. "You don't understand how it is when the crescent moon rises."

I couldn't say his words didn't disturb me, but I also couldn't say I didn't love him.

"Help me understand, John."

He shook his head.

"Was I just bait to you?"

"That was King's idea. I didn't even know what he'd done until you showed up with the picture." He took a deep breath, then let it out slowly. "Touching you made me feel alive again. So even though it was wrong, I was selfish. I guess I haven't changed all that much."

"You just gave up the only chance you knew of being cured because I asked it of you. That doesn't sound very selfish to me." He didn't answer. "I know the worst, John, and I still love you."

"No you don't."

"Don't tell me what I feel." My hand tightened on the letter opener. "You're a werewolf, but maybe I could live with that."

John's smile was sad. "I won't sentence you to hundreds of nights alone, wondering where I am, if I'll come home. I won't deprive you of the blessing of children just to have you with me." He cupped my cheek, and I rubbed my face against his hand. "But most of all I won't watch you age and die while I remain exactly like this."

I hadn't thought of that. Still—

"You'd rather have nothing than as many years as we could of something?"

"Yes."

"I didn't think you were a coward, John."

"Think again," he said, and walked out the door.

I was so shocked I didn't immediately follow. Big mistake.

Katie had disappeared into the crowd in an instant. John disappeared in a single beat of my heart.

36

I DIDN'T FIND him; I didn't really expect to. John had been outwitting *Jäger-Suchers* for over fifty years. A PI from Philly didn't stand a chance.

I ended up sleeping one last night in my room above Rising Moon. King returned as I was packing. He stood in the doorway, beneath the worthless horseshoe. "Watch your back, girlie."

"I'll be fine," I said. Though I didn't feel fine. I felt bruised, battered, deep down achingly sad. I was going to miss John for the rest of my life.

"Your sister could be anywhere," he continued. "She might come after you."

"I hope she does."

"She ain't Katie. She *will* kill you."

I pulled out my letter opener, turning it this way and that, until the light caught the silver and sparkled. "No," I said, and met King's eyes. "She won't."

King peered at me for several seconds. "You've changed."

"The whole world's changed."

K ING SPENT THE night in Rising Moon with a base-ball bat across his lap, protecting the place against looters. I figured I was safer there than any-where. In the morning, I'd catch a plane to Philly. In the meantime, I needed to figure out what I was going to tell my parents. Certainly not the truth.

Bright and early, there was a knock on the door of the club. Sullivan stood on the stoop.

I was tempted to sneak out the back and head straight for the airport. From the expression on King's face, he expected me to.

Instead, I opened the door, then moved as far away from the detective as I could get and still be in the same room. His gaze lit on my packed bag, then lifted to my face. "You're going?"

"Yes."

"What about your sister?"

He didn't remember what Katie had become, what she'd done to him, and that was good. I wished I didn't.

"I don't think she's here." I figured Katie was as far away from New Orleans by now as she could get.

"Something's changed." Sullivan fidgeted, uncom-fortable. "I did something or said something that's made you . . ." His gaze met mine. "Hate me."

He had, but I couldn't explain it to him. He deserved the oblivion Elise and the *Jäger-Suchers* had provided.

Sullivan was a good man once more, and he'd go on to do great things.

"I don't hate you," I lied. "But I have to go home."

"It's Rodolfo," he said.

"Yes."

He nodded as if he'd expected as much, then crossed the room to take my hand. I flinched; I couldn't help it.

Why couldn't I cut Sullivan the same slack I'd cut John? Why couldn't I see that the beast who'd hurt me wasn't the same man as the one in front of me? Perhaps because I'd never seen John as Henri, but I had seen Sullivan as Satan.

Or perhaps it was because I'd never completely trusted John, sensing something in him he was holding back. But I had trusted Sullivan; I'd felt safe with him. For Sullivan to turn on me, even though it hadn't been *him,* had been devastating. I doubted I'd ever get over it.

Sullivan dropped my hand, but he was still too close for my comfort, and I inched out of his reach.

"I was sick," he said. "I don't remember things. I'm taking a leave of absence from the force until I feel more . . . myself."

"That'll be good."

I wondered momentarily if he'd give up on his quest for the serial killer, but I kept my lip zipped in case Edward had purged the NOPD of the case. From what I'd seen of Edward, he probably could.

Our good-bye was awkward. He wanted to hug me; I didn't want him to, and he knew it. We shook hands, and as soon as he left, I did too.

• • •

B ACK IN PHILLY, life just wasn't the same. How could it be? I hadn't been kidding when I'd told King the whole world had changed.

Now I knew that evil could lurk behind every smiling face. The night held horrors I easily imagined. I'd seen them, touched them, almost become them.

In the first hour back in my parents' company I lied to them so many times I lost count.

"The DNA was Katie's," they greeted me as soon as I walked in their door.

I'd completely forgotten we'd sent evidence to the crime lab.

"Uh, yeah," I said. "The bracelet was found at the jazz club Rising Moon."

"Katie had to have been in New Orleans after she disappeared from here," my father said.

"Yes."

She had been, just more recently than we'd thought.

"So she must be alive."

My parents were conveniently ignoring what blood on a bracelet might mean, and I decided to let them.

"Sure," I lied.

Katie wasn't alive. Not really. She wasn't even Katie anymore. However, I couldn't tell my parents that, so I began to avoid them.

My job bored me. My friends too. Suddenly I didn't fit in in the place I'd been a part of my whole life. I spent most of my time searching the Internet, trying to find a trace of Katie somewhere. That is, when I wasn't looking equally hard for a trace of John.

When Edward called and offered me a job, I jumped at the chance.

"You're going to hunt for your sister anyway," he said. "Why not do so with the resources of the *Jäger-Suchers* behind you?"

I couldn't think of a single reason.

The night before I was scheduled to leave for J-S training, I watched the sun set from my window and sighed.

"You need to stop searching for me, *chica*."

I spun around, the pure silver knife I'd bought to replace the letter opener in my hand. John stood just inside the room.

He didn't look much better than I did. Oh, his black pants were pressed and his white dress shirt was spotless, but he was pale, with dark circles under his eyes; he'd lost weight too. He'd shaved off his goatee, but his five o'clock shadow darkened his jaw, making him appear both dangerous and a little bit sad.

"Who said I was searching for you?"

"Elise." His smile did not reach the deep blue eyes I just couldn't get used to seeing. "The woman knows everything."

I scowled, not only at the knowledge that he'd spoken to her and not to me, but at the revelation Elise knew so damned much. I shouldn't be jealous—the two of them couldn't even touch without getting a migraine—but I was.

"She told me to come here," John said.

My spirits fell even further at his words. He hadn't come because he couldn't bear to be away from me any longer, he'd come because Elise had told him to.

"You'll never move on with your life unless you see the truth," he continued.

"What truth is that?"

"I'm a monster, Anne," John began to unbutton his shirt. "And I always will be."

"I know what you are. I don't care."

"You don't really know."

The shirt slid to the floor; the fading sunlight glistened across his beautiful skin. He unzipped his trousers; the sound ripped through the heavy silence.

"You don't know," he repeated, "because you've never really seen."

He kicked off his shoes, shucked his pants, then stood before me completely naked. I couldn't even enjoy the view, because he was making me very nervous.

"What are you doing?"

"What I should have done in the beginning." He glanced at the window. "Only a few more minutes."

I followed his gaze. The sun had disappeared; the moon would soon rise.

A crescent moon.

My fingers tightened on the weapon, and John nodded. "Keep the knife handy. You never know what an animal might do."

"I don't need it." I slapped the thing onto the table. "You won't hurt me."

"Dammit, Anne! Don't be a fool. Pick that up."

I backed away from the table. "No."

Fury flashed across his face, sparked in his eyes, and for a minute, I was uneasy. My unease increased when he strode forward, grabbed the knife and came toward me.

Despite his being stark naked and gorgeous, all I

could do was stare at his long, supple artist's fingers wrapped around the hilt.

"You're holding it," I said.

"So?"

I lifted my gaze from his hand to his face. "That knife is pure silver, John. Every last inch."

He frowned, opened his fist, and stared at a palm that should be smoking but wasn't, then he looked out the window. The crescent moon hovered just above the horizon.

"What the—"

Before I could protest, he pressed the flat of the blade to his chest.

Nothing happened.

The knife clattered to the floor. "The—the curse is broken," he said.

"Just like that? How?"

"I'm not sure. Let me think." John turned away, seeming to forget he wasn't wearing any clothes. I didn't mind. "Mawu said I had to commit the ultimate sacrifice."

"And her great-grandson times ten said you had to kill all the werewolves," I pointed out. "You haven't."

"Maybe both methods are true."

"You didn't die. Lately."

"The ultimate sacrifice was never my life," he said slowly, "because it wasn't worth saving."

"I hate it when you say that," I muttered.

He ignored me. "In not killing Katie, I gave up my chance to be free, and in doing so *was* freed."

"I don't understand."

"The ultimate sacrifice, for me, was losing any chance I had to break the curse."

Why do we always think the biggest sacrifice is our lives? There are other things that mean a whole lot more.

Love. Happiness. Family. A future together. Did John want those things too?

"You're cured?" I asked. "You're sure?"

"I'll go to Montana, turn myself over to Elise. She can run all her tests and make certain I'm human, but—" He looked at the moon again. "I don't hear it calling me. I don't feel the pull. I don't have a taste for—" He stopped, cleared his throat, shrugged.

"Blood?" I asked, and he nodded.

John bent and picked up his pants. While he dressed, I waited for him to say something, anything, about us, but he didn't.

I couldn't let him walk out the door again without knowing how he felt.

"After you go to Montana," I blurted, "and Elise proves you're human, what will you do with the rest of your life?"

John lifted his head and his gaze met mine. I couldn't read his eyes any better now than when he'd hidden them behind dark glasses.

Then he reached out, snaked a hand around my waist and tugged me close. He brushed his lips across my brow, laid his cheek against my hair. "I love you, Anne. You're the only thing that's ever mattered to me in two lifetimes."

His arms tightened; at last I felt like I belonged somewhere, with someone.

"I'll probably never be a cheery fellow," he continued. "I'll always remember what I did. I'll always need to atone."

"How?"

"I hear you're working for Edward." I nodded. "should too."

"But your music—"

"Can be practiced anywhere. There're clubs in every city in the world, and being a musician is a good way to get to know a certain element in most of them You think Edward will hire me?"

"Yes."

Edward was no fool. He never had been. He'd see the advantages.

"Where should we live?" I wondered.

John lifted his head, touched my cheek. "Do you really have to ask?"

TWO MONTHS LATER, after John had passed all of Elise's tests and was declared human again, we went through J-S training together, then got married in the Crescent City. We moved into John's apartment and let King manage Rising Moon.

Once I'd looked at New Orleans and known I would never fit in. Ancient, ghostly, and magical, with the echoes of jazz floating on the sultry air, the place had become as much a part of me as it was a part of John. I couldn't imagine living anywhere else.

However, we weren't there very often. Edward sent us to cities across the United States and Europe. We went everywhere together. The werewolves were up to something; they always were.

Katie had disappeared completely; I wasn't sure we'd ever find her. But I'd never stop trying.

HE AWAKENS SOMETHING WILD IN HER...

Stay tuned for the next *Nightcreature* novel from
RITA Award–winning and *USA Today* bestselling author

LORI HANDELAND

HİDDEN MOON

COMING SOON FROM ST. MARTIN'S PAPERBACKS
ISBN: 0-312-94917-0